IN
ICE

New York Times & USA Today Bestselling Author

CYNTHIA
EDEN

Published by Hocus Pocus Publishing, Inc.

Copy-editing by: J. R. T. Editing

CHAPTER ONE

She'd never intended to be a predator, but life had other plans.

Delilah "Lila" Darrow kept her spine straight and her chin up as she walked across the crowded ballroom. She was conscious of the click of her heels—she shouldn't have been able to hear that click, not over the band's passionate music, not over the murmur of voices that filled that cavernous space—yet she did. Two inches, spiked, they tapped on the floor with every step she took.

The heels weren't her normal style. Neither was the dress that fit her like a second skin. The dress cost more than her first car, *not* that she'd paid for the dress. It was a loaner, just like the shoes. Cinderella was at the grand ball, and, come the stroke of midnight, the fake trappings would disappear, and she'd slip back to her normal life.

But it's not midnight yet. And you have a job to do. Makeup had been carefully applied. Highlights put into her hair. The new haircut was stylish and sexy, and she could feel her hair sliding across her shoulders with every step that she took. Delilah didn't glance to the left or right as she advanced. She didn't need to look around her.

Her prey waited dead ahead.

Archer Radcliffe. Tall, muscled, looking far too gorgeous and sinful in his perfectly cut suit. He was rich as hell, wickedly smart, and, quite possibly...a killer.

Archer wasn't alone as he stood near the bar. A man like Archer was rarely alone and that was part of the problem. Getting close to him, getting into his inner circle, wasn't the easiest task in the world. Luckily, Delilah didn't particularly *like* easy. She enjoyed the thrill of a good challenge.

She would enjoy bringing Archer to his knees.

At that moment, he looked up and his gaze— dark from a distance—locked on her. She saw the slight stiffening of his jaw. The faint flaring of his eyes. She thought he might do a sweep of his gaze down her body. After all, the fancy dress was designed to show off her assets. But he didn't let his gaze shift. He just held her stare.

Her steps didn't falter. She knew what would interest Archer. She knew how to draw him close. And close was exactly where she intended to get him.

Never looking away, Delilah continued to advance. Her heels kept clicking and she could feel the vibrations, just as she could feel the too fast drumming of her heart. If Archer saw through her, if she messed this up, then all of her careful work would be for nothing.

It can't be for nothing.

As she closed in on him, the man to Archer's right kept talking. Archer inclined his head toward the fellow, but Archer's gaze never left Delilah's face. The closer she got, the more she could see that Archer's eyes *weren't* just dark. Though she knew that, of course, from his file—the file she'd carefully created. The file that told her exactly what Archer liked. The file that told her how to become the perfect woman to enchant him.

To obsess him.

If Cinderella had been able to access the tech that Delilah possessed, she wouldn't have needed to worry about catching the prince's eye at the fancy ball. She would have just baited him and gotten Prince Charming to fall straight into her web.

Gold. That was the real color of Archer's eyes. Not brown. Battered gold that gleamed as she got within five feet of him.

Five.

Four.

Three.

The man with Archer stopped talking, as if he'd finally realized he'd lost the attention of his audience. Archer had turned fully toward Delilah. One strong hand gripped a champagne flute—the champagne appeared not to have been touched. His expression was absolutely unreadable. A light growth of stubble covered his strong jaw, but she was fairly certain she'd seen his jaw tighten a moment before.

Two feet.

And...

She stopped in front of Archer.

One dark eyebrow rose. "Hello."

Play it right. Do this.

"I don't believe I've had the pleasure..." Archer began.

"And you won't," she finished for him. "Because unlike everyone else in this room, I'm not here to bow down to the great Archer Radcliffe."

The man to his right—a guy with carefully tousled blond hair—seemed to choke on the champagne he'd just lifted to his lips.

Without glancing away from her—that golden stare of his was truly quite disconcerting—Archer reached over and slapped his companion on the back. "That is disappointing to hear," Archer noted with a faintly amused twist to his sensual lips. Up close, he was even more attractive. It seemed a sin for one man to be so diabolically gorgeous. Perfect jaw. Long, straight blade of a nose. High forehead that was punctuated by a faint widow's peak. So much dark hair. Thick and luxurious, twisting just a little with a natural curl.

Archer had an undeniable, almost animalistic sensual allure. A vibe that seemed to roll off him. A vibe that had, no doubt, served him very well over the years. She was sure that vibe had made plenty of panties hit the floor.

The gorgeous killers are always the most dangerous ones. They just seduce their victims into surrendering.

Archer stopped slapping his companion. His gaze finally swept over her. But the golden eyes didn't heat. Just remained impassive. "If you're not here to bow, then why are we having this conversation?"

Why, indeed? "It's mine. I'll be taking home the Princess's Tear." A ridiculous name, but, whatever. The Tear was a huge diamond scheduled to go up for auction that night. Because the whole elaborate ball routine? It would end with an auction for the rich and bored. The Tear was the highlight of the event, and she knew that Archer was in attendance just to get his strong, tanned fingers on it.

He smiled at her. For a moment, her breath seemed to freeze.

Dangerous.

That smile of his...it was slow and wicked and hot. Another weapon in his arsenal. "I don't think so," he told her softly.

Delilah shrugged. "We shall see." Instead of backing away, she took a step closer. So close that she could touch him, so she did. Her hand rose and her fingers pressed to his chest. Her voice dropped as she said, "Archer Radcliffe, I'm here to take you down."

She felt him tense beneath her touch. She also felt something else—something she had very much *not* expected. A jolt of sensual awareness seemed to fly through her body like an electric charge. It started in her fingers—the fingers that pressed so carefully to his chest—and it pulsed up her arm and *through* her. It was a surge that she didn't want.

He was prey. A target. Not someone who was going to have any sort of personal—

His smile widened. "I do like a challenge."

Yes, she knew that about him. *We have that in common.* That was why she was setting her stage. Baiting her trap. Delilah wanted to snatch her hand away from him but that move wouldn't work with her setup. "And I like to win." Her lashes lowered to conceal her gaze.

"That's something we have in common." His words seemed to echo her thoughts.

She released a slow breath. From her research, she knew that the great Archer never lost. *You will this time.* If she could find the evidence to seal the nails in his coffin, Archer would go down.

"I'll see you at the auction." Delilah let her fingers trail down him—slowly—then she began to turn away.

He caught her wrist. His hand flew out in a lightning-fast move to curl around the fragile bones on her wrist. Beneath his touch, she wondered if he felt the sudden racing of her pulse. Unfortunately, that was a reaction that she could not control.

"You're not getting away that fast," he murmured.

I have no intention of getting away...yet.

The band began to player a slower, more romantic song.

"How about a dance?" Archer's voice was mild. Faintly amused. "You know, before you rip the Tear away from me and leave me a sad, tragic mess at this lovely event."

I will leave you a sad, tragic mess. His words had been mocking. Her intention was not. He was literally falling right into her trap. She hadn't thought it would be this easy.

Delilah forced a shrug of one shoulder. "I guess I have time for one dance. But I hope you're a good partner. I don't like to be disappointed."

He laughed. And, dammit, his laughter was a warm and sensual sound. The man was too lethal.

And you know that's true.

"I will endeavor not to disappoint you." His voice dropped. Went molten. "In any way."

Her lashes lifted. She stared at him. Saw the sexual intent in his eyes. He was still holding her wrist, so she knew he felt the fast racing of her heart, and Delilah wondered just how deliberate him grabbing her wrist had been. She'd been wearing a cool, careful mask, but he would now know—thanks to the fast rhythm of her pulse—that she wasn't nearly as controlled as she pretended to be.

A worthy adversary. Tread carefully. "Promises, promises," she replied.

"I'm not a man who gives empty promises."

The blond who'd been watching the byplay between them cleared his throat. "Um, hello."

Delilah turned her head toward him.

"I'm Oz Whitlock."

She knew exactly who he was. Oz Whitlock, attorney. He'd graduated at the top of his law class at Yale, had been best friends with Archer since the first grade, and his primary job was to make sure that Archer stayed out of trouble.

He was very good at that job.

He was also someone she'd prefer to keep at a distance.

"I didn't catch your name," Oz added.

Because she hadn't given it. She stared steadily back at him.

"A mysterious and beautiful woman who doesn't wish to offer her name," Archer inserted into the silence, voice smooth. "I am enchanted." He still had his hold on her wrist. "This is one of those situations," he added to Oz, "when I believe I have to enact our old first-sight rule."

Oz shook his head. "Like I didn't see that coming."

"Glad we're clear. Now, if you'll excuse me, a dance is waiting for us." Archer led Delilah onto the dance floor. People immediately backed away to give him room, and Delilah was conscious of all the considering stares flying their way.

He'd ditched his champagne flute, pushing it onto a waiter's tray, and now both of his hands were free. One gripped hers—lightly, as if he feared holding her fingers too hard—while the other rested on the curve of her waist. Even with her two-inch heels, he towered over her. He was big and obviously strong. She could see the strength in his wide shoulders and powerful chest, but Archer danced smoothly. Elegantly.

And he held her as if she was some kind of treasure. Ever so carefully. Ridiculous, of course. She wasn't a prize. She was punishment.

"What's the first-sight rule?" The question just sort of spilled from her. Not what she'd intended to say at all.

He laughed.

Little shivers slid through her. *Dangerous*. So very dangerous.

"Ah, now, surely you've heard of the rule before?" He spun her effortlessly. The room whirled, then he brought her back up against him. "Two men, one incredibly gorgeous woman. Whoever sees her first..."

Her shoulders stiffened.

"Gets her," he finished.

"I am hardly some *thing* that you get." Sharp. And she just stopped dancing. Right there on the dance floor.

Voices murmured near her. A twitter of gossip.

"No," Archer replied, and he didn't seem to care at all that she'd brought their dance to a complete standstill. If anything, his eyes gleamed. "I think you are someone who must be won."

Delilah laughed. "No, I'm not that, either. Your thinking is highly outdated—and unamusing." She made to move away—

But he still held her hand, and he pulled her right back.

"My deepest apologies." A statement that was as smooth as silk. He began to dance again with her. Light, easy steps. "I certainly did not mean to offend you. I merely wanted you to know that I think you're incredibly beautiful, and I am very, *very* interested in you. That's why I basically told Oz to go fuck himself."

Her steps faltered. Her ankle had twisted in the stupid heels. She fell forward, and his arms immediately curled around her. "Got you," he said.

No, I have you.

"First-sight rule. It means I saw you first, so he has to fuck off."

Her head tipped back. She was pretty much plastered to him, *not* part of the plan. Stupid shoes. "And if I'm not interested? What if I want *you* to fuck off?"

"Is that what you want? Because if so, just say the word."

Instead of answering, she pulled her mask back into place. Let her body sway against his. Anyone watching would not realize that she hadn't even known how to do a simple box step two weeks ago. Luckily, she was a fast learner.

His hand was still at her waist. She could feel the heat of his touch through her dress.

His hand shifted a bit. Stretched. The back of her dress dipped low, sliding to the base of her spine, and his fingers brushed over her skin.

More electricity. The kind she hadn't planned for, dammit.

"Unusual," Archer murmured.

"What is?"

"The way I feel when I touch you. It's like sparks fly under my skin."

Her breath caught because he'd just described *exactly* how she felt.

"That kind of reaction doesn't happen often. Actually, I'm not sure it has ever happened before. Makes me think that if we were in bed together, we'd be incredible."

"We're not in bed together." Her voice was steady. Amazing. "We're dancing." They were in a ballroom. Surrounded by strangers. So why did she feel like they were alone?

His fingers slid to her hip. *Away* from her skin. "Why do you want the Tear?"

"Because it's beautiful. I like beautiful things." Lie. She didn't care at all about beauty. Give her scarred. Give her different. Give her savage. She'd take that any day of the week over a fake perfection. "Why do *you* want it?"

"Because it belonged to my grandmother. My father gave it to a mistress years ago. She promptly sold it, and I've been searching for it ever since."

The honest answer surprised her. "Sentimental value?"

"Don't I strike you as the sentimental type?"

"No." Not at all. "But you do strike me as the possessive type. If you think something belongs to you, I believe that you will do anything necessary to keep your prize."

His head tilted toward her. His eyes narrowed. Such a deep gold. Very unusual color. "Insightful. You should remember that about me." His low words sounded like a warning.

They probably were. "I'm not going to back off. I want the Tear." Lie, lie. The Tear was a means to an end. He was that end. *I want you.*

The song was winding down. The dance had come to an end.

"I don't back off, either, and I usually get what I want."

The music stopped. The band was taking a break. No, not a break. It was probably time for the auction. Delilah had deliberately arrived late so that she would only have to stay a short time at the event. She slowly pulled from Archer's embrace.

"Don't I get a name?"

Cinderella hadn't given her prince a name. She'd just left him with a fancy slipper. He'd been resourceful enough to track her down. Granted, he'd used all his guards and power, but he'd gotten the job done. "Why kill the mystery?"

"Because I want to see you again."

And someone is taking the bait.

Pleased, Delilah offered him a slow, sensual smile. It was one she'd practiced in her mirror over and over again until she'd gotten it just right. "We don't always get what we want." With that, she turned away. Kept her back straight. Kept her chin up. And she left Archer Radcliffe standing alone in the middle of the dance floor.

Step one, complete. Archer was falling into her trap.

She just had to be careful. Her heart still beat too fast. Her body seemed to quake a little. Archer was supposed to get caught in the illusion. She wasn't.

Delilah glanced back.

And found Archer's golden gaze locked on her.

CHAPTER TWO

"It happens to the best of men," Oz said with a sigh. "Sure, you can have good luck. You can be hooking up with super models left and right and you can think you are on top of the world and then—bam. Rejected." He clapped a hand around Archer's shoulder. "You'll get used to it, I promise."

The auction was underway. Some paintings had already been sold. An ancient vase. A ruby necklace.

He waited in the back, standing and watching the crowd, while his annoying companion hammered at him. But Archer wasn't looking at Oz. His attention was on the woman who sat—perfectly poised and ever-so-elegantly—in the front row.

His mystery lady. "I want her name."

"Oh, man, I wanted it, too. Did you see how she—"

"I'm telling you to work your magic and *find* out her name. She's registered for the auction. That means her name is written down somewhere. This is an invitation-only event. I want to know who she is. I want to know where she lives." *I want to know everything.*

"Um..." Oz cleared his throat. "Got to advise you, as your attorney, that seems a little stalkerish. If the woman isn't interested, I get it— hurts the old pride. But you have to move on."

The Princess Tear had just been brought onto the stage. A man with graying hair, a slight paunch, and a glinting pinky ring motioned to the Tear. "Our highlight of the evening!" he boasted. "Who would like to start the bidding on this wonderful—"

"Twenty thousand."

The bid had come from the woman in the front row. *His* mystery woman.

"Oh, shit," Oz whispered. "She was for real."

"Bidder Thirteen has just said she would like—"

"Twenty-five thousand," Archer announced as his voice cut through the announcer's words.

The announcer's attention jumped to him. The man's eyes seemed to double in size. "We have twenty-five thousand," he said and swallowed. "Do I hear—"

"Fifty." Bidder Thirteen had her paddle in the air. "Fifty thousand is what you hear." Slowly, she turned to look over her shoulder and stared straight at Archer. And she smiled at him.

His eager cock immediately jerked in reaction to that slow, taunting smile.

"She did not come to play." Oz's tone held a note of admiration. "Damn. I think I am in love."

"Get over it," Archer snapped flatly. He was also not there to play. "Sixty thousand."

Voices rose. A nervous, excited rumble.

"Is it even worth that much?" Oz muttered. "Seriously, let's just take a moment to—"

"Seventy," Bidder Thirteen said without looking away from Archer.

He smiled at her. Truth be told, he hadn't anticipated the auction would be this much fun. There was very little in his life that *was* fun these days. "Eighty."

"Oh, my." The announcer's voice brightened. "Do I hear ninety?"

"In-fucking-sane," Oz rasped. "Stop. I don't think that's worth—"

Archer gave a small, negative shake of his head.

Bidder Thirteen smiled. She obviously thought that Archer's head shake had been directed at the announcer. She thought wrong. It had been for Oz because the guy needed to shut the hell up. That necklace? It was worth everything. Not just one diamond, but three in a perfectly shaped cluster drop. A necklace that had been in his grandmother's family for ages, until his father had just tossed it away like it was some useless trinket.

His father had always been good at tossing things away.

"Going once," the announcer boomed. "Going twice—"

"Ninety," Bidder Thirteen's cool voice declared.

Archer took an instinctive step forward. "One hundred grand."

Her eyes narrowed.

He winked at her.

Red immediately flushed her well-sculpted cheekbones. Her delicate hand lowered as she brought down her bidding paddle.

The silence in the room seemed to stretch as Archer stared at his mystery woman. He could practically feel the tension in the air. It was getting thicker and deeper and—

She smiled. A real, beautiful bloom that took her striking features and made them absolutely gorgeous.

"Sold to Mr. Archer Radcliffe! And, sir, I guarantee, you will not be disappointed with this purchase. And on behalf of the charity committee, I would like to thank you for your substantial bid."

Bidder Thirteen didn't look upset with her loss. In fact, she appeared pleased as hell.

Archer realized that he'd just been played.

***

The air held a faint chill. Unusual for Miami. The nights were rarely cold. Instead, the heat would grab you and hold tight. The air would be thick and heavy. Like a rough touch.

Archer slowly closed in on the woman who was about to head down the stone stairs and out of his life. They were outside of the plush ballroom, on the balcony that overlooked the beach, and she was using the opportunity to sneak away.

"Not so fast." He stepped into her path, slipping from the shadows.

She didn't give so much as a start of surprise.

Because she knew I was here the whole time.

"Sorry you didn't get the Tear. You certainly should get points for effort." Her scent—absolutely delectable and bewitchingly feminine—wrapped around him. "I expected you to stop bidding around fifty thousand."

She laughed. "I know. That's why I kept going."

Surprise pushed through him. "What?"

Her hand lifted. She gave his cheek a little pat. "I told you I was here to take you down."

Yes, she had. But she'd also said she wanted the Tear.

"The money from the auction went to support a charity that helps runaways. Helping those who need us is certainly a worthy thing to do." For a moment, steel entered her voice. Emotion. It was quickly smoothed away. "A man like you—a man with ever-so-deep pockets—he should be expected to pay richly for the things that he wants." Her left hand gripped a small, glittering clutch. She hadn't possessed that clutch before. Archer knew she must have picked up her bag from the check-in area before slipping outside.

"You were deliberately driving up the bidding."

Her hand fell away from him. "Was I?"

She'd just freaking admitted it. "What if I'd stopped? What if I'd left you high and dry and owing for the diamond?"

Her head tilted as she seemed to consider the matter. "That would have been unfortunate. Especially since I have no way to pay."

He'd been conned. Beautifully and completely.

"Not like it would have happened, though," she continued blithely. "I made sure to learn just how much you wanted the diamond. Our chat on the dance floor was very enlightening."

Anger pulsed inside of him. It was cold, the way his rage always was. The way *he* always was. "I'm not the kind of guy you want to fuck around with."

"No? And here I thought you wanted me to fuck you. That was certainly the impression I received during our dance." She wet her lips. "Guess that was my mistake. Too bad." She moved around him. Took a step down the stairs.

"What game are you playing?"

She kept going down the stairs. "Not a game." Her voice drifted back to him.

"Bullshit." *She conned me.* She'd played her role so perfectly that he could not help but be impressed. And intrigued. Usually, events like this one bored the hell out of him. No, correction, he *usually* avoided events like this one. He didn't have a lot of time for bullshit in his life. Most of the people in that ballroom had been staring at him with fear in their eyes. *All* had been whispering about him.

He'd only come out because he wanted that Tear.

Now though, he'd found something else— someone—that he also wanted. *And she isn't going to just slip away.*

Pausing half-way down the stone stairs, she looked back up at him. The full moon shone down on her and revealed her features. Not classically beautiful, but more striking—the first thought he'd had upon seeing her in the crowded ballroom. Once you saw her, you could never forget her. Delicate jaw. Sculpted cheekbones. Plump lips designed to drive a man to madness. Wide, deep eyes.

"If I were Cinderella, I'd leave a shoe for you. You could be Prince Charming and follow me as you promised me a life I'd never forget."

Automatically, his gaze dipped to her heels. Fuck-me shoes if he'd ever seen them. *Or maybe, fuck-off shoes.* Her dress stopped at mid-thigh, revealing legs that were truly glorious. Legs that he could imagine wrapped around his hips—or thrown over his shoulders—all too easily.

"But you're not Prince Charming." A new note had entered her voice. An edge of tension. "And I'm not Cinderella."

He bounded down the stairs after her. "You shouldn't play with me. You do not want me for an enemy."

"How do you know what I want?" Husky.

The question had his shoulders tensing. *I know what I want. It's you.* He wanted her more than he'd wanted anyone in a very long time. And every confusing, tricky word she uttered just increased his need to know more about her.

"The money went to a deserving charity," she continued with a roll of one shoulder. "You got back your heirloom. Win, win. Why would you be my enemy because of that?"

He was right beside her. He wanted to reach out and touch her. Instead, his hands clenched into fists. "If you're not Cinderella, then who the hell are you?"

"Back to that, are we?" A low, amused laugh. "Why don't you just call me the wicked stepsister? Think of me as the one the slipper doesn't fit."

She still wasn't giving him a name. What she *was* doing—driving up his curiosity. And, dammit, his attraction.

"It's been an...experience meeting you," she noted with a little nod. "I don't think I will be forgetting you anytime soon."

He knew he wouldn't be forgetting her. At all. He—

"Good night, Archer," she whispered as she pushed up onto her toes. Her hand rose and curled behind his head, and she tugged him toward her. Toward her mouth.

The kiss happened before he could even think. One second, he was plotting about what to do with her, and the next—his mouth was on hers. And she was kissing him with a careful, skilled passion. With total control. Licking lightly with her tongue in a technique he knew was designed to drive him crazy.

Fine. It *was* driving him crazy. She tasted rich and decadent. Her mouth was soft and lush, and all he wanted to do was pick her up and get lost in her. Right then. Right there.

She'd just cost him one hundred grand. She'd schemed. Lied. Tricked him.

And now she was trying to seduce him.

So he let her. What the hell? The night was certainly different. It was—

She pulled back. "Not bad." Her fingers touched her lower lip. Was it his imagination, or did her fingertips tremble just a bit? "But I've had better."

His jaw clenched.

She turned and walked down the stairs. She still gripped the clutch.

Cinderella didn't leave a shoe behind for him. She didn't even glance back. But then again, she wasn't Cinderella.

And he wasn't a fucking prince.

He waited until she was gone, then he slowly opened his hand. When she'd been kissing him, he'd taken the liberty of slipping his hand inside that tiny clutch of hers. So small that there had only been room for her ID, keys, and some cash.

He looked down at her ID. Brought out his phone. Shined his light on it.

No, she wasn't Cinderella.

She was Delilah Darrow, and she'd just played with the wrong man.

***

She'd kissed him. So not part of the plan. But she'd done it. A spur of the moment thing. A move designed to wet his interest. To get under his skin.

Except he'd gotten under *her* skin. She'd felt the power of that kiss resonate through her body. She'd wanted to get closer to him. Wanted to rub against him. Hold him tight. And let go of her control. She'd wanted to kiss all of her inhibitions goodbye—something she never, ever did—and just hold on for the ride.

Absolute madness. Her reaction to him was way, way over the top.

Is this how the others had felt? The other women who had fallen prey to Archer? She knew what he was—correction, what he *could* be—and she had no business lusting after him. You didn't lust after the monster in the dark. You didn't get turned on when he touched you. When he kissed you.

Not unless you were screwed up in the head. Or as twisted as the monster.

The limo pulled to a stop in front of her place. She didn't wait for the driver to come around and open her door. Delilah surged outside.

"Miss—"

"Thank you." She pulled money out of her clutch. Pushed it into his hand. "You were great tonight. Fabulous service." The limo had been part of her cover. Not like she could arrive in her old VW convertible.

Delilah didn't wait to see the driver climb back into his car. She was already heading for the door to her home. Not fancy. Not glamorous. Just a standard two-bedroom house with a sweeping front porch and colorful pentas in the flowerbeds. Their scent teased her nose as she rushed up the steps and headed for the door. In moments, she was inside. Safe.

Her first order of business was to kick off the shoes. To stalk barefoot across her floor. Would Archer take the bait that she'd left for him? She'd given a fake name and number at the auction. The number would link to the cell phone she'd gotten just for use with Archer and—

A hard knock shook her front door.

She spun around. Frowned. The driver? Had she left something in his limo? Delilah hurried toward the door. Pressed her nose to the wood and looked through the peephole.

When she'd come inside, she'd automatically flipped on her porch light. It shone down—not on the limo driver—but on Archer Radcliffe.

Oh, no.

He knocked again.

She grabbed for her entrance table. Took out the item she needed from the top drawer, put it behind her back, and only then did she swing open the door. "Stalker much?"

He smiled at her. That smile of his sent an icy shiver right down her spine. "Hello, wicked stepsister."

"What are you doing here?"

His hand lifted.

She tensed.

But when his fingers unfurled, Delilah just saw her driver's license. How in the hell had he gotten that?

"Much better than a glass slipper. It conveniently contains your address." His head cocked. "By the way, what's behind your back?"

Her breath was coming too fast. Too hard. Archer Radcliffe—the monster in the dark—was right in front of her. They were alone. He didn't have his guards or his friends or his power to protect him.

"Delilah..." He seemed to taste her name. "I found you."

"Yes," she agreed. "You did." And then she brought her right hand up from behind her back—the hand that gripped her gun.

She pointed the weapon straight at him.

CHAPTER THREE

Archer looked at the gun, then back up at Delilah's face. The gun was trembling because she was trembling. And for an instant, he'd caught the flash of fear in her bright eyes before Delilah had carefully schooled away that emotion. "I have to tell you," he said, quite seriously, "you are fascinating to me."

A furrow appeared between her brows. "When a woman aims a gun at you, it shouldn't fascinate you. If you're smart, it should terrify you."

Fair enough. "Consider me terrified."

"Is *everything* a joke to you?"

He advanced on her. "Hardly."

"*Stop.*"

"Are you going to shoot me?" He didn't stop, not until the gun was pressed to his chest. "I have to warn you, things will get messy if you fire. This close, my blood will go all over you. It will also splash off these pretty white walls of yours."

Her lips parted. Now wasn't the time to notice how plump and luscious her lips were. But, dammit, he noticed.

"You're crazy," she breathed.

Perhaps. "I have my lawyer running a background check on you even as we, ah, speak." *Or as I stand here with a gun at my chest.* A turn that he had not expected this night to take. "Oz knows I'm here. Not like I left without telling anyone where I was going. If I turn up dead, I'm afraid you'll go to jail." A sad sigh. "You'll spend the rest of your life locked away. An utter waste if you ask me. Someone as gorgeous as you are shouldn't be locked away from the world."

"I won't go to jail if it's self-defense," she returned without missing a beat. "A stranger followed me home. Pushed his way inside my house. You *are* inside right now."

He was. "I'm no threat to you."

She laughed. A mocking sound. "So you always stalk women? Steal their driver's licenses? Show up in the middle of the night on their doorsteps?"

No, that wasn't his typical routine. "I want to offer you a job."

Delilah squinted at him.

"I'd be happy to tell you about the benefits and salary package, but how about we lower the gun first, hmm? My fascination is starting to wear a bit." He kept his tone mild, but his body was tense. If he thought that she was going to pull that trigger, he'd have to take the weapon. He prepared to—

"*I'm* not a killer." Delilah lowered the gun.

But the tension he'd felt had just gotten all the worse because there had been no mistaking the emphasis she'd put on the *I'm*. Obviously, he knew exactly what the lovely Delilah was implying. *As if she was the first.* "You shouldn't believe every story that you hear."

"I don't." She had the gun at her side.

"So what...you think I'm the big, bad beast?" He smiled.

She didn't. "Yes. I think you're Archer Radcliffe. A man with more money that God. A man who was linked to the disappearance of his fiancée two years ago. All the evidence points to you as being guilty as hell when it comes to her, but here you are, standing in my house, uninvited, and making me feel not the least bit reassured by you."

He looked over his shoulder. The door was still open. "Does it make you feel safer to have it open?"

"Why are you here?"

He turned his focus back to her. "You're an actress."

"Excuse me?"

"Everything you said and did in the ballroom—then later at the auction—it was all designed to capture my attention. You could not have played the scenes more perfectly. I do applaud your talent." He was also sure that when Oz was done digging, his lawyer would turn up intel to show that Delilah Darrow was quite the skilled actress.

"You think that tonight was all some elaborate show?"

It would be nice to shut the door. To sit on her overstuffed couch. To relax. Actually...fuck it. He strolled toward the couch. Unknotted his tie. Tossed aside his coat. Made himself comfortable.

"What in the hell are you doing?" Delilah didn't move from her position near the door. The still *open* door.

She should close it. Trouble could walk in at any moment.

Oh, wait. I already did walk in.

Archer rolled back his shoulders. "I know about acting. I have to do it every damn day. Between you and me, playing the dick gets old. But hey, if it's the image people want, you have to give it to them, am I right?" A long exhale. "Maybe that's why I can see you so well for what you are. We're the same."

"We are *nothing* alike." A lift of her chin. A narrowing of her gorgeous eyes. Blue eyes. Electric blue. When he'd looked up and found her gaze on him, it had been as if he'd taken a punch to the gut.

Now probably wasn't the time to tell her how incredible he found her eyes to be. Especially when she huffed out a breath—

And dramatically announced, "We're not alike because, for one thing, no one suspects me of murder."

"Yet," he couldn't resist saying. "No one suspects you of murder *yet*. But you *are* the one holding the gun so who knows how this night will play out?"

She inhaled sharply, and when she did, the bodice of her dress lifted up—moving those truly fabulous breasts of hers to optimum temptation level.

But tonight wasn't about temptation. No matter how interested one part of his anatomy might be. His dick was way too focused on Delilah. "I'm not a killer."

She merely lifted an eyebrow. A cute, elegant arch.

"Someone hired you tonight. Someone who wanted you to get close to me and...what, exactly?" It wasn't as if this was the first time someone had tried sneaking in his life. PIs and paparazzi had dodged him for months after Vanessa had vanished. "Learn all my secrets?"

"Do you have secrets to learn?"

Of course, he did. So many secrets that sometimes, it felt as if they were suffocating him. "Everyone has secrets. I'm sure you keep plenty close to your heart."

She swallowed. "No one hired me."

Hmm. Those words seemed to hold the ring of honesty. Intriguing. "So you just set on your own to hunt me? What, were you bored and looking for some entertainment?"

She gave a little start at the word *hunt*.

He decided to focus on that tell. "You're some sort of vigilante? You think it's your job to take down the big, bad Archer Radcliffe?"

Slowly, she shut the front door. The soft *click* seemed overly loud. Her fingers flipped the lock.

So you feel safe being locked in with me?

Delilah strolled toward him. It was in that moment that he realized she'd lost her shoes. She was smaller, more delicate, and she also had the most adorable toes—and toenails topped with black polish.

He was staring down at her toes when Delilah asked, "Are you bad?"

More than you realize. His gaze slid up her body. "We're all a little bad. But I'm not a killer." He let those words sink in and then added, "And you're going to help me prove that."

She stared at him with eyes that *couldn't* be real. Had to be contacts, right? Before he could ask, she threw back her head and laughed. The laughter was rich and warm and Archer found himself leaning forward. Sitting on the edge of the couch as that warm sound seemed to draw him closer to her.

"Oh, Archer...only in your *dreams* would I help you."

Funny she should mention dreams. He had the feeling she'd be starring in quite a few of his.

"It's a win, win offer for you." *My mysterious lady.* Soon, he'd have every bit of information available on her. "I will give you the chance to have an all-access pass into my life. You can search my home and do whatever snooping you want to your heart's content."

Her head tilted. "You can't be serious."

He was. Desperate times and all that. Not that he let his desperation show. He never did. As he'd told her, he had a role to play. He was the controlling, arrogant bastard. A true dick. "I am basically always serious. Ask any of my associates." He didn't say friends. He didn't have friends. Not even Oz counted as a *friend.* "I have need of someone with your skill set."

She put the gun onto a nearby table, evidently deciding he wasn't a threat. Or at least, not a threat at the moment. "What skills would those be?"

"You can act like you want me."

A faint stiffening of her body. "Is that something you need? A woman to *pretend* that she desires you? You're that hard up?"

Currently, he was hard, but that was a different story. "Women are attracted to me, whether they think I'm the devil or not. Having a few billion in the bank helps with that situation. I've found that if you have enough money, most people don't give a damn about what you've done."

She rolled her eyes. "How wonderful for you."

He would *not* smile at her. And the fact that she was obviously not impressed with anything about him, including his money? *Makes you sexy as sin, Delilah.* "You look right."

Her stare shot to him. "Excuse me?"

"Oh, come on." He motioned toward her. "Don't act like you didn't dress with the plan of being the perfect woman to capture my attention. You *look* like the women who are photographed on my arm. You'll fit in. Be the perfect camouflage."

"You *are* a total asshole."

"I've been told that before." He waited a beat. "But what I am not...is a killer. Despite speculation to the contrary." He let his gaze dart around the house. Nice furniture. Not expensive, but attractive. Homey. A few framed photographs, including one on the mantel of a younger Delilah—he could see the bright blue eyes from across the room.

So...not contacts.

In the photo, Delilah had her arm thrown around the shoulders of another—

Delilah stepped into his line of sight. "A lot of people think for certain that you murdered Vanessa Byron."

"And you're one of those people." A nod. "That why you took the acting job? Tell me, was it Vanessa's sister who hired you? She's the one who pops up in the news every few weeks, screaming that I used my money to get away with murder."

"I told you already, no one hired me."

So she wasn't in the mood for truth. "That's disappointing." It was. He rose, slowly. Closed in on her. Without the shoes, he towered over her much smaller frame. "If we're going to work together, we need honesty between us." He stopped about a foot away from Delilah. Her sweet smell flooded his nostrils.

Good enough to eat.

His nostrils flared. "We'll be lying to the rest of the world, but in order for the con to work, we have to be truthful with each other."

"I do not understand you."

He reached into his pocket. Pulled out his card. "It's late. I don't want to risk you pulling a gun on me again." *And I want to get that file on you before I say anything else.* "Come to my office tomorrow at ten. I'll explain everything."

She looked at the card, then at his face.

"Take it," he urged. "Promise, I won't bite."

She grabbed for the card. Their fingers tangled and that electric surge fired through him once again.

"Another reason why you are perfect," he murmured. "I don't have to fake it. When I tell the world it's hard to keep my hands off you, I'll mean those words." The fact that his desire for her was real would help to sell the story.

Delilah snatched the card away from him. "What do you want from me?"

"Come see me tomorrow. Find out." His stare dropped to her mouth. Utterly delectable. "I'll protect you," he heard himself say. "But it will be dangerous. You need to know that. You'll be putting yourself in the killer's crosshairs."

Her lips parted. She backed up a step. "What?"

"Tomorrow." *Leave.* Because if he didn't leave...he could feel his control cracking. A situation that never, ever occurred. He didn't lose control. Didn't let his mask fall. He handled his business. He got shit done. Nothing—no one— touched him. "Ten o'clock. If you're not there, then I can assure you that you will never have access to my life again. Whatever grand plan you were working, you'll just have to consider it a failure." He turned away. Headed for the door.

"What if the only grand plan I had was to push you into donating more money to charity? Not like I did anything illegal. I made some bids. You bid higher. Big deal."

They both knew much more had gone down. Once more, he heard himself say, "Fascinating." He wasn't sure he'd ever met anyone quite like her.

That's why she will be perfect. He flipped the lock. Turned the knob but didn't leave. "She wasn't my fiancée."

"Excuse me?"

"The media got that wrong. *You* have it wrong. I never intended to marry Vanessa Bryon. In fact, we broke up shortly before her disappearance."

"Uh, that *doesn't* make you look any less guilty."

What in the hell will? But he didn't ask that question because he knew the answer. Finding out what had really happened to Vanessa— finding the person who had really hurt her—*that* would finally clear his name. "Make sure to turn on the alarm when I leave," Archer advised her. "You never know who's waiting in the dark." He left. Didn't look back. If he looked back, he might do something absolutely foolish.

Like try to pull her into his arms.

Like kiss her.

***

Delilah slammed the door shut behind Archer. Her heart raced, and her fingers trembled as she secured the lock *and* the alarm system.

He'd followed her home.

He'd left her driver's license on the table. She'd slammed his business card down on top of it moments before. Her body felt revved up as adrenaline poured through her.

He hadn't threatened her. He'd seen through her lies but hadn't seemed the least bit angry. As for the job offer, what in the heck had that been about?

She peeked out of her window. Saw him strolling down the sidewalk. He moved easily, as if he didn't have a care in the world. A long, black car waited at the end of the drive, idling. The driver had been out there the entire time?

You never know who's waiting in the dark.

No, indeed, you didn't. Delilah didn't move until the long, black car pulled away from her house. The breath she'd been holding released on a sigh. Even though he was gone, she swore that she could still *feel* Archer in the house.

I pulled a gun on Archer Radcliffe. And he'd...offered her a job?

What. In. The. Hell?

Not the reaction she'd expected from him. She made her way to the bedroom. Sat down at her desk and fired up her computer. Her fingers poised over the keyboard as the events of the night ran through her head again and again.

It didn't take long for her to navigate her way to the location of her private group. She didn't even get to post a message before the first DM appeared.

Did he take the bait?

She'd been the bait. Her aim had been to capture Archer's attention. Considering he'd shown up at her house, yes, she'd say he'd taken the bait. But he'd also taken control. A very, very dangerous thing. Her profile on him had indicated that Archer was a control freak. A man who never let emotion deter him from his goal.

A man who had cold-bloodedly killed his fiancée?

I never intended to marry Vanessa Bryon. In fact, we broke up shortly before her disappearance.

Delilah stared at the screen. Her fingers typed out a response. *Consider the bait taken.*

Except, he'd been the one to give her the business card. To dangle a partnership, of sorts, right in her face. He knew she suspected him. The whole *world* suspected him. Suspected him. Feared him. Still needed him because people didn't turn their backs on a man with that much money.

No wonder he goes nearly everywhere with his lawyer. Just one of the many guards who were always close to Archer. In order to get to the truth she sought, Delilah had to get past the guards. She had to get close to him.

He was offering her an all-access pass. Because he thought he could manipulate her. Silly man. She'd built her life on manipulation.

Consider the bait taken. She'd be at the meeting tomorrow. And if he wanted to *pay* her to take him down, she'd take that cash. If he turned out to be guilty, then she'd take his freedom.

And no slow, sexy smile was going to stop her. After all, the devil was supposed to be sexy. Seductive. Even as he led you down a path of destruction...

Delilah wasn't in the mood to be destroyed.

***

Two hours later...

Delilah jerked upright in bed. Her heart raced, and a fine sheen of sweat coated her body. Her hands grabbed for the sheets.

The dream had been so real. It had shattered her straight to her core. She could still feel little after-shocks rushing through her. She had nightmares all the time. Side-effect of the job. And her past. But...

But this hadn't been a nightmare. Even though it had starred a monster.

Slowly, she eased back down into the bed. She could still feel a quiver in her core.

A freaking sex dream. An unbelievably good, body-shaking dream.

Her eyes closed.

And Archer's slow smile flashed through her mind once more.

CHAPTER FOUR

She wasn't an actress. At least, not a professional one. Archer sat behind his desk, his hands gripping the arms of his chair, as Casey, his assistant, led Delilah Darrow into his office.

She wore black today. Black blouse. Form-fitting black pants. Black heels. Her hair was loose around her shoulders and those electric eyes of hers met his without any hesitation.

Just like before, his reaction to her was instantaneous. His dick immediately hardened.

His enemies had often said that he had ice that flooded through his veins. That he didn't get emotional about anything. That, of course, went along with the story that circulated—the story that said he'd cold-bloodedly murdered his fiancée. *Only she wasn't my fiancée.* But everyone seemed to believe that he'd walked up to her, maybe sliced her throat, and then took his time disposing of her body. He'd committed the perfect murder because he hadn't let emotions get involved.

Vanessa Byron had supposedly been threatening him with a scandal. He'd made the problem disappear. Just as he'd made her disappear.

"Do you need anything else, Mr. Radcliffe?" His assistant looked at Archer, then motioned toward Delilah. "Uh, miss, would you like some coffee?"

"I'm fine." She didn't take the seat across from the desk. Instead, she moved to stare out at the window. "Killer view."

Archer felt his lips curl. "Nothing else, Casey. Please just see to it that I'm not disturbed."

"Absolutely." He hurriedly backed out.

Casey was still relatively new. His last assistant had run away about a month ago because...working for a murderer had just become far too stressful for Tammy. She'd told him those exact words. Told the whole company as she'd screamed them at the top of her lungs.

But she hadn't seemed to care that he might be a murderer when she'd tried to seduce him. She'd only cared when he rejected her.

He was so over this shit.

He swung his chair toward Delilah. "I wasn't sure if you'd appear today."

"Well, I figured if I didn't show up, you'd just pop up on my doorstep again. I'm trying to cut down on unexpected late-night visitors." She turned to face him. "But I don't like to waste time, so...?"

"You're not an actress."

Her nose scrunched. Oddly cute. "Did I claim to be one?"

"I made an assumption. My mistake. But other than doing some theater in high school..."

Her shoulders stiffened.

"You've had no professional training," he concluded. His right hand lifted. Tapped against the edge of his desk. "Tell me, how fun was it to perform the role of Desdemona?"

"Getting strangled by my lover? Not exactly a highlight but I did get a standing ovation."

Damn. She was going to keep him on his toes. He'd thought the casual comment would throw her off guard, make her realize he now knew far too much about her, but she'd just shrugged like it was nothing.

She needed to stop fascinating him.

"Am I supposed to be impressed that you know how to use the Internet and do a search on someone?" Her eyes widened. She made a clicking sound with her tongue. "Shocking. What a genius you must be."

"My search was a bit more thorough."

"Of course. Because if you aren't throwing your money around to tear into an unsuspecting woman's life for shits and giggles, then what is the point of being so wealthy?"

"You don't like me."

Another shrug.

"You think I'm a killer." His hand moved away from the desk. Clenched near his lap. *Like I don't get accused of this crap every other day.* "Have you and your friends decided that I'm next on your hit list?"

Caution stole across her features. "My friends?"

"Um. That online team you have. You and your group, sitting at your computers, trying to solve crimes. I guess I was the next name on your list?"

She surged toward him, then seemed to catch herself. "You're mocking me."

"And you're hunting me. Hardly something that I find amusing. Especially when you are wasting my time."

Her mouth opened. Closed. Her delicate nostrils flared. "You're the one who asked me to show up today. If anyone is having time wasted, it's me." Her breath came fast. A little too fast. Finally, he'd surprised her by knowing about her team. He'd have to give Oz a bonus for uncovering that particular detail.

Archer's head cocked as he studied her. "You think you can catch killers."

"I don't *think* I can. I know that I can. I've done it before. I've solved four cold cases. Cases that the cops had stopped investigating. I found the bodies. I have helped to get killers arrested. This *isn't* some game to me." Now she stalked toward him. Her hands flattened on the desk as she leaned toward him. "This is real life. *My* life."

Only the desk separated them. "This is your life because you're a reporter. You like to chase stories."

Her delicate nostrils flared once more. "I prefer the term investigative journalist."

"Um, I'm sure you do. You report under the name of Lila Darrow. Mostly web pieces. With a face like yours, I'm surprised that you aren't on every TV in the country."

Anger flashed on her face. "I'm not looking for a spotlight. I just want to do my job."

Her job. Now they were getting someplace. "Yes, about that…"

"My background made me a prime candidate to focus on true crime. In college, I studied coursework in psychology and criminal justice. I—"

"You're obsessed with killers. You like to pick apart their minds. See what drove them to commit crimes. You try to understand their motivation and behavior. Try to see if they're sane or just completely crazy. And you do all of this under the guise of writing your stories." He leaned toward her but didn't rise from his chair. Not yet. "You were examining your killers. Learning all about them, writing their stories, and then, bam, you started hunting them."

"I started hunting the missing. *They* are my focus. When I find the missing, they just happened to lead me and my—lead *me* to the killers."

Interesting. She'd almost said "lead me and my team"—he was sure of it, but she'd caught herself. "So for you, it's about the missing?" And finally, he rose.

She stiffened but didn't back up.

The damn desk was in the way. He wanted to be closer to her. But when he was close, Archer had to fight the urge to touch her. When he'd danced with her the previous night, his fingers had skimmed against the skin of her back. Her skin had felt like the softest silk.

Be careful. Skin that soft will bruise easily.

"I want the missing to come home," she responded doggedly.

He was sure that she did. "Because your sister never came home?"

Red stained her cheeks. "Do you think bringing up my sister is going to hurt me? I knew before I walked in that you would find out about her. When you search my name, the first hit has to be about her."

Yes, it did. The photograph he'd glimpsed before on her mantel—a smiling Delilah with her arm thrown around the shoulders of a blonde who'd appeared to be about the same age. Delilah's fraternal twin.

Layla Darrow had disappeared five years ago. Despite a massive search, she'd never been found.

"I'm sorry about your sister," he said gruffly. "Losing her must have hurt very much."

Her lashes—thick and dark—swept down to cover her eyes. "I'll find her one day."

Yes, he believed that she would. "I can help finance that search."

Her lashes flew back up.

"As you have pointed out, I have way too much cash. I can help finance your search efforts."

"Are you trying to bribe me? Is that what you did before? Bribe people so your problems vanished?"

She was so fucking gorgeous. And she clearly had the lowest possible opinion of him. An opinion she wasn't hiding. "Are you going to be a problem for me?" he asked coolly.

"One hundred percent. Consider yourself warned."

"I'm shaking." He wasn't. If anything, he was like a damn moth drawn to the flame that was Delilah.

Those bright eyes of hers narrowed. "You will be shaking."

He put his hands on the desk. Settled them right next to each of hers. But he didn't touch her. He wasn't ready for that electric jolt again. Not until they had an agreement in place. "It's not a bribe. It's a payment for a job. You shouldn't run around accusing people of crimes like bribery without evidence. You might piss off the wrong person with an allegation like that."

Her plump lips pressed together.

"You look at me, and you see a killer." He knew exactly what she saw when she stared at him. Unfortunate. Too many others saw the same thing. Archer was tired of that shit.

"You don't know what I see," Delilah fired back.

"You have me in your sights. You're here to take me down." Not like she'd be the first. The others had failed. So would the lovely Delilah.

But she shook her head. "No, I'm here to find Vanessa. That's my first step. I told you, I look for the missing."

"And you think you can find her by getting close to me? By wearing a sexy dress and putting yourself in my path?" He raised his eyebrows and let the doubt seep into his voice. "Come now, that is hardly—"

"You followed me from the ball. You couldn't let me get away. How do you know that is not exactly what I intended to happen?"

His gaze sharpened on her.

"I don't normally wear dresses that cost more than my first car—that was a loaner last night—but I needed it because I knew you would only be drawn to a certain type of woman."

He would have been drawn to her no matter what she wore. Fuck the dress. "Not true at all."

"I had to wear the right dress to get inside the big, fancy party. Not like I had one of those thousand-dollar invitations. You were there. I had to be there, too. Then I had to make sure I captured your attention." She glanced around the office. "I'd consider it captured."

Damn straight it was. Archer was completely locked on her.

Her bright gaze returned to him. "You like a challenge. I gave you one from the first minute I spoke. I made sure you were amped up and ready for the auction. Drove your emotions to the edge. You see, the rest of the world may think that ice runs through your veins, but I know differently."

"And how the hell do you know that?" Like he didn't realize what the others said about him. *Ice cold bastard.*

Her hand lifted. Her palm pressed to his cheek.

The damn jolt slid through him. His eager cock surged toward her. *She is so much more dangerous than I expected.* Or maybe he'd just gone too long without a lover. But it was hard to let anyone close when you knew everyone was working an angle.

Delilah offered him a tight smile. "How about we just say that I know my monsters?"

"I'm not a monster." *Is that what she thinks I am?*

"You're a passionate man, Archer. You do value control above all else. But when your control breaks, I suspect it can be a terrifying sight to witness."

"If you're afraid of me, why are you touching me right now?" Why the hell was he enjoying her touch so much?

A sharp knock sounded at the door. Before he could say anything, it flew open, and Oz popped his head inside. "Archer, we need to go over—*oh.*"

Archer and Delilah were inches apart. She was cupping his check. For all the world, he knew it looked as if they were about to kiss. Behind Oz, he could see Casey's straining features.

"I told him you were busy!" Casey called out. "So sorry, boss!"

"Normally, he's never too busy for me." Oz grimaced. "But I can see this is a different circumstance. My mistake. I'll come back." He yanked the door closed.

Perfect. Archer could not have set the scene better if he'd tried. But he didn't let his satisfaction show. He was still working an angle with Delilah. There was no point in revealing all of his cards to her yet.

Her hand slowly slid away from him. For an instant, he could have sworn he felt the warmth of her touch linger on his skin. When you were cold all the damn time, you enjoyed a bit of warmth.

"One hundred thousand dollars," he said deliberately.

She blinked. "That's what you paid for the Tear last night."

It was. It was also... "That's what I'll pay you."

Delilah took an unsteady step back. "I'm trying to make certain that I follow along correctly here. Are you attempting to *buy* me?"

"I'm offering you payment for a job. I told you, I can help you continue that fun crime-solving gig you enjoy so much."

"Don't mock me." Flat. For the first time, real emotion broke through her voice. "Nothing I do is a joke. Real lives are on the line. Real people."

People like your sister? He nodded. "Fair enough. I apologize."

Her gaze turned suspicious.

"You wanted to catch my attention last night. You made yourself into—what did you call it—"

"I became a woman you'd want."

He didn't touch that statement, but the truth was...*I would want you anywhere, any way. Anytime.* "Others saw the same thing when we were together last night. They saw our attraction."

"Our?" She pounced on that word choice.

He had to laugh. "Really? Going to pretend that you didn't feel it, too? You might hate my guts, but when I had you on the dance floor, you trembled in my arms." He waited for a denial.

None came. Interesting. It would work well for him if she didn't deny her attraction. *And this way, I know it's not one-sided.* Not that he intended to do anything about that desire. As alluring as the fantasy of fucking her on his desk was...there were other matters that had to come first.

But she'd be incredible spread out for me on—

"Get to the point." Delilah lifted a slender wrist and stared at her watch. "I have other things to do today. I can't just entertain a bored billionaire forever."

She had bite, and he enjoyed it. "You're perfect. You're exactly who I need at my side. For one hundred thousand dollars, I want you to pretend to be involved with me."

"Excuse me?" Her mouth had dropped.

He waited for her to pick up her lovely jaw from the floor. "You heard me. I spoke quite clearly. You'll pretend to be involved with me."

"Are you that hard up for a date? Granted, you haven't been tied romantically to anyone in quite some time, but I was sure you picked up the random one-night stand here and there."

"I manage to have sex just fine when I want it, thanks. This isn't about sex." He let his gaze slide over her delectable body. "Sorry to disappoint you."

"Disappoint me? *Disappoint me?*" Her voice rose.

It's nice to see her lose control. "I said I wanted you to pretend to be involved with me. Pretend. I don't pay for sex. Never have. Never will."

"Tell that to the bimbos who let you throw diamonds at them."

His jaw locked. "If we have sex, it will have nothing to do with the current arrangement we are making."

"We are *not* having sex."

Archer shrugged, as if the matter held no importance for him. "I need everyone else to think that we are passionately involved. That I need to have you close to me at all times. You will move into my house. You'll accompany me to every important function I attend."

Delilah nibbled her lower lip. "You understand this isn't normal, correct?"

Nothing about his world was normal. "In exchange for doing this, you'll have an all-access pass to my life." He turned away from her. Walked to the window. His hands fell down to his sides. "You can poke and prod and do your best to find evidence that proves I'm a cold-blooded killer."

A shocked silence filled the room behind him.

"But you won't find that evidence," he continued as he stared outside. "Because despite what you think—what so many think—I didn't hurt Vanessa. I have no idea where she is." Though he would very much like to find her.

"You were the only suspect named by the police."

He could see the grim reflection of his smile in the glass. "Come now, you know I was only a *person of interest*. That's not the same as being a suspect."

"Isn't it?"

"The person who hurt her is still out there."

"How do you know she *was* hurt? If you didn't do it, then maybe she just ran away...wasn't that one theory you told the police?"

How he knew she'd been hurt—he would get to that momentarily. "I want to draw out the person who made Vanessa vanish." He turned back toward Delilah. "I thought you might be interested in assisting with that process."

Her hair slid over her shoulders as her head tilted. "How will you draw this individual out?"

"By having a new victim for him." He stared at her. Waited.

Her brow furrowed. "Me?"

"Yes. I have an idea about why Vanessa was taken. And it is a whole lot less about her and more about me."

Delilah rolled her eyes. "Oh, shocker. Everything is about the billionaire...in his own mind."

He let that jibe pass. "If the attacker thinks that I have grown close to someone else, if he thinks that I'm moving forward, it is my belief that he will come out again. He wants to hurt me. That's my theory. To hurt me..." His sentence trailed away as he waited for her to connect the dots.

"He...what? Targets people you're close to?" Her laughter was bitter. "Nice. Way to make yourself look all innocent and tortured."

He returned to his desk. Opened the top drawer. Reached for a manila file. He pulled out the paper inside and slid it across the surface of his desk.

Delilah sidled closer. Frowned down and read the words that had been typed on the page... "You don't get to love." Her head whipped up. "What the hell is this?"

"It's a note I found on my bed after I saw Vanessa for the last time."

Her jaw tightened. "This wasn't in any of the reports I read from the police station—"

And how had she gotten access to those? A question for another day. He had to get her cooperation first, then he'd see just what all Delilah and her team had discovered. "That's because the police don't know about it."

"Uh, why not?"

"Because it was printed on my personal computer. At my home. Because my fingerprints were the only ones on it. Because the cops would have thought that I'd just created the damn thing myself to throw off suspicion."

"*Did you?*"

"No." Curt.

"How do you know only your fingerprints were on it?"

"Because I had it checked."

He put the paper back in the envelope. Carefully replaced the envelope in the drawer. Shut it.

"Is...is this why you haven't been seriously linked—romantically—to anyone since Vanessa vanished?"

One of the reasons. He nodded. "If I'm right about this—"

"If you're right, you have a stalker. A person who thinks to control everything that you do. A person who doesn't believe that you have the right to be with anyone else. A person who had access to your home."

A person who will pay. "If I'm right," he continued doggedly. "Then when I move you into my life, he'll attack."

"I'm assuming you *will* have protection on me?" Cool. Careful. "Not like I want to be the next one to vanish."

He stared into her eyes. The most incredible eyes he'd ever seen. "That won't happen." Gruff. There were a few important differences between her and Vanessa.

Difference number one...*Delilah will know a killer is coming.*

Difference two...*Delilah won't be fucking around on me.*

Archer cleared his throat. "It's win, win for you. You get an all-access pass to my life, and you also get one hundred grand. If this is some con I'm working, surely an investigative journalist like yourself will figure things out fairly quickly. You'll catch me in a lie. You'll find evidence I hid. But if you don't find that evidence, if you see that I'm being truthful with you..." He continued to hold her stare. "Then maybe you and I can make this partnership work. Maybe we can find the attacker. Maybe we can find Vanessa. Maybe we can make this all end."

Deliberately, Archer moved around the desk and closed the distance between them. He saw her shoulders tense, but she didn't retreat. He kept closing in until he was right before her. His hand lifted. "Do we have a deal?"

Her gaze darted to his hand. Up to his face. He didn't let his expression alter. He'd grown far too skilled at hiding his emotions. He didn't sound as if it mattered to him whether she took the deal or not. Didn't act as if his future hung in the balance. He merely waited, with his hand outstretched...

Until her fingers curled around his. Until that electric jolt fired through his body.

"We have a deal," Delilah agreed.

CHAPTER FIVE

Had she made the worst mistake of her life? Possibly. Time would certainly tell. If she'd entered into an agreement with a killer, Delilah knew that the truth would be revealed very, very soon.

It wasn't as if she planned to let her guard down around Archer. Quite the contrary. She'd be extra careful with him.

Delilah began to tug her hand back.

His grip tightened. "I will, of course, require confidentiality for the time being. Not like I want you going out and posting online about your new undercover assignment."

"I plan to save my reporting until the end of our relationship."

"Relationship?" Archer repeated as his brows rose.

"You know exactly what I mean." His hand was strong, and she could feel faint calluses along his fingertips. She hadn't expected the calluses, not from a guy like him. He sat in this fancy office, in that leather chair, all day. Everyone catered to him.

I won't be like that.

"We do need the world to believe we have a relationship. So a certain amount of public displays of affection will be warranted," Archer mused. His gaze turned considering. "Don't worry. Nothing too extreme. If we go overboard, *then* the media will suspect something is off."

Because he was always so careful. So in control. No sloppy PDA for him. A careful holding of the hands. An arm around the shoulders. Not like he'd ever be caught nearly fucking someone in a hallway. Hardly the style of Archer Radcliffe. "Don't worry. I can handle PDAs." Now she tugged again to free her hand. "No one else is here right now, though, so how about letting me go?"

He looked down at her hand. Almost seemed surprised to still be holding her. Slowly, he let her go. As her hand pulled back, his fingers slid along her inner wrist. A careful caress. One that had her breath giving a fast jerk.

She immediately put her hands behind her back.

"You should pack up whatever you need from your rental house." He turned away. Paced back around his desk. "You've only been there a few weeks, so it's not like you have a sentimental attachment to the place."

She didn't have a sentimental attachment to many things. "You've obviously got a top-notch investigative team at your beck and call. How come they haven't found this mystery guy for you?"

He glanced back at her. "They tried and failed. I thought it was time to attempt a different method. Then you ever-so-conveniently walked into my life in that delectable dress of yours."

Her chin lifted. "When did you realize I was working you? Was it when I started bidding?" Just so she could know for next time. Delilah liked to learn from her mistakes.

"It was the moment you walked into my line of vision. I knew immediately that you weren't like the other women in the ballroom."

She stiffened. He'd insulted her? "If you think I'm not good enough to belong with that crowd, then how the hell do you plan to pass me off as your new love interest?"

Now he whirled to fully face her again. "I never said you weren't good enough. What gave you that idea?"

He'd given her that idea. Delilah glowered.

"Oh, right." A nod. "I said you weren't like the others. You misunderstood what I meant. Your gaze wasn't calculating. You didn't have boredom and pretentiousness clinging to you like cheap diamonds."

"Wow." Delilah rocked back on her heels. "Someone doesn't like his friends."

"Those people weren't my friends. They were the individuals who happened to be in my world."

She tucked that tidbit away for further study—later. "I'll pack my stuff. Then what?" Deliberately, she kept her voice all casual and relaxed. In truth, she felt as if she might jump from her skin at any moment. He didn't realize what he was doing, the opportunity he was providing, but it was far too good to pass up.

A chance to get straight into his life? To talk to everyone close to him? Everyone who'd been close to Vanessa? Oh, hell, yes. And he wanted to *pay* her? One hundred grand?

She'd take the money. Take the chance. And if he turned out to be guilty, she'd be taking him to jail. This wasn't amateur hour. She wasn't some dewy-eyed co-ed with dreams of changing the world. *Been there, done that.* That girl had died a hard death...

The same day her sister had vanished.

Delilah had worked hard—damn hard—to study and learn and master as much as she could. She'd trained with police, shadowed a PI for half a year, taken multiple martial arts classes, spent two months tracking with a bounty hunter. Anything—everything. She'd wanted to learn as much as she could. She had contacts all over the US. All over the world.

Innocence wasn't something she could afford in this world, so she'd given that up long ago. She knew you couldn't trust people. That you could take nothing—no one—at face value. Her guard would not be lowered.

She *would* get this case closed.

Ever since her sister had vanished, Delilah had worked to bring home as many of the missing as possible. To date, she'd brought home two women, one man, and one boy.

They'd all been dead. But the families had still needed the closure, even if finding the bodies had broken Delilah's heart.

"I'll give you until six to pack, then I'll come to pick you up tonight. Do you have another suitable dress?"

"Suitable...for what?"

"The opera."

"We're going on a date?" That was the first step?

"We're going to catch attention. There is a special showing tonight. If you don't have a dress, I'll send one over for you."

"I'm fine. Thanks. I'm sure I have something that will work." Maybe. Possibly. If she dug deeply into her closet.

A nod. "I'll send something over."

"Uh, did you *hear* me?"

"In fact, I'll make sure you have an entire new wardrobe. It will be necessary, I assure you."

"Whatever. It's your dime." He wanted to throw fancy clothes at her? *Have at it.* When they were done, she'd keep what she wanted. Sell or donate the rest. "Not worth arguing about."

He blinked.

"What?" Her eyes narrowed. "Why do you look at me like I have two heads? You do that, quite a lot."

"Just trying to figure you out."

"Good luck with that." But wasn't she doing the same thing? Trying to figure *him* out? "See you at six." She turned for the door. Took about three steps. Stopped. "You understand this is crazy?"

She *felt* him closing in behind her. "Absolutely. I'm rather surprised you agreed so easily."

Why not agree? It gave her what she wanted. He knew that. "I would have done it for fifty thousand." Delilah just tossed that out as she peered over her shoulder at him.

"And I would have easily paid two hundred grand."

Well, damn. Unwillingly, she felt her lips curve. "Next time, I'll ask for more."

His features tightened. It was a subtle, slow thing. A faint hardening near his golden eyes. A flexing along his hard jaw. A hollowing of his cheeks. "There will be no next time. You aren't vanishing."

Certainly good to know. She swallowed because her throat had suddenly become very, very dry. "Try to pick out some nice things, will you? And black is my favorite color."

"I'll remember that."

She should go. Why was she staying? She was playing him. He was playing her. The game was incredibly dangerous, and yet she felt...drawn to him. Pulled.

So bad.

She focused forward again and took more steps toward the door. Her hand reached for the doorknob.

"The show starts the moment you step foot outside this office."

"And here I thought it had already started."

"Just giving you a final chance to change your mind." Those low words almost seemed like a taunt. Or maybe they were supposed to be a warning. Either way, it didn't really matter. She'd agreed to the plan. She didn't intend to cut and run now. He'd learn that about her, soon enough. She didn't give up.

After all, it's been five years, and I'm still looking for Layla. I will never give up on her.

Delilah pulled open the door. The assistant with the stylish glasses was behind his desk, and his head immediately bobbed toward her.

But Casey Wilkins wasn't alone. The lawyer, Oz, sat on the edge of Casey's desk, swinging one Italian-leather-clad foot.

He had to know who she was. He'd been in on the research, hadn't he? One of Archer's guard dogs. So she gave him a tight smile. One that showed her teeth.

But she felt a warm hand close around her shoulder. "I can't wait to see you tonight." Archer's voice. Intimate and low. He turned her toward him. "Don't keep me waiting." And his head lowered toward hers.

Oh, damn. The show was most definitely starting. Apparently, Archer wanted his assistant to get the picture that they were a couple. Was Casey an office gossip? Was that the deal? Was—

Archer's mouth pressed to hers and her spinning thoughts just...halted.

Everything seemed to still around her. Even the air itself seemed to settle for a moment. Her body had gone tight.

His lips brushed carefully against her own, and her mouth parted.

Sell it.

Her mouth parted, and her tongue dipped out toward him. He gave a low growl in the back of his throat, and his hands slid around her. He pulled her against his body, and, oh, wow, but he must be in the mood to *sell it,* too, because she could feel the hard length of his arousal pressing up against her.

Archer Radcliffe, a man she could have sworn was made of stone, was aroused. He was holding her tightly and kissing her with an almost savage grace. Skilled and passionate, just the right touch to make her ache and need.

She was woman enough to admit that her knees felt a little jittery. She could also admit that kissing him was no hardship. In fact, this was the best kiss she'd had in ages.

And it had better not be coming from a murderer.

She jerked back at the thought. Her hand flew to her lips. Lips that were warm from his mouth. She could still taste him, dammit. To herself, she could admit that Archer tasted very, very good.

But when did I start thinking he might not be guilty?

The answer flew through her mind...

Last night.

Her breath whispered out. Her hand moved to caress his stubble-covered cheek. "Don't keep *me* waiting." With that, she turned and sashayed off. She gave her hips a little extra roll because— what the hell? Why not?

Delilah didn't glance back. She jabbed the button for the elevator. When the doors opened, the space was blessedly empty. She slipped inside. Turned and pressed her back to the wall. As the doors closed, she had a perfect view back down the corridor—back to Casey's desk. Oz still sat perched on the edge. As for Archer, his hands were shoved into the pockets of his pants and his gaze was on her.

Possessive. Almost predatory.

The doors closed.

***

"Ah, Arch? Mind if I take a moment of your time?" Oz asked, voice smooth. "Got a wee bit of business to discuss."

Archer turned back to his office. The door was open. "Come in."

"Thanks so much," Oz announced. "I think Casey was getting tired of amusing me. Later, Casey." He followed Archer inside. Shut the door.

Leaned against it.

Archer settled in behind his desk. He rolled back his shoulders.

"So..." Oz announced with a long sigh.

Archer looked up at him.

"So...are you fucking insane or what?"

CHAPTER SIX

The limo arrived at her house at exactly 5:58 p.m. A little early, but Delilah was ready. She had her rolling luggage bag—the large one—at her side and her laptop bag hung over one shoulder. She waited on the porch. Did that look too eager?

She didn't really care.

The limo driver came toward her. There was no sign of Archer.

"Hello, ma'am." The driver was young, with sandy-blond hair and a slightly crooked grin that flashed one dimple. "I'm Daniel Gates. You can call me Danny."

"Hi, Danny."

"Let me get the bags for you." He reached for her laptop.

But she shook her head. "I like to keep this one close, but I'd appreciate some help with the luggage."

"You got it." He began to wheel the luggage down the sidewalk. His curious gaze darted over her. "The, um, boss is in the limo. He was just finishing up a call."

"Sure. Totally get it. Why bother to leave the vehicle and act like a gentleman?"

Danny stopped. Gaped. "You...ah..."

She opened the back door to the limo. Peered inside. "Hmm. Seems like the phone call is over." Because Archer was reclining back against the leather. Looking as if he didn't have a care in the world.

You'd better care. "My dates usually come to the door for me," she told him crisply. "They don't just pop up in cars to collect me and wait for *me* to come to *them*."

Danny was behind her. She heard the nervous tap of his feet.

"It was a rule my dad had, you see. One that stayed with me even after he passed away." She wouldn't think about how her dad had withered right in front of her eyes after Layla's disappearance. He'd viewed himself as their protector. And to be unable to protect his daughter...Her chin rose. She was bending toward the open door and giving Archer a cold smile. "He said that any man who thought he could take out one of his daughters had damn well better walk to the porch and introduce himself."

Archer inclined his head. "My mistake. Would you like a do-over?"

She had no idea what possessed her, but Delilah heard herself say, very definitely, "Yes." With that, she turned away. Almost bumped into Danny.

He was still gaping at her. "Y-you are not like his other dates."

"God, I hope not." She nodded. "Thanks for the help with my luggage. I really do appreciate it." Then she made her way back to the porch.

She heard footsteps behind her. Not the nervous taps of Danny's feet, but the heavy, solid tread that she knew belonged to Archer. She turned on the porch. Straightened her shoulders. Put a friendly smile on her face.

Archer closed in. The sun was starting to set, and streaks of gold slid across the sky. He stalked toward her with a predatory grace. He was dressed in a tux, looking expensive and sinfully gorgeous, and she was far too conscious of her own attire. The silky dress that fluttered lightly with the faint wind. It dipped off one shoulder, and the fabric hugged her bust and waist, only to flare at her hips. The silk tumbled down her legs. Her high heels gave her a few extra inches, and she'd pulled her hair up into what she thought was a rather elegant twist. She'd had to watch the how-to video for that twist online seven times before she'd managed to perfect it.

He stopped at the end of the sidewalk. Didn't climb the three steps that led up to her porch. His head tipped back as he gazed up at her. "You look beautiful."

That was nice. Way better than him just sitting in the back of a closed limo while she scurried out to him.

"I should have brought you flowers," he said, voice roughening. "That was my mistake. Next time, I will be better prepared."

"You don't have to bring me flowers. You *do* have to get out of the damn car. I can't have my dad rolling over in his grave."

His eyelids flickered. "I'm sorry about your father."

So am I. He'd been her rock. Her gruff, tough-on-the-exterior dad who had always been a complete marshmallow to her and Layla.

That's why he blamed himself. Because he thought if he'd just—

"I think I would have liked him," Archer continued as he seemed to consider things. "No damn way I ever want my daughter rushing off into a car with some guy I haven't even seen."

"When I was sixteen, my date came to pick me up for prom." Why was she telling him this? But she was. And he was listening, raptly. "My dad was sitting on the porch swing and cleaning his gun."

Archer's lips curled.

"My date didn't get within two feet of me all night. He wouldn't even dance with me." The memory was so clear. "When I got home that night, my dad was still waiting up. He always waited up for us to come home."

But Layla never did.

Sadness pulled at her. "You can be so careful. You can try to make all the right choices, but bad things will still happen no matter what precautions you take and blaming yourself just doesn't do any good."

His hand reached out. Caught hers. His grip was careful. Comforting. Since when was Archer the comforting type? But he was—or rather, he was trying, with her.

For her?

"Do you blame yourself?" he asked softly.

For Layla. And for her dad. Yes, she did. Because she was a lot like her father. Delilah cleared her throat. "I don't like flowers. You don't need to bring me those." She hadn't planted the ones that were around her house. They'd already been there when she moved in. Delilah didn't have a green thumb. Flowers died on her, and dead flowers just reminded her of all the flowers that had come to the house—for days, for weeks—after Layla vanished. Flowers that had withered as the time passed.

"If you don't want flowers, then I'll bring you diamonds."

She could only shake her head. "It's not real, Archer." Soft. For his ears alone. "You're already paying me plenty. You don't have to—"

"It has to look real, doesn't it?"

Yes, she supposed that it did.

"Delilah." He said her name like a caress.

A little shiver shot over her.

"Would you please do me the honor of attending the opera with me tonight?"

"I would." She eased down the steps. He kept his grip on her hand, and she didn't mind. That little jolt had hit her when they touched, and she knew they were probably going to have to address that issue, sooner or later.

The issue that when we touch, we're electric.

The attraction between them was undeniable. Sex would probably be fantastic. *Not* that she intended to find out. The kiss they'd shared at his office—a kiss she'd *refused* to think about during the day—had left her more shaken than she cared to admit. A simple kiss wasn't supposed to make your whole body quake. It wasn't supposed to drive your hormones into overdrive.

It had.

Danny held the limo door open for them. She slid inside. Finally took off her laptop bag. Archer followed her in and then settled right beside her. The heat of his body immediately seemed to envelop her.

Danny shut the door.

"In my defense, it was a two-million-dollar real estate deal."

She tilted her head. "If you want it to look real, you'll have to drop everything for me. That's what a man who is completely obsessed with his new lover would do, right?"

"But we both know that's never the kind of man I've been." He settled back against the seat as Danny got the car moving. "I'm not exactly known for being ruled by passion."

"No, you're supposed to be cold-blooded."

He laughed. A rough, deep rumble that made her stomach twist.

"I suppose," Archer returned slowly, "that's one kind way of putting things."

"And an unkind way?"

"I'm a bastard who doesn't care about anyone or anything but myself. I fuck when I feel the urge, I cut dead the people who annoy me, and I am ruthless when it comes to getting what I want. My emotions are never involved. They don't rule me. I rule them."

I cut dead the people who annoy me. She tensed. "About the cutting people dead part...That's probably not something you want to say when you're trying to convince me that you aren't guilty of being involved with your ex's disappearance."

"Like I told you before, we'd broken up before she disappeared."

Her lips parted in surprise. "You said you'd broken up *shortly* before the disappearance." A pause. "Just how shortly before?"

"The last time I saw her—that was when we broke up."

Her heart did a hard lurch in her chest.

"I didn't even tell the cops. Knew it would just make me look worse."

Oh, damn. "Why are you telling me?"

"Because I am going to be as honest with you as I can be, and in return, I want you to be honest with me. I value honesty. I don't want people close to me who are lying. I've had more than enough of that to last me a lifetime."

She wasn't lying to him...exactly. She also wasn't telling him the full truth. Delilah had an agenda that she was working, and she sure as hell wasn't magically at the point where she trusted him completely. "Honesty requires trust." She could give him that much, and he could interpret it however he liked.

His head tilted. "Then I guess I'm showing you that I trust you."

"Why? We just met. And I lied to you at the very beginning of our relationship." *Relationship* still felt odd to say.

"Yes, you did. So now I know what you look like when you lie."

Unease slithered through her. "I'm supposed to buy that you are extraordinarily good at reading people? You think you know all my tells and you know me?"

"I think I am learning a great deal about you. More every moment."

They'd gotten off topic. "Why did you and Vanessa break up?" She wanted to get back to the case. Back to their whole reason for being together.

"How many people are on your team?" he asked her.

"*Excuse me?*"

"The online group—your friends who've worked with you on the other cases you've closed. How many people are there?"

With an effort, she kept her breathing nice and slow. She was interrogating him, and, in turn, he was interrogating her. "It varies, depending on availability. Some people help a little on a case. Some help a lot. We all have other commitments. Other jobs. We do what we can as time allows."

"And who are these people?"

Tread carefully. "How about I answer your questions if you answer mine?"

He looked at his watch. She saw the flash of the glowing dial. "We have a little time before we get to the opera house."

"Why are we going on a Thursday night? I would have thought more people would be there on a Friday—"

"It's a special event tonight. VIPs only."

She huffed out a breath. "Of course. Your life is a whole VIP event."

"No, it's not."

For an instant, she could almost feel the anger in him. She inched to the side.

"You smell good," he murmured. "Like lilacs."

"How..." He was right. Her lotion had been lilac scented. "That's quite the nose you have."

"My mom had a garden when I was a kid. I'd help her plant her flowers."

The visual was just—"That's hard to imagine. The mighty Archer Radcliffe getting dirty in a garden." While she had no green thumb, apparently, Archer did. *Surprise number one.*

"My mom didn't mind dirt. And she liked being with me." Said softly. "But when the cancer got too bad, she wasn't able to go outside. So I would plant the flowers on my own, and when they bloomed, I'd take them to her so that she could see them, smell them, and smile one more time."

Delilah swallowed.

"When she lost her sense of smell—a side-effect of the treatment—she'd still just like to touch the flowers. They always made her smile."

His mother had died when Archer was ten years old. Delilah had already known that cancer had taken his mother away, but reading those facts online wasn't the same as hearing him talk about his mother's garden.

After her death, Archer's father had married three other times. Three much younger wives before he'd had a heart attack and passed away.

Archer had been twenty-one when his father died. His father had been found in a hotel room with a woman who was *not* his wife. His father's exploits had been tabloid fodder for years.

And Archer is so different. So controlled.

"I'm sorry about your mother." Her hand reached for his. Squeezed. "It sounds like you worked very hard to make her happy."

He stared down at their hands.

She probably shouldn't have touched him. She started to pull back, but his hand flipped over and caught hers. Held tight.

"Be very careful."

Delilah sucked in a breath. "Excuse me?"

He looked up at her. "Most of the stories about me are true. *Most.* I didn't hurt Vanessa. That shit isn't on me. But I am a cold-blooded bastard. Don't think I'm anything else just because you hear a sob story and you feel sorry for me."

Anger flared inside of her. "I don't feel sorry for you, and I *know* you are a bastard. You might as well have it written in neon letters on your forehead." An exhale. "But even cold-blooded bastards can love their moms. From all accounts, your mom was someone very special and kind, and I am sorry that she passed." A faint pause. "When you said you were sorry about my dad dying, I didn't immediately jump onto the 'oh, he must pity me' bandwagon, so maybe you should just settle down."

"Settle down? Right." He cleared his throat. Let her go. "I'll try to do that." He eased back into the seat. Looked out the window.

"If we're going to make this work, we need to get along."

"I don't always play well with others."

Yeah, she got that. *Big neon letters.* "I'll call you on it when you're being an asshole, and when I'm invading your space too much, you can call me on that." She knew that she could be pushy. One of her faults—and one of the reasons she'd had success as an investigative journalist.

"I don't mind you in my space." A soft, rasping admission. "Quite the opposite."

She was not sure how to respond. To get back on firmer footing, Delilah blurted, "Our Q & A session. How about we get back to that before we arrive at our destination?"

Not like they could have a lot of time left.

"Ask your questions."

"Why did you and Vanessa break up?"

"Because I found out she was fucking someone else."

That would be a reason. Check. "Who was he? How did you find out?"

"My turn."

She blinked.

"My turn to ask a question. We were going back and forth, remember?"

"Technically, mine were just follow-ups," she muttered. "Because your answer was incomplete."

Deep rumbles of laughter slid from him.

That laughter made her feel all tense and achy. No, correction, he did that.

"Who are the closest members of your team?"

She licked her lips. "It's not like we meet for coffee every Thursday. This is an online group. People use screen names. Aliases. Help comes and goes at different points."

"Yes, but this is *you*. You don't trust strangers. You would have dug into their lives and only let the people you had vetted into your inner circle. I want to know who they are. I want to know the people you rely on most."

"I'm not telling you that."

His head turned back toward her. "Because you don't trust me yet?"

"Because this is the first day of our new partnership and you want me to basically turn on people that I've worked with for years." A shake of her head. "That's not happening. That's not how I operate. I protect them. They protect me." She tensed as she waited for his anger.

Instead...

"Good answer," he murmured.

"Excuse me?"

"Will you be as protective of me, once I've proven myself to you?"

Her tongue darted out to wet her lips. "That's a second question."

"You didn't answer the first one."

He had a point. "If you prove yourself, then, yes, I will be protective of you. I tend to be protective of friends."

"Friends." He seemed to taste the word. "Is that what you think we'll be?"

The back of the massive limo suddenly seemed very, very small. The atmosphere far too thick with tension. There was a sharp awareness between them, and as she stared at him, Delilah knew she wasn't going to lie. "I very much doubt that."

"Why." Not a question. A demand.

She answered because she felt like answering. Not because he'd demanded a response. "Because I don't have sex dreams about my *friends*."

A heavy stillness came over him.

Get this conversation back on track. "That was two different questions. At least. So it's back to me. How did you know that Vanessa was cheating?"

"Because she told me. Told me that she'd finally found someone who fucked her like she mattered."

Her eyes widened. "Okay..." Delilah cleared her throat.

"She hated that I never lost control. That I never wanted to take her up against a wall or on a desk or in an elevator or in the back of a limo..."

Her hand smoothed over the limo's seat.

"Those were her words, on that last night. She said *he* was different. Always out of control and wild and he was what she needed. *I* wasn't that kind of guy."

Delilah's heart drummed too hard in her chest.

"I didn't love her." Flat. "She knew it. It was more of a business relationship than anything else. She fit in my world. I gave her every expensive present she wanted."

Goose bumps rose on Delilah's exposed arms. "That sounds cold."

"Cold enough for one of the Ice Breakers to handle?"

She'd walked straight into that one. But his question made her realize he had dug far deeper into her life than she'd realized. *The Ice Breakers.*

That was what she and her team called themselves. They took the cold cases, and their aim was to break them wide open. Sometimes, they succeeded. Sometimes, they didn't.

"Have you ever made love in the back of a limo, Delilah?"

He was just asking question after question, wasn't he? "No."

"What about on a desk?"

"Is this an invitation?" Her crisp reply.

"Funny," he muttered. "Because I never thought I'd be tempted to fuck someone in my office, but then you walked in this morning, and all I could think about was getting you up on my desk and driving as deeply into you as I could go." Rough lust thickened each word. "Vanessa never knew me—not the real me. Or she wouldn't have wanted my control to vanish."

Her heartbeat was getting faster and faster.

"I can all too easily imagine fucking you on a desk. Against a wall. In a limo." A pause. "Anywhere I can get you. Just so you know, you're not the only one who had dreams last night. You starred in every one of mine."

Her goose bumps were long gone. The back of the limo was hot. She should ask Danny to adjust the air.

"Is this going to be a problem?" Archer asked.

"Your dreams?" *Or mine?*

"I thought it would be best for me to tell you how I feel before we step out of the limo and the world sees us."

The limo *was* slowing. Dammit. So much for getting more questions answered.

"I want you." Deep. Low. "I think I want you more than I've ever wanted anyone, and that reaction is quite...surprising. No, wrong word. Unsettling."

He wanted her—because she'd set him up to want her. She'd researched him ever so carefully and the first night, she'd deliberately been everything he wanted. "You fell for an illusion."

"Did I?"

"I'm not who you think."

The limo stopped. Through the dark glass, she saw the throng of people waiting. VIP night. The big event. She was sure that reporters would be on scene because the fancy red carpet had been rolled out for the high-profile attendees.

She'd never walked a red carpet before. *I had better not fall on my face.*

"You're exactly the woman I want. But we can keep things an illusion, if that's what you prefer. Just put on a show." He leaned closer. Dropped his voice lower. The door would be opening soon. "But what *I* want...it's you. Naked and moaning my name. Digging your nails in my back. And coming for me over and over again."

Her panties were getting wet. *Dammit.*

Danny opened the door. Lights flashed. Archer slid out of the limo and gallantly offered his hand to her. She sucked in a deep breath, schooled her features, and took his hand.

It was, after all, showtime.

Archer leaned toward her.

She pulled him closer. Whispered, for his ears alone, "If I fall on my face as I walk this carpet, I will be so pissed off."

He laughed. Warm and fast. And murmured back, "Don't worry. I swear, I won't let you fall."

***

The bastard wasn't alone.

Archer Radcliffe exited the limo with a lazy grace, and he reached back into the limo with a casual hand.

Then she appeared.

A woman wearing a stunning, pale blue dress. A woman with poise and grace and a warm, sexy smile. Archer swallowed when he looked at her. His fingers linked with hers. He tugged her to his side.

Kept her close.

Reporters were shouting questions. She ducked her head closer to Archer. Said something that caught him by surprise. Something that had Archer laughing.

Archer's head turned. He looked down at the woman with the smile on his face. In his eyes.

No! A cry of rage. *No, you sonofabitch! You don't get to do this to me!*

Archer Radcliffe did *not* get to fall in love. He did not get to find someone to stand beside him. He did *not* get to have a single fucking second of happiness.

He. Did. Not.

CHAPTER SEVEN

"Who is your date tonight, Archer?" A shout from a dark-haired, male reporter.

Archer opened his mouth to reply—

"Delilah Darrow," she answered, voice smooth.

He'd wondered if she would worry about those reporters uncovering *her* identity. Apparently, Delilah didn't give a shit. She'd just proudly announced herself to them. Within minutes, Archer knew they'd be investigating her on the Internet. Attempting to find every bit of dirt that they could.

Someone else asked, "How did you two meet?"

The red carpet had been part of his plan. He'd wanted pictures of him and Delilah spread far and fast. The best way to do that? Be seen at a public event. Before entering his partnership with Delilah, he'd had no intention of coming to this show. As soon as she'd agreed to his deal, he hadn't been able to get there fast enough.

I want everyone to know she's with me.

"How did we meet?" Delilah repeated the question.

He should have come up with a quick cover—

"I was investigating him," Delilah announced.

Some of the reporters frowned.

"Investigating him for what?" A fast, hard question from someone in the back of the crowd.

Delilah offered a wicked grin. "For murder, of course."

Archer put his arm around Delilah's shoulder and drew her close. *What in the fuck are you doing?*

The reporters weren't shouting. They were looking uncomfortable. Nervous. Trying to figure out if she was serious or not?

"Archer, I don't want us to be late for the show. I've never seen an opera before." She'd turned toward him. Was staring up at him with her incredible eyes.

For a moment, he lost every damn thought in his head.

Holy shit, she is dangerous.

He finally managed to nod, and he guided her away from the reporters.

The shouts started when they'd only taken a few steps.

"Do you think Archer was involved in Vanessa Byron's disappearance?"

He kept walking. Kept looking forward. This was necessary. It was what he'd planned.

He still hated it.

"Do you think he killed Vanessa?"

He would not look at them. They could take their pictures. They could post whatever they wanted. They always had. He'd tried proclaiming his innocence. Tried *proving* it again and again.

But no one had listened. No one had given a damn about his side of the story.

They'd been too ready to crucify him.

"Did he bury her body?"

No, hadn't buried her body. Hadn't done *anything* to her.

"How does it feel to be dating a murderer?"

Delilah stopped walking.

They'd almost made it to the entrance of the opera house.

But she turned her head. Stared up at him. He knew his jaw was tightly clenched, and he'd been grinding his teeth together. Shouting his innocence did no damn good. He knew. He'd tried over and over until he'd just...

Stopped.

But Delilah can help me. We can draw out the killer. I know he's there. I know he's watching.

Just as he knew that Vanessa *wasn't* just missing. She was dead. An enemy in the dark had killed her because he'd wanted to hurt Archer.

"Is it always like this for you? I have to confess, I've never been on the receiving end." Her voice carried only to his ears.

He forced a shrug. "This is an easy night." It was. Things had calmed down considerably in the last year.

"Huh." Her head slid back toward the reporters.

He got a very, very bad feeling. "Um, Delilah..."

She slipped from his hold. Moved toward the pack. Put her hands on her hips. "Have any of you tried to find Vanessa?"

They were filming her. Taking her picture.

"Have any of you done *anything* to find the missing woman or are you so busy trying to get some sensational story about Archer that you don't care about what really happened to her?"

They started shouting random shit again.

He could have told Delilah to save her breath. They weren't going to listen to—

"What's it like to be dating a murderer? Isn't that what one of you asked?" Delilah fired out that question.

A blond with an avid expression leaned forward. She'd asked the question.

"I wouldn't know," Delilah added coolly. "Because the man I'm with tonight was never charged with a crime. Never charged. Never tried. Never convicted. And if you throw around accusations that say otherwise, I think that is hitting pretty damn close to slander. But then, you'd probably want to ask the lawyers at Radcliffe Industries about that, wouldn't you?"

Archer could not look away from her. The whole time...ever since Vanessa had vanished, no one had publicly taken his side.

She reached back. Took *his* hand. "I'm with Archer because he's my partner. As for the rest of your questions? You're asking the wrong ones. Why don't you try asking more about Vanessa? Why don't you try to help *her* come home?" She gave a disgusted shake of her head. Swung back toward Archer. Then she gave a little start when she saw his expression. "Archer?"

Immediately, he locked down his emotions. *A mistake. Don't let it happen again. Keep the mask up.*

She crept closer to him. "You okay?"

"Yes." His voice was a growl. Too rough and hard. "We need to get inside."

There were more shouts from the reporters. Curious glances from the others walking on the red carpet in their expensive evening attire. People who'd come not for the show, but to see and be seen.

Isn't that why I'm here? To start putting the pieces in place.

Except he hadn't quite counted on his growing response to Delilah. Wanting her was one thing, but the way he felt...*This isn't about desire.*

It could be about something far more dangerous.

They didn't speak again, not until they were settled in his private box and he was sure no one could overhear them. She sat down and glanced over the edge of the balcony's railing. Gave a little wince. "That is a long way to fall."

He sat beside her. "What was that all about?"

"It's about gravity. You go over the edge and you are going to smack hard into the people below you." She was still gazing down below.

But he realized she was *studying* the crowd. Looking at all the faces out there.

He leaned in even closer. Brought his mouth next to her ear. "I thought you believed I was a killer." His breath blew lightly over her.

A little shiver skated down her body. He was so close to her that there was no way for him *not* to feel that telltale movement.

"It's still something I'm considering," she muttered.

But he didn't believe her. She'd defended him on the red carpet. And he didn't know how in the hell to respond to that.

"Are you sure my laptop is going to be safe in the limo?" Delilah asked suddenly as her head swung back toward him.

She almost clipped him. He eased back, just a little, to avoid that collision. "It's perfectly safe. Danny will ensure no one gets inside the vehicle." She'd been very reluctant to leave her bag behind. "All your files are on there?"

"Well, yes."

"The files that make me look guilty."

Her head tilted. "I have considered the possibility that you might be innocent. If I hadn't considered that option, do you think I would be here right now?"

God, she was so fucking beautiful. Those eyes of hers seemed to see straight through him. "No one defended me before."

She blinked. "No one? Not even your lawyer?"

"Oz gets paid to do his job." For the right price, Oz would defend anyone for anything. "You're different..."

"I'm getting paid, too, in case you forgot."

When it came to her, he forgot nothing. "You didn't have to say a word to the reporters. You know how they work." Hell, she *was* one of them. She could probably play them with one hand tied behind her back. "Why did you do it?" The question was driving him crazy—as crazy as she drove him.

"Because I don't like bullies. Because they need to focus on Vanessa." A delicate exhale. "Because maybe I think you might be innocent and to see what you've gone through for the last two years...it really pisses me off."

Was that a lie? Or the truth? Dammit, he'd thought he could tell when she was lying. But—

Does it even matter? Because he finally had someone who'd stood proudly not just *by* his side, but in front of him. She'd shielded him. Gone to bat for him. This wasn't about their partnership. This was about her. "I'm going to kiss you right now."

"Why?" Breathless. Her gaze darted to the side, then back to him. "Because people are watching?"

Sure. Whatever. If that was what she wanted to think...

His head lowered toward her mouth. And some primitive, possessive instinct rose in him. "It's not about the others." He shouldn't say this. Shouldn't even think it. "It's about *you.*"

His mouth took hers. Her lips parted for him, and his tongue swept eagerly—greedily—inside. He pulled her closer. Didn't care who might see them. Didn't give a damn about anything but the way she felt against him. Her taste was pushing him to the edge of reason. The soft, sensual movements of her lips and tongue...

A growl built in his throat, and he wanted more. He wanted everything. He wanted to lift her onto his lap. Shove up her dress. Fuck her right there.

This isn't me. This wasn't the controlled, civilized man that he'd tried so hard to be. Or rather, the civilized man that he wanted the world to see.

Delilah made him want to wreck his control. She made him want to let his true self out. A guy who wasn't civilized. Who didn't follow the rules. A guy who took and took and let the rest of the world go screw itself.

She moaned softly. The sound drove him on. Archer kissed her harder. Deeper. His hand slid around the edge of her dress. Moved up her delicate ribcage. Inched toward the soft curve of her breast—

She pulled back. A faint gasp slipped from her. She stared at him. Her lips were red and plump from his mouth. Her eyes wide, startled. A pink heat stained her cheeks.

He wanted her mouth again. He wanted *her*.

The lights flickered.

Shit.

Reality returned. He was in his freaking box. Hundreds of people were below. Eyes were on them. He swallowed, twice, and eased back into his seat. His damn dick shoved hard against the front of his pants. *This turned on, just from a kiss.*

Not just any kiss, though. A kiss from Delilah.

Her fingers went to her mouth. She looked away. Glanced across at the other box on the opposite side of the opera house.

I can still taste her. And he liked her taste. No, he loved it. Wanted more. *Will have more.* Archer gripped the arms of his seat as the house lights began to dim.

"There's a blond-haired woman in the box on the other side of the building," Delilah said, voice husky. "I swear, I think she's glaring at me."

He looked toward the box.

Before he could find the blond, the house lights died away as orchestra music began to fill the air.

***

She was not making it until intermission. Delilah tried to keep her eyes on the performers—they were fabulous and amazing, and their voices could do insane, incredible things—but her attention was most definitely elsewhere.

It was on the man beside her. On the man who'd kissed her like he needed her more than air. On the man who'd said he didn't get controlled by his passions, yet he had her ready to rip his clothes off—right there. She'd been ready to jump him in the opera box, for goodness' sake.

Yeah, right. Like goodness had anything at all to do with it. More like wickedness. She'd wanted hot, fast, dirty sex with him. The wild rush of release. And, embarrassingly, she'd been pretty close to release.

Just from a kiss. Insane. Impossible.

Get it together, Delilah. She'd just...gone too long without a lover. Truth be told, she couldn't exactly remember how long it had been for her. At least a year. Her body was in some kind of overdrive, and her feelings for Archer, her attraction—it was just magnified.

She was so lying to herself. *I just want him.* So badly that she still quaked.

Why did I speak up to the reporters? She'd known the reporters would realize who she was—any reporter worth her salt, and surely, there would be *some* good reporters in that crowd—would do a little research. Delilah's identity would have popped up sooner or later, and they would have seen that she focused on true crime stories. Missing persons' cases.

So she'd thought to head the reporters off by admitting she'd gone to Archer first. But protecting him? Coming to his defense? That hadn't been part of her grand plan.

The plan had derailed because...

They pissed me off. Archer had been all stoic, but she'd seen the stiffening of his body. She'd caught the haunted look in his eyes. And she'd had to speak.

I am getting in too deep with him. Yes, she'd had her questions about him from the beginning. And the fact that he'd *asked* her to help him in his hunt? That certainly made him look *less* guilty, and her instincts were screaming at her, actually urging her to *trust* him.

But her instincts had been wrong before. When her emotions got involved, it was hard to be detached and clinical. *And my emotions are definitely getting involved.* This wasn't just about desire. Desire she could handle. This was—

Delilah shot to her feet. "I need to go to the restroom." Yep. She needed some space from

Archer. Some space to clear her head. "I'll be right back."

His head turned toward her. "I can escort you." He began to rise.

Her hand pushed down on his shoulder. That strong, broad shoulder. "Nope. Got it. I'm a big girl. I can handle this on my own." Then she, yes, pretty much fled from him. She shoved aside the curtain to get out of his VIP box, and her heels click, click, clicked as she rushed to the restroom.

***

Archer's phone vibrated. He'd turned off the ringer so it wouldn't interrupt the performance, but he'd been expecting a call from one of his investigators. He pulled the phone out of his pocket and frowned at the screen.

He needed to take this call. Since Delilah was gone...

He slipped from the box. Hurried toward the stairs. He'd find a spot where he wouldn't disturb anyone. Where *he* wouldn't be overheard. He'd make it fast. His steps rushed over the stairs.

He'd be back before Delilah returned to the box. She'd never even realize he'd left.

***

There was a large waiting lounge in the bathroom. Technically *before* you got to the bathroom. A waiting area that was separate from the stalls. A fancy place with plush couches and soft, classical music and flickering candles.

Delilah rushed past that space and went straight to a sink. She yanked on the water and threw a few drops at her overheated face. *Get a grip, woman.* It had just been a kiss. Granted, it was definitely one of the best kisses she'd ever had, but it had *only* been a kiss.

A door opened behind her. Heels tapped on the floor. Someone moved through the lounge. Came toward the stalls.

Delilah glanced at her own reflection in the mirror. Her eyes were wide. Her lips swollen. Her cheeks flushed. She looked like someone who had been well and truly kissed.

"You shouldn't fuck him."

At that stark announcement, Delilah swung around. She found a blond in a sleek, red gown glaring at her.

"He's a monster. You fuck him, and he'll do to you *exactly* what he did to Vanessa."

Before the house lights had dimmed, Delilah had caught a glimpse of this woman across the opera house. But they'd been too far away for her to clearly make out the lady's features. Now that she had an up close view, Delilah instantly realized the woman's identity.

Tiffany Lassiter. Vanessa's half sister. Delilah had tried to speak with Tiffany numerous times, but Tiffany had refused her. Every. Single. Instance.

Delilah reached back. Turned off the water. Grabbed a paper towel to dry her fingers.

"Did you hear me?" Tiffany surged closer with an aggressive lunge that she probably shouldn't be making in those heels. "He'll do the same thing to you."

Delilah tossed away the towel. "What did he do to Vanessa?"

"She didn't want him any longer. But Archer wasn't going to let her just leave him." Her hands clenched at her sides. "No, no one leaves Archer."

A cloud of fury and pain seemed to circle Tiffany. "I'm very sorry about Vanessa," Delilah said softly. She cleared her throat. "My name is Delilah Darrow, and I've tried to talk to you before about—"

"I know who the hell you are." Snarled. "And I know what the hell you think you're doing—you think you get to poke and pry in everyone's lives and get your big story and be some kind of superstar."

Her hands pressed to the sink behind her. The porcelain felt cool to the touch. "That isn't what I think at all."

Tiffany's left hand flew up, and she pointed at Delilah. "You aren't going to make him look like some poor victim that we should all pity. You won't turn him into the hero of this tale."

"I—"

"You won't." With that, she spun on her very high heel and stormed away.

Delilah realized that she was gaping. She snapped her mouth closed and shook her head. *Not* the reaction she'd expected from Tiffany Lassiter. She'd...shit...*what did I expect?*

When she'd first reached out to Tiffany, she'd felt a sense of kinship with the other woman. *Because I know that it's like to lose your sister.*

She'd wanted to help Tiffany. Not stir up old fury and pain. Delilah shoved away from the sink. She'd explain. Get Tiffany to understand.

But when Delilah exited the restroom, there was no sign of Tiffany. She looked to the left. To the right. Nothing. She figured she could only be a few steps behind the other woman. Delilah's stride was quick as she hurried forward. If Tiffany had gone back to her box, she would have gone down the hallway to the right.

Delilah went to the right. She walked past the top of the stairs—stairs that curved and led to the lobby below.

"I won't let you."

At those low words, Delilah froze. "Tiffany?" She started to turn back. She was right in front of the stairs—

Something hit her shoulder. A hard, powerful shove. Delilah surged forward. Her heel—the stupid, too high heel—caught the edge of her dress and suddenly Delilah was hurtling through the air. She grabbed for the banister, but her body was moving too fast. She missed it.

And slammed down the stairs.

CHAPTER EIGHT

He heard a thump. Another. A faint groan. Archer shoved his phone back into his pocket and hurried across the marble floor of the lobby. Automatically, he glanced up, looking toward the second level of the theater, and a glittering, massive chandelier caught the light and sent it dancing across the ceiling.

Another groan. So soft.

He turned the corner. Almost stepped on a high-heeled shoe.

Cinderella lost her slipper. He bent down. Reached for the shoe. He wasn't at the opera with Cinderella, and he damn well preferred his wicked stepsister.

"*Help...*"

His head whipped up. A woman was sprawled half-way down the staircase. Not just any woman—

Delilah. He raced toward her even as a roar of fury broke from him. He rushed up the staircase. "Delilah!"

She winced. One of her delicate hands had a death grip on part of the banister. "Managed to...catch myself. After half the steps." A wince.

"Where are you hurt?" His gaze scanned over her. Then his hands followed suit. He touched her carefully. Tenderly. "Where—"

"Nothing is broken. Just bruises. Probably lots and lots of lovely bruises."

His roar had attracted attention. A security guard appeared at the bottom of the steps. "Sir? Ma'am? What happened?"

"She fell," Archer snarled. "We need a medic to check her out." Because Delilah couldn't know if she'd broken anything or not. He wanted a trained medical professional checking her. Screw it. "I'm taking you to a hospital."

Delilah pushed up to her feet. "No."

"Yes," he snapped right back as fury and what could have been fear pumped through his blood. "You're getting checked out. You just *fell* down the stairs—"

A shake of her head.

Why did she keep shaking her head at him? He was not budging on this point. She would be checked out. Dammit, if she hadn't caught herself, she could have easily broken her neck—

He stopped the thought. Just shut it down. But the image was already in his head. An image of Delilah, lying at the foot of the stairs, with her lovely neck twisted.

No.

Delilah put one hand on his chest. Leaned in close to him. "Get me out of here, Archer."

Hell, yes, he would. He—

"I didn't fall." Her lashes lifted. She was far too pale. All of the color had leached from her cheeks. Even her gaze didn't seem as bold and bright. "Someone pushed me."

A cold fist closed over his heart.

***

"So, the carrying thing is nice. Don't get me wrong. I love that you feel compelled to now carry me everywhere we go, but it's totally unnecessary." One of Delilah's arms hung around Archer's neck and her head pressed against his shoulder. "Gorgeous house, by the way. Big enough for you and half an army, am I right?"

"Do not push me." Low and growling.

"But it gives me joy. Pushing you, I mean. Makes me feel better about the header I took down the stairs." She tried for a lighter edge to her voice.

His stubble-covered jaw just hardened all the more.

And the lighter edge failed. Apparently, it was very, very hard to lighten the mood after an attack.

Archer had insisted that she talk to the security guard. Then the cops. And he'd also been adamant that she get thoroughly checked by a doctor. The doc had just backed up what she'd already suspected—bruises would come. She'd be sore. But no broken bones. She'd been lucky.

She wasn't dead. Bones weren't shattered. So, yes, Delilah *did* feel lucky. What would have been even luckier? Catching the sonofabitch who'd shoved her. "The cops didn't believe me, you know."

"I fucking know." He turned to the right. Took her inside what looked like a den. Carefully lowered her onto a brown leather couch. But his hold lingered, as if he didn't want to let her go.

I don't want to be let go. Because he had been holding her as much as possible. He'd carried her into the hospital. Carried her out. Kept a grip on her wrist when they'd been in the limo. Stayed at her side every moment.

And I wanted him there. "It really sucks when people don't believe you, doesn't it?" she murmured.

His lashes—thick and long—slowly lifted. His golden gaze held hers. "Yes. It sure as hell does."

He was close enough to kiss. All she had to do was lean forward just an inch, maybe two.

His gaze dropped to her mouth. Lingered. The gold seemed to heat. Delilah could feel heat rising in her own body, too. Sex should be the last thing on her mind. Oddly, it wasn't. *How messed up is that?* Maybe it was the adrenaline. Or the whole near-death drama bit. Maybe it was from being in his arms so much. Or—

Or maybe it's because I know he's innocent.

Someone had pushed her, but it couldn't have been Archer. He'd rushed *up* the stairs to her. Whoever the hell had pushed her—that person had been on the second level of the theater. No way it could have been him.

But Delilah did believe she'd gotten the shove because she'd been at that opera house with Archer. And if someone was willing to attack her because she was with him...

Did that same someone attack Vanessa?

Archer's lips pressed together. His gaze darted up to meet hers. Then he backed away. "I want to hear every bit of the story again."

She kind of just flopped on the couch. Her shoes were long gone—one of the reasons Archer had insisted on carrying her—and her dress rode up to expose her legs. Like Delilah cared. *Other things to worry about.* So what if he got to see her thighs? "Not much of a story. I was walking past the stairs. I thought I heard a voice, so I stopped."

"What did the voice say? You didn't tell the cops that part."

"Because I couldn't be sure I heard correctly. I just heard *something*. A whisper." She stared up at his ceiling. Her hands pressed over her stomach. It quivered and twisted. She wasn't ever going to forget the rush of fear she'd felt when she flew over those stairs.

"What do you *think* the voice said?" He stood by the couch.

Her head turned. She took a good look at him. His fancy clothes were wrinkled. He'd left his coat in the limo. Jerked open the top two buttons of his dress shirt. His hair was tousled, not perfectly styled, because he'd raked his fingers through it over and over again. "I *thought* the voice said, 'I won't let you.'"

His eyes immediately turned into slits. "Won't let you do what?"

That was the rub. "So...I, um, might have engaged in a small conversation with someone before my fall."

Tension slid through his body. Through the whole room. Everything suddenly seemed way more dangerous. "What conversation? You didn't say anything to the cops about a damn conversation."

"Yes, well, I didn't tell them because I was waiting to say this to *you*."

He squinted at her as if she'd gone mad.

She hadn't. "It's part of our investigation and I thought you and I could handle things better. If the cops went after her, she'd just clam up with them."

He put one hand behind the cushions near her head as he knelt beside the couch.

Oh, wow. He was certainly much closer.

And his other hand? It was brushing against her thigh. Maybe flopping on the couch hadn't been the best idea, after all. Now she was all caged by him.

"What in the hell are you talking about?" Archer's words were murmured. Almost husky like an endearment.

Delilah frowned. "Is that how you sound when you're really mad?" Low and sexy and growly?

"It's how I sound when I'm attempting my best not to scare you, but still trying to get you to tell me *everything*."

That was interesting. Her hand rose. Pressed to his cheek. "I'm not scared of you."

A shudder worked the length of his body. "You could have died tonight."

"The odds weren't high that I'd break my neck. It was just a tumble down a few steps." Delilah tried to play it off but, truthfully, she had been terrified.

"You don't know what could have happened." Still low. But rougher. "Who did you talk with before you fell?"

She swallowed but kept touching him. Almost stroking him. As if she was trying to soothe him. Crazy. *She* was the one who'd had the push down the staircase. "Tiffany Lassiter followed me into the women's room."

"What?"

"She was in the box across from us. Remember the blond I mentioned? It was her. She saw us making out, and I think she felt duty-bound..." *Or some kind of bound.* "To warn me." This was where things got tricky. *Fine. Things had been tricky for a while.* "At first, she was telling me that I would wind up like Vanessa."

"That will *never* happen." A guttural vow.

"I certainly hope not." She could not look away from his golden stare. "Vanishing isn't on my agenda. I never want to wind up like Layla." Wait. She'd meant to say Vanessa. That she never wanted to wind up like *Vanessa*.

But...

But the truth had come out on its own, and it hung heavily between them. Delilah saw the knowledge in his eyes and prepared for him to say something to her that would be some sort of weak statement about understanding or how he was sorry or—

His head turned. His lips brushed against her palm. Once. Twice. There was an odd care to his caress. A tenderness she hadn't expected.

Then his head turned back. His gaze returned to meet hers.

And in his stare...she saw...*I know. I know what you meant. I know.*

She wet her lips. "That was, um, how the conversation started, but right before she stormed off, Tiffany told me that I wasn't going to make you into some hero."

"Never been accused of that before."

No, she didn't think he had. "It took me a few moments to go after her. I wanted to talk." Time for full disclosure. "I *tried* talking to her before, but she refused to meet with me. I was hurrying after her, thinking she'd gone back to her box, and that was when I thought I heard the voice." A frown pulled at her brows as Delilah tried to remember. "But I think the voice came from downstairs." Those last few moments were a bit blurry. "That's why...I was turning toward the staircase. I thought the voice came from below." *Tiffany's voice?* "Then someone shoved me."

"You're sure you didn't fall?"

She shot upright into a sitting position. Moved fast and he had to jerk back. Delilah swung her legs over the edge of the couch. "The cops thought I imagined it. So did the guard. I don't need you doubting me, too."

"I just asked if you were sure."

She lurched to her feet.

"Don't." He curled his hand around her.

"I don't need you to carry me. I need you to believe me. I felt a hand on my shoulder. A strong, hard *push*. Then I went tumbling. I tried to catch myself. Missed on the first attempt." She could remember the world spinning. The hard drumming of her own heartbeat. The pain that had radiated from her hip when she'd slammed into a step. "But I caught hold on my second try. That was when you entered the scene." Rushing in like some sort of roaring lion.

So much for him being controlled. *I can see past that lie now.*

"You never saw who pushed you?"

"No. I just saw you, coming from the *bottom* of the stairs, so I know it wasn't you. I know you didn't do it."

"I wouldn't hurt you." Low. Rough.

She sucked in a deep breath. "That's good to know."

"I am not a killer. I didn't hurt Vanessa. That last night, I told her goodbye. She walked the hell away. That was the end of the story."

"The story isn't over." Wasn't that obvious? "What happened tonight was about you. Not like I have a line of enemies out there. No one has come for me before now." Before the first night that she'd been on his arm. Except, this wasn't the first night, was it?

She'd been with him the night before, too.

Two dates. "We should see if anyone was at the charity ball *and* at the opera."

A slow nod. "I already know one person who was."

The sinking in her stomach told Delilah who this person would be. "Tiffany?"

"Yes. She tends to have a way of showing up wherever I am."

"Because she blames you for what happened to her sister."

He laughed.

Her brow furrowed. Laughter hadn't been the reaction she'd expected.

"No, that's not the reason."

"Then what is?"

Eyes glinting, he said, "She wants to sleep with me. She wanted that before Vanessa and I were together, and she wanted it after, too. Vanessa hadn't even been gone a month before Tiffany was at my house, trying to get in my bed."

Her lips parted. Delilah couldn't quite figure out how to respond.

"Considering that I was suspected of killing her sister, I thought that reaction was a bit...off."

"Damn off." Her shoulders squared. An ache immediately rushed through her and she winced.

His eyes narrowed. "Delilah?"

"Can you call me Lila?" Absently, she reached up to rub her shoulder. "That's what my friends call me."

"But we aren't friends."

Her hand stilled. There had been a note in his voice—almost sensual... Her head lifted. Her gaze met his. "We're partners."

"Sure. But I also want to fuck you, and I don't typically go around wanting to fuck my business associates."

She let her breath slide in and out. "You are a very blunt man."

"I've found that being blunt saves time." His attention was focused completely on her. "Now you know exactly how I feel, so if you decide you want to wander into my room in the middle of the night and jump my bones, have at it." His gaze never left her face.

She ignored the fierce pounding of her heart. "You just made a joke."

"Did I?"

She had no idea. Maybe? "I'm going to bed. No, correction, I'm taking an extremely long, hot shower, and then I'm going to bed. I don't predict any bone jumping on my agenda, but I do thank you for the option." Delilah took a step forward, then bit her lip. "Yeah, so...ahem. Where is my room?"

He pointed toward the curved staircase. "Second floor. Right hallway. Door number two."

"Wonderful. More stairs. Just what I was hoping for." Squaring her shoulders—dammit, the left one really ached—she headed for the stairs.

But he scooped her into his arms before she'd taken more than a handful of steps. He picked her up easily, showing the savage strength that was hidden beneath his expensive clothes. Automatically, her arm curled around his neck.

"No protest?" he asked.

Zero protests. She was tired and achy, and a bed sounded like paradise. "You want to carry me up? Have at it. But if you drop me, I will be exceedingly unhappy." It seemed only fair to warn him.

Soft laughter came in response. At the unexpected sound, her head turned. Their faces were so close.

Close enough to kiss. Not that she was planning to kiss him. When she kissed him, all kinds of things happened. Things like her body heating. Her breasts aching. Her yearning and wanting.

His laughter had already faded. "I was afraid." A low confession from Archer. "When I saw you on the stairs, I was afraid you'd been seriously hurt." His hold tightened on her. "That was never part of my agenda. I didn't expect..." He stopped. His jaw flexed. "I didn't expect this so soon."

"Neither did I. But obviously, this person has been watching you very, very closely." Something that should make them both wary. "The attacker has stayed close the whole time. And you were right, having a woman come into your life set off a chain reaction." A very dangerous and immediate one.

"Do you want out?" He watched her carefully.

"No, but I do very much want to catch the person who thought it would be fun to give me a shove."

"So the hell do I." His gaze dropped to her lips. Heated. The gold seemed to blaze as he looked at her mouth.

She wet her lips. Oh, hell. Why had she done that?

Archer's stare went even hotter.

The seconds ticked by. He kept holding her. She kept thinking about how it felt when his mouth took hers. When she'd first started this case, first started investigating Archer, she hadn't planned on her reaction to him. She *shouldn't* have felt any real reaction. Everything should have been faked.

It wasn't.

"Are you real?" he rumbled. "Or just who you think I want you to be?"

He was talking about the first night. The way she'd known how to deliberately bait him. "Do you think I'm making you want me?"

"You breathe, and I want you."

That was incredibly blunt—and honest.

And I feel the same way. "This isn't a normal reaction. The...the attraction between us is very strong."

"I think *strong* is a weak word." He pulled his gaze from her mouth. Headed for the stairs. Carried her up easily. Didn't show even a little strain.

Color me impressed. "I felt better when I saw you." A stark truth that made her uncertain. "I was scared, and then you came running to me, and I felt safe." When he was supposed to be the bad guy—the monster—yet the sight of Archer had made her feel like she'd be okay.

He reached the landing. Turned to the right. Went past the first door. Stopped at the second. He still held her.

"You can..." Her voice had gone all husky. Not deliberate. "You can put me down now."

Slowly, he did. He lowered her until her bare feet touched the floor. Her body brushed against his. Her arm slid from behind his neck, and her fingers moved to curl around his shoulder. "Thanks for the lift up the stairs."

"Your bags are inside already. The luggage and the laptop."

Handy.

"If you need me at all during the night, I'll be right next door."

Oh. That *was* close. "I'm sure I'll be fine." She reached back. Opened the door. Let it swing inward behind her. "Good night."

He didn't move. "I don't think of myself as a violent man."

Certainly another point about him that was good to know.

"But I intend to absolutely destroy whoever it was that sent you tumbling down those stairs." His hand lifted. Curled under her chin. "And I swear, you will *not* be hurt again. Not on my watch."

She'd know to be on her guard, twenty-four, seven, too. Delilah hadn't expected an attack so soon. Her mistake. She made it a point not to repeat mistakes.

Why did the attack come so soon? Was it because she and Archer had been seen together two nights in a row? Because he'd kissed her in such a public manner when she knew that type of display hadn't been typical of his romantic interactions in the past?

His thumb brushed across her lips in a light caress. "I discovered something quite startling tonight."

"What's that?"

Instead of answering, his head lowered. His lips took hers. Tenderly. So gently. A caress more than a kiss.

Her left hand rose and gripped his arm. Now she was holding onto him with *both* hands, and Delilah pulled him ever closer. Her lips parted, and her tongue swept out. She wasn't particularly in the mood for some gentle, little good night peck. If he was going to kiss her, then they were damn well going to *kiss*.

The desire ignited between them, just as she'd known that it would. Need flooded through her body and had her rubbing against him. She could feel his arousal—thick and full and long—and she knew he wanted her just as badly as she wanted him. His taste was incredible. His skillful, wicked tongue made her go wild. She heard a moan and realized it was her own, and she didn't care. She wanted to keep kissing him.

No, no, she wanted a whole lot more than a kiss.

And because of that, Delilah pulled back.

He had a hot, predatory look about him. Lust burned in his eyes. "What do your lovers call you?"

Her brows pulled low. "What?"

"Your friends call you Lila, but what do your lovers call you? Because sooner or later, I *will* be your lover."

She wanted to call him a cocky bastard, but the truth was...

Sooner or later, I will be your lover, Archer. They both knew they were crossing lines. They both knew the desire between them wouldn't be ignored.

His hand slid over to tuck a lock of hair behind her ear. After her tumble on the stairs, her hair had come loose from its ever-so-careful twist and now slid over her shoulders. "Forget what they called you," he rumbled. "Doesn't matter a damn to me. You'll be my Delilah."

My Delilah. There was a dark, possessive edge to Archer's words.

Then he stepped back. "If you need me, call out," he said once more.

Because he would be in the room right next door. Check.

He turned and walked away.

"If you need me," Delilah raised her voice, "then just shout. I'll come running to your rescue."

He stilled. After a beat, he glanced over his shoulder. "You know, I believe you would."

"Isn't that what partners are for?" *I can still taste him. I want him.*

"No one has come running for me before."

"Then you were hanging around the wrong people." Obviously. "Good thing that's changed." And, before she could do or say anything else— like jump those bones he'd mentioned before— Delilah retreated into the bedroom. She firmly shut the door.

Two hours later, she screamed for him.

CHAPTER NINE

"*Archer!*"

He lunged out of bed. Rushed out of his bedroom and nearly ripped Delilah's door from the hinges as he fought to get to her. Delilah's voice had been high-pitched and threaded with pain.

No one fucking hurts her!

He slammed his hand into the light switch and illumination immediately flooded in the guest room as he searched for the threat. Archer was more than ready to kill.

Except, there was no threat.

Delilah was in the bed, the sheets tangled around her legs. She wore a black tank top, black panties and—

"Don't just stand there! Help me!" She let out a pain-filled moan and grabbed for her thigh. "Cramp. Stupid, terrible, painful *cramps*."

From the fall. Shit. He should have rubbed her down before bed. He lurched forward, like a puppet pulled by strings, and reached for her. Archer sat on the edge of the bed, and his hands moved hers so that he could reach the tight area.

As soon as he began to rub the tense muscles, her breath hissed out.

He froze. "Am I hurting you?" *Never want to hurt her.*

"Do *not* stop." Her head fell back against the pillow. "I tried to get out of bed a few minutes ago, thinking I could try to walk some of this off, but I almost fell. Please just...help me."

"Always." He worked her carefully. Tenderly. Her skin felt like silk beneath his touch. The muscles beneath the silk were tense and hard, and his fingers circled over those sore spots. He stroked and worked, trying not to think about the fact that her panties were inches from his hand. Or about the fact that she wasn't wearing a bra beneath that little tank top. He could see the tight thrust of her nipples against the fabric.

She needs you. Keep your shit together. Stop ogling her.

A moan trembled on her lips. "Thank you. So much better. I just...I couldn't make it stop myself."

He would rub her all night long if it helped. He kept at it, and her stiff muscles eased beneath his fingertips.

Her eyes drifted closed.

"Does anything else..." Shit, but his voice was grating and rough. Archer cleared his throat and tried again. "Does it hurt anywhere else?"

Her lashes lifted. Slowly. Languidly. "My shoulder. Part of my back. I, um, hit that side when I went down. But you don't have to—"

"Roll over."

"Archer?"

"Princess, roll that sweet ass over. I'm going to take care of you." The way he should have taken care of her earlier. But, no, he'd been a selfish prick and he'd let her go off on her own into the guest room. After that fall, her muscles must be aching constantly. Hurting so badly that she hadn't been able to sleep.

He couldn't do much for her, but this—*this* he could do. "Roll over," he ordered again.

"Only because I really hurt," she grumbled.

Hell, even her grumble was sexy. The problem was that he was finding *everything* about Delilah to be sexy. When he'd originally come up with his plan, everything had seemed so easy. Delilah knew the score, so she could help him set the scene. There would be no confusion about what was happening between them. No mixed messages. They'd work together. And, he'd, yes, *use* her to get what he wanted. Because he was a selfish bastard who often used people in order to get what he wanted. It was the way he'd always been.

She turned onto her stomach. "It was the left shoulder," she told him as her head moved to a comfortable position on the pillow. "Then down a few inches."

His fingers curled around her shoulder. So delicate. He was careful here, so very careful. "I have some cream I can put on for you. It will help with the stiffness."

"Right now, I just want your fingers." Husky. "God, that feels good."

She felt good. His jaw locked tight as he went to work on her. Stroking. Kneading. Not too hard because he didn't want to injure her anymore. Just enough to help ease the pain. She stretched beneath his touch.

He kept his eyes on her back. Not her pert ass. The ass that was so close to him.

Swallowing, Archer leaned over her a little more. His fingers slid down, moving the inches she'd indicated before as he tried to work out the tension. *And ignore my giant dick.*

"That feels so great. Didn't realize the mighty Archer Radcliffe was a massage therapist on the side."

"I've got lots of secret skills." He tried to make his voice light. Utterly failed. Light just wasn't him. The words came out as more of a rasp than anything else.

And his fingers edged around her side as he stroked her. Accidentally touched the curve of her breast because she'd turned a bit—

They both froze.

The sound of her breathing—his—seemed far too loud in the bedroom.

"I, um, think that I'm good now." Delilah rolled fully toward him. "Thank you."

His hands moved. Caged her body when they pressed into the mattress on each side of her. "I can..." Shit, he sounded rough. "I can put that cream on your body. It will help with soreness."

She nibbled on her lower lip. Her gaze traveled down his body. "You're just wearing boxers."

"You screamed. I was afraid you were in trouble. Not like there was time to waste getting dressed." And there was no way she could miss the massive erection currently tenting his boxers. It was what it was.

And her gaze *was* currently on his dick.

Time for him to move back. He started to rise.

Her hand flew out and curled around his wrist. "You know, I think I'm still a little sore. Can you work me for a few more minutes?"

I can work you all night long. Not the right reply. He jerked his head in agreement. Was it her back? Was that where she needed—

Her hand pushed his toward her upper thigh. "It hurts here."

His fingers spread over her thigh. Rubbed. "Here?" Her skin was so freaking soft.

Her breath caught. "Actually, a little higher..."

His fingers slid up. "Here?" His voice was even more of a growl. His fingers were near the edge of her underwear.

"Y-yes..."

There was something about her voice. His gaze lifted. Caught hers. Saw the desire in her stare and felt all the air leave his lungs. "*Delilah?*"

"Maybe a little higher."

*Fuck, fuck, fuck...*His fingers eased under the edge of her panties. She was wet. Hot. Incredible. Her legs parted more for him, giving him better access as his fingers stroked her. First her clit—he strummed her clit and she arched back against the bedding with a little moan.

Gorgeous.

He just had to dip a finger into her. Just one...

His index finger slid inside. Inside the hottest, tightest heaven he'd ever touched.

The damn panties are in my way.

His hand pulled away from her.

"Archer?"

He yanked the panties down her legs. Tossed them somewhere—they landed on the other side of the room, and he didn't give a shit about them. What mattered to him was Delilah. A Delilah who was naked from the waist down. A Delilah who'd asked for him to touch her.

So touch her, he would. First with his fingers. He learned every inch of her tender core. Learned what made her gasp. What made her quiver. Learned that she was so incredibly, insanely tight as he pushed first one finger, then another into her and thrust them, again and again into her heat. His thumb trailed over her clit.

Her breath came faster. Harder.

It wasn't quite enough for him. Or her.

So maybe she needed a different type of touch.

He repositioned himself. Put his mouth *on* her. Licked her clit. Tasted her. And didn't stop—didn't stop using his lips and his tongue, didn't stop tasting and taking and *devouring* until Delilah came against his mouth. She jerked beneath him, her whole body jolted, and his name broke from her.

He kept licking her. Tasting her pleasure. Getting damn near drunk off her.

She fell limply against the mattress. His head slowly lifted. His dick was hard and aching for her. He wanted to rip aside his boxers and plunge deep into her. He wanted to make her call out his name again. Over and over.

He wanted her to need him. To want him more than she wanted anything else.

The way I want her right now.

And because he wanted so much...because it mattered...*so much*...He slowly pulled away from her. Pulled away, climbed from the bed, and rose to stand near the mattress.

Her gorgeous eyes blinked up at him. "I— Archer?" She reached for the covers, as if embarrassed. She should never be embarrassed. She was perfect.

He caught her hand. "I want you."

Her attention shifted to the dick shoving toward her. The dick that was very close to her face.

I want her mouth on me.

She licked her lips. "I can, um, see that."

"When I fuck you, I don't want you to still be wondering if I'm a killer."

Her stare flew back to his.

"Women have fucked me since Vanessa disappeared. I know what they thought. I *don't* want that to be you." He wanted so much more from her. "Just over twenty-four hours ago, you burst into my life. And your plan was to bring me down."

Just over twenty-four hours...

Weird. It felt like she'd been in his life so much longer. "Maybe it's still your plan," he continued, voice grim. "Maybe you're still working your angle, doing all the things that just make me want you more, even as you plot to get my ass tossed in a jail cell."

She didn't deny the charge. Didn't confirm it. Just stared at him with eyes so bright and solemn.

"When we fuck, you'll know who I am."

"I know who you are."

He raked a hand over his face. He wasn't explaining this shit well and staring at a naked Delilah was damn well not helping with his thought process. In fact, staring at a naked Delilah made it hard for him to think of *anything* but fucking her. "Try to get some sleep." Gruff. "We'll talk more in the morning. Start digging. Find the truth."

He swung away from the bed. If he didn't leave now, he would be climbing back into that bed. Denying himself something he wanted very, very badly? That wasn't part of his nature. Frankly, the shit sucked. But he was *trying* to prove something to her.

He wasn't a monster. He didn't just take and take and take in this world. No matter what the tabloid stories claimed.

"You have the wrong impression of me." Her voice was quite calm. Strong. It reached him just as he was about to cross the threshold and leave the guest room. "Probably because, as you said, it's only been a little over twenty-four hours...and I just let you go down on me."

And I want to go down on you again. And again. Her taste was addictive. Spicy and sweet at the same time.

"I don't normally jump into bed with men I've just met."

That was fucking excellent to know.

"And in case you're not real clear on it, let me help you out...you had your mouth on me. If you think that didn't involve trust, if you think that didn't involve me letting myself be incredibly vulnerable with you, then you need to rethink the whole situation. Because *that* was about trust. It was me showing you how I feel."

He whirled back to face her.

She'd yanked a sheet from the bed. Wrapped it around her body, toga-style, as she stood and glared at him with the regal grace of a queen. "It wasn't like I just did it so I could see what wicked skills you had with your mouth."

His hands fisted—only so he would stop himself from reaching out for her. He was *trying* here. Trying hard to be more than his normal, selfish bastard self. *She was pushed down the fucking stairs.* Delilah had been through one hell of a night. And if he took her...

"You think I'm not *seeing* you?" Delilah asked him as she tossed back her hair and notched up her chin. "Because I am. I already had background on you before I ever said the first word to you. I knew more about you than most of your lovers ever did. When it comes to research, I am very, very thorough."

"Yet you still thought I was a killer."

She took a step toward him. Seemed to catch herself. "Did I? Or did I just ensure that I got close to you? That I got in your world? Because here I am, in your house, with complete access to you. Maybe I didn't think *you* were the killer. Maybe I just thought you were the key."

His eyes narrowed.

"I already know you better than anyone else did," she continued clearly. "And I'm learning more and more about you with every moment that passes. If you were truly a cold-blooded ice king, then I think we would be wrecking the bed right now."

He wanted to be in that bed. Wrecking it.

"But I think there is so much more to you than you've let the world know. Every now and then, your mask cracks, and I *see* you."

No, she didn't. "Good night, Delilah." Once more, he whirled for the door.

"I like what I see. *That's* why I wanted you tonight."

He didn't look back again. Couldn't. He hurried away from her while his self-control was still in place. She didn't get it, but his control had been hanging by a thread. All it would have taken was one freaking minute more, and he would have pounced. He could have lifted her up. Ripped away that sheet. Taken her against the wall.

Taken her and never let go.

He slammed closed the door to his bedroom. Marched to the en suite. He ripped on the shower—using the ice cold water because he needed to cool down. But then he turned his head. Caught his own reflection in the mirror. The hard features. The blazing eyes.

I like what I see.

His expression hardened. She had no idea just what a true bastard he was. Soon enough, though, Delilah would learn the truth.

***

The push had been a mistake. Too soon. Too sloppy. A surge of emotion—anger—had taken over. Delilah Darrow had just been right there.

It had been so easy. So tempting.

Until Archer had rushed in like some knight to the rescue. Who the hell did he think he was kidding? Everyone knew what Archer was. Just because he hadn't been convicted, it didn't mean the world didn't believe he was guilty.

If it weren't for the fact that he'd been born into too much damn money, he would have been a pariah. But the sad truth was that too many people would overlook the crimes of the rich and powerful.

So in order to hurt them, you had to attack the things they truly valued.

But you didn't value Vanessa. I thought you did. I was wrong.

Because Archer had *never* looked shattered after Vanessa's disappearance. Never shown his rage or fear. Oh, no, not the controlled Archer fucking Radcliffe.

He'd kept his mocking mask in place through the investigation. Through the scandal. Through everything...

Until tonight. Until he'd been holding tightly to Delilah and carrying her out of the opera. His rage had been clear to see. So much fury because she'd been hurt.

He'd never been furious about Vanessa. Hadn't given a damn when she'd cheated. Even when the stories had filled the air—the accusations about him had flown—Archer hadn't shown his fury.

Not until his new lady had taken a tumble down the stairs.

Yes, the shove had been impetuous. A mistake that *could* have proven costly, if anyone had seen the attack. But, something important *had* been learned.

Archer had a weakness.

And I do love it when the bastard is weak.

CHAPTER TEN

"I figured you would come calling, sooner or later, Archer." Tiffany Lassiter swung around from her carefully poised position on the balcony at the expensive restaurant and offered him a wide smile. "You're just lucky I was in the mood to—" She broke off. Frowned.

Delilah waved at her. "Hi, there. Fancy seeing you again."

Tiffany's mouth opened and closed—very fish-like—as she gaped at Delilah.

From behind the lenses of her sunglasses, Delilah watched her prey. Having a chat with Tiffany had been item one on her agenda for the day. And since Archer had been sure the woman would be willing to meet him for a private breakfast, that little chat had certainly been easy to arrange at the upscale spot by the shore.

Archer had used his connections to make sure a private space would be waiting for them at the restaurant. It was currently right during the big mimosa brunch, and Tiffany clutched a tall champagne flute in her white-knuckled grip.

"I didn't know this was a three-some," Tiffany announced with a sniff.

"It's not. It's a two-some." Delilah motioned between herself and Archer. "He's with me, so give up those dreams, honey, and just sit yourself down."

Instead of sitting, Tiffany moved to dramatically storm past them.

Cute move.

Cute, right up to the moment when Archer stepped into her path. "I have been kind so far," he noted quietly with an implacable expression. "I haven't ruined you with the backers you have in this town. I've let you keep the art gallery you enjoy."

"Ruined me?" A laugh that was a bit too high. "As if you could."

A nod from Archer. "I could."

Goose bumps rose onto Delilah's arms. There was something about Archer's voice...*I believe him.* Like Delilah, he was wearing sunglasses. They made him look handsome and sexy, and the sun glinted down from overhead even as the waves crashed into the nearby shore. The hostess had made sure they were the only ones on the balcony dining area. Plenty of privacy, and not a whole lot of room for Tiffany to run, especially with Archer blocking her path.

Tiffany's stare swung to Delilah once more. "I tried to warn you. Do you *see?* Do you see what he's really like?"

She was seeing plenty. "Where did you go last night, after you delivered your dramatic threat to me and ran away?"

A sniff from Tiffany. "Back to my box. Where else would I have gone?" She chugged the rest of her mimosa. Slammed the empty flute down on a nearby table.

"You didn't go back." Archer's voice was smooth. "I checked with an attendant this morning. He said you never returned to your box."

"Fine. So I left. I wasn't feeling the best. I *might* have had a bit too much to drink, so I went home. Why the hell does it matter?" Red stained Tiffany's cheeks. "Is it a crime to leave a boring production? My ears were burning."

Watching Tiffany carefully, Delilah said, "Someone pushed me down the stairs last night."

Tiffany laughed.

Archer tensed.

Delilah just kept staring at the other woman.

Tiffany's laughter slowly faded away. "Wait. You're serious?"

Did it look as if she was joking?

"And you think it was *me?*" The waves crashed harder as Tiffany's voice rose. "I don't even know you."

"True. But you still saw fit to stalk me into a bathroom and deliver threats." Delilah rolled one shoulder in a shrug. "So when I get attacked, you can see where I might want to have a little chat with you about the situation."

Tiffany backed up a step. "I didn't push you. I left with Harrison Walker. He was right outside and waiting for me. Don't believe me? Just ask him. We had a very long, busy, and strenuous night together."

"How wonderful for you." Delilah's considering stare swept over the other woman. "If that's true, why not just say that to begin with? Why lie about going back to your box?"

"Why not lie? I don't have to tell you my personal shit. Again, I don't know you."

This woman was...interesting. "Do you lie often?"

"Every chance I get," was her fast reply.

Delilah nodded. Now they were getting somewhere. "So then you lied to the police. When Vanessa disappeared and you told them that you'd heard Archer threaten her, that was a lie?"

"I—"

"When you went on gossip shows and talked about how he had such a fiery temper—how you'd seen him erupt into jealous rages, that was a lie?"

Tiffany's nostrils flared. "I don't like you."

The feeling is ever so mutual. "That just hurts me. Super deep inside." Delilah's head tilted to the right. "Wait, no, it doesn't. My bad."

Had Archer just smothered a laugh? She slanted him a glance, but his face appeared inscrutable. Her attention darted back to Tiffany. "I have to give you credit. You are a very impressive actress. I mean, last night, I thought those tears I saw in your eyes were real."

Tiffany narrowed her eyes. There was no sign of any tears. "What in the hell do you want from me?"

"I want to find your sister. That's what Archer and I both want. See, he's tired of everyone calling him the monster. And if the cops can't handle the case—it sure seems as if they've given up on her—then we're going to take over."

"You and what army?" Tiffany laughed. The sound seemed even more brittle than before.

"That is an old joke, and not the least bit funny." Delilah took a step forward. Her voice lowered as she said, "She was your sister. Don't you want to find out what happened? Don't you care?" This she just didn't get. "How do you sleep at night knowing that she could be out there hurt or dead or—"

"Vanessa didn't give a damn about me. I felt the same for her. We were *half* sisters, and trust me, that half meant nothing. So our moms happened to screw the same guy once upon a time. Big deal. Doesn't create some big, emotional connection for me."

"Obviously. Or you wouldn't have tried to screw your sister's ex." Delilah deliberately delivered that line.

Tiffany's cheeks flamed even redder as she gaped at Archer. "You *told* her?"

His hands were shoved into his pockets. "You put yourself—naked and uninvited—in my bed. Yes, I told her."

Tiffany let out what sounded like a strangled scream and she stormed forward. She shoved at Archer. He stepped back.

"How did you get into Archer's house?" Delilah called her question quickly, before Tiffany could vanish.

Tiffany tensed.

"You were uninvited, so that meant the door wasn't opened for you. You let yourself in. I've seen the security at Archer's place. I know how tight it is. How did you get inside?"

Tiffany swung toward her. "I used a key."

"What key?" From Archer. Low. Hard.

"Vanessa's key, all right? I took it off her ring because she was gone, not like she needed the thing. And she'd mentioned the security code to me, so it wasn't hard to get inside." Tiffany huffed out a breath. Her shoulders sagged a little bit as she mumbled, "You think I'm a total bitch, don't you? Because I don't care about her."

Well, Delilah *was* leaning toward that assumption.

"But at first, I thought Vanessa had just cut out of town. Found another rich dumbass—no offense, Archer, but you were just another in a long line—to finance her life. Figured she'd taken off for Mexico or the Cayman Islands or some other fabulous place." She swallowed. She brushed back a lock of her hair with fingers that trembled. "Sooner or later, Vannie would post a pic of herself on some sandy beach, and we'd all realize she'd just left in a cloud of drama because she *enjoyed* doing that crap. Enjoyed playing with people's lives. I didn't think anything bad had happened."

Two years had passed. There had been no pics of Vanessa on any beaches. "And when you went on those talk shows?"

"Someone had to play the grieving family member. If I wasn't gonna do it, who would?" Tiredly, she let her shoulders drop. "It was only as more time passed that I realized Vannie wasn't coming back."

Archer moved closer to Delilah. His arm brushed against her. "You think Vanessa is dead."

"I think..." Tiffany's lips twisted. "I think nothing has been posted to any of her social media accounts in two years. I think she would never, ever go media silent this way. She liked attention too much."

"I didn't hurt her," Archer said.

"Sure you did. You never loved her. You never love anyone. And you think that doesn't hurt?" A bitter smile. "Try again." With that, Tiffany spun and stalked away. This time, she didn't stop—well, except to grab another mimosa from the waiter who'd just started walking toward the balcony dining area.

She took the mimosa and kept going.

***

"The first thing I did was check her phone." Archer lowered into his chair and studied Delilah as she made herself comfortable on the edge of his desk. She just hopped up there like it was the most natural thing in the world and began to casually swing one high-heeled foot. "I knew the cops were trying to track the phone, but I had more resources. My name was being dragged to hell and back, so I thought if I could find her, I could prove that I'm innocent."

Her head tilted. Her hair brushed over her shoulder. "You thought she'd just run away, too?"

"No, no, I didn't. Because I found that fucking note, and I knew she'd been seeing someone else. Disappearing without a trace—that wasn't her style. Tiffany was right. Vanessa always loved attention. She always found a spotlight. To just slip away...it never fit."

Delilah nodded and seemed to mull over his words. He took that time to study her. He wished that he knew what she was thinking. Had the scene with Tiffany helped his case? Delilah had seen right through the other woman. Archer had known that a breakfast meeting would be Tiffany's weakest time. Truth be told, he knew she was usually hung over in the mornings, so that time was when she was least likely to keep up her act and her lies.

So many people had bought her lies.

"You never found out who Vanessa was sleeping with?"

"Not definitely, no. But I had one very strong suspicion."

She stared back at him.

He got lost in her eyes.

She waved one hand toward him. "Um, Archer, this is the part where you do *not* leave me in suspense. You keep talking."

Right. Yes. Damn embarrassing. He cleared his throat. "You have really nice eyes."

Her eyes widened. "Thank...you?"

He was an idiot. "Harrison Walker."

Her mouth opened. Quickly closed. "Wait a minute. The Harrison that Tiffany mentioned? The guy she slept with last night? That Harrison?"

"Yeah. Harrison and I go way back. He has a history of liking to screw me over." *And of liking to screw the women I date.*

"Well, yes, let's move him to the top of the suspect list." She hopped off the desk. "I'll make plans to talk with him today and—"

"The hell you will." He curled his fingers around her wrist before she could dart away from him. "There's no fucking way I want you near that asshole."

Her brows flew up. "Have you forgotten exactly what we're supposed to be doing?"

No, dammit, he had not. "Harrison is a charmer. You—"

Laughter sputtered out of her. Unlike Tiffany's laughter, Delilah's was warm and robust. "*You* don't need to worry. I can handle myself."

But he did worry. "We stay together. *That's* the point of this ruse. To make people think I can't keep my hands off you." His hand was on her right then. His thumb kept sliding along her racing pulse. The racing pulse told him she wasn't as unaffected as she wanted him to believe. "You want to question him, then we'll do it together. I know where he'll be tonight." Friday night. No way would Harrison not show at his usual spot. "We'll plan to make our paths cross."

Grudgingly, Delilah turned back toward him. "This is going to involve another evening dress, isn't it?" She did not sound enthused.

"It might." Actually, it wouldn't involve a fancy dress. But sexy? Hell, yes. They'd hit Harrison's club. A club known for rather infamous reasons in the right—or wrong—circles.

A sigh escaped from Delilah. "At least my nightlife is picking up."

Did that mean she hadn't been dating anyone recently? His research on her had turned up no serious boyfriends, a fact that had made him ridiculously pleased. But just because she didn't have serious men in her life—dumb assholes—it didn't mean that Delilah didn't have someone waiting in the shadows for her.

Too fucking bad. I have her now.

"Archer, you're getting that weird, intense look again. The one that tells me you have all kinds of dark thoughts spinning through your head."

He did have dark thoughts. They were mostly about wanting to make Delilah forget every other guy who'd been with her before she'd come into Archer's life. He didn't want to think of another man driving his fingers into her. Putting his mouth on her. Hearing her moan as she came—

"Are you going to share with the group?"

His breath sawed out. Hell, no, he wasn't about to share those particular thoughts. But he could distract her. "There's something else you should know," he said. His thumb continued to caress her. Why stop? He enjoyed touching her. "I didn't give Vanessa a key to my house."

A furrow appeared between her eyebrows. "You were engaged—"

"She didn't have a key to my place. She didn't live with me. And I told you already, we weren't engaged. That was something that was overhyped, on her end. Vanessa got tired of waiting for me to propose—Vanessa gave me those exact words, she was *tired*—so she sped things along by leaking the news of our supposed engagement to a reporter down here."

"And you let the story stand?"

"There wasn't a chance to set the record straight. Doing it afterwards—hell, no one believed anything I said at that point, anyway."

She nibbled on her lower lip. "Then where did she get a key?"

"That is quite a good question."

"*Why* didn't you give her a key? You were dating, even if you weren't engaged. Couples exchange keys all the time."

"I don't. I'm very private. I am very careful about the people I let into my world."

Her tongue swiped over her lower lip. "*I'm* in your world. You've known me for a few days, and I'm living in your house. Something you apparently didn't let her do."

Yes, Delilah was very much in his world.

"Why?" she asked starkly.

Because you're the right one. Not that he could tell her that. A man didn't get to say shit like that without seriously scaring a woman like Delilah. "We're partners, remember?"

Her breath whispered out. "Last night, I think we were more than that."

Yes, they had been. He rose from the chair. His body brushed against hers. "Do you regret it?" *Don't. Don't regret it.* He had wanted her more than he'd wanted—

"I regret that we didn't finish."

Those words had his heartbeat thundering in his ears. Lust blazed through him. When Delilah was close, Archer was discovering that he was always on the sharp edge of desire. But for her to say those words...for her to stare into his eyes...

I regret that we didn't finish.

He could feel his self-control cracking. "Delilah..."

"Too bad you're not the type to go for sex on a desk." Her head tipped back. "Maybe next time."

Want her.

His hands locked around her waist. He lifted her up, put her down on his desk, and stepped between her spread legs. He was the type to have sex with her any damn place he could get her. He'd tried playing it slow and steady with her. Screw that tactic. She wanted him? She was going to get him.

He took her mouth. Thrust his tongue past her plump lips as he tasted her. A ragged groan built inside of him. His hand flew to her thigh. Her skirt had hiked up, and it was far too easy to slip his fingers under that skirt and go up higher. To find the silk of her panties and stroke her and feel her getting wet through the fabric for him.

His cock shoved at the front of his pants. Her hands slapped down on the desk. Something fell. He heard a clatter. Didn't care. His mouth tore from hers, and he began to kiss a hot path down her throat.

"*Archer.*"

He was touching her through the silk of her panties. Needing to be *in* her.

"Archer, I want—"

The office door flew open. "How many damn closed-door meetings are you having this week, man?" Oz announced as he stormed in and—

Stopped.

Archer's head whipped up. He glared at his lawyer.

Oz's jaw dropped. "Oh, shit."

Delilah grabbed Archer's shoulders. Then immediately shoved him back as she tried to close her legs and get off the desk. But he was still between her legs and *not* in the mood to move. "Out," he snarled at Oz.

Behind Oz's shoulder, Archer could see the shocked face of his assistant. Casey should have stopped Oz before he ever stepped one foot inside Archer's office.

The timing is shit. You have no idea how much pain I am going to bring to you both. They'd just fucked things up for him...when he'd been too close to fucking *her.* "Out...*now.*"

Oz jerked back and nearly slammed into Casey. Then Oz hauled the door shut behind him.

Archer's breath rasped in and out. His head turned back to Delilah.

Her cheeks were flushed. Her lips trembled, and embarrassment coated her features. "Let me down."

Dammit, dammit to hell! He backed up and went to help her down—

She jumped off the desk. "I can see why the office sex scene...um, doesn't appeal." She smoothed her skirt. Her hair. "OhmyGod. The one time I try—"

His hand curled under her chin. "The one time?" he repeated. He wanted her mouth again, but he understood that Oz had shattered the mood.

Her long lashes lifted. Her gaze met—held—his. "I don't sleep around. My last lover—I was with him over a year ago."

A year? *Then there is no one in the shadows.* No one in his way. Delilah would be his.

"I get that things have moved fast for us," she added.

Not fast enough for me. If he'd had his way, he would have been *in* her right then.

"But my reaction to you isn't what I'd call typical."

She could be playing him. The more he learned about Delilah, the more Archer realized how dangerous she was to him. Perhaps she was still working her angle and she was determined to draw him into her web. If so, the act was sure as hell working.

And she was a far, far better actress than Vanessa or Tiffany.

But he didn't want to believe that she was faking. He wanted to believe her words because... "My reaction to you isn't typical, either. In fact, I worry you can be someone who makes me lose control."

She pressed up onto her tiptoes. Her cheeks were still flushed, but Delilah whispered, "Promises, promises..."

He was having her mouth again. His head bent.

She dodged away. Sidestepped and hurried to the bathroom that connected to his office. "Go see what your buddy wants. Maybe it's about our case. I'll, um, freshen up real fast and be right out."

He wanted to tell his *buddy* to screw off. But Delilah had already vanished into the bathroom. The door shut with a click. Swiping his hands through his hair, Archer marched for the office door. He yanked it open and found Oz sitting in one of the waiting chairs near Casey's desk.

Oz looked at his watch, then back up at Archer. "That was quick."

"Do *not* start with me right now. Get your ass inside."

"You got it. My ass is coming inside." He saluted and rose to his feet. Oz didn't say another word until they were inside Archer's office. As soon as the door closed, and Oz did a quick sweep and realized that Delilah was in the bathroom...

Oz closed in on Archer. Keeping a faint, polite smile on his face, Oz softly gritted, "I warned you about that woman. What in the sweet hell are you thinking?"

CHAPTER ELEVEN

Sex on a desk. What in the hell had she been thinking? Or, no, the problem was that she *hadn't* been thinking. This whole case was way, way out of control, and Delilah knew she had to pull things back.

Falling for her mark? That wasn't an option, yet here she was still shaking and quaking in a bathroom because she'd almost had sex with Archer.

He's innocent. Her belief in him kept growing. The more lies she uncovered, the more she wanted to prove his innocence. And the more dangerous things became. Emotions clouded logic. Emotions made a person sloppy. She could *not* let her emotions get involved. It was bad enough that desire was burning through her.

Her phone vibrated, and Delilah hurriedly yanked it out of her skirt pocket. She'd almost forgotten about it. Her finger slid over the screen, and she read the text. *Do you have an update?*

Her hold tightened on the phone. No, she wasn't ready for an update.

Three dots appeared, and Delilah held her breath as she waited for the next text.

Any news on Vanessa?

She had to reply. To remain silent would just push him to be more curious. Quickly, Delilah typed...*Nothing I can use yet. Will sign on later to talk with the group.*

Delilah could hear the faint murmur of voices beyond the door. Schooling her features, she straightened her shoulders, tucked the phone into her pocket once more, and headed back into Archer's office.

Sure, she flushed when Oz glanced over at her—with a knowing gleam in his eyes—but she kept her spine straight and merely lifted an eyebrow as if this kind of thing happened to her all the time. *Ha! Not even close.* "You have utterly horrible timing," Delilah announced to him coolly. "Has anyone ever told you that before?"

Oz blinked, then gave a quick bark of laughter. "To be perfectly honest, yes. I have heard that a time or two." He headed toward her and offered his hand. "Oz Whitlock."

She took his hand. Felt the steady strength of his grip. Noted the assessing quality of his stare. "Delilah Darrow. But then, I'm sure you already know that. You were one of the ones doing the investigation on me, yes?"

He shrugged and released his grip on her. "It's my job to protect my client."

Was there the faintest edge of a threat in Oz's words? Delilah thought there might have been. "And you believe I'm a threat?"

"Aren't you?" Polite but...

Something about his eyes.

"No, Delilah isn't a threat." Archer's firm reply. "But she is something special." He closed in on her. He wrapped one arm around her waist and pulled her against him. "So you *will* be on your best behavior with her, Oz. This isn't a courtroom. I don't need you on the attack."

Oz inclined his head. "Wow. We are certainly moving...swiftly, shall we say? I'd heard a rumor that she spent the night at your place, but I thought that had to be wrong. We all know how gossip can distort things, and you don't usually let strangers stay over."

"She's not a stranger." A smooth retort from Archer.

"Yes, you two certainly seemed very well acquainted a moment ago." Oz glanced toward the desk.

Her jaw tightened.

"Don't make me kick your ass." Archer didn't sound quite as smooth when he delivered that threat. "Because I will do it. You don't disrespect her. Sure as fuck not when I am standing right next to her."

Oz's stare jumped back to him. "Are you serious right now?"

"Doesn't he look serious?" Delilah asked. She turned her head and studied Archer's hard profile. Nodded. "He appears quite serious to me."

Archer winked at her.

"What. The. Fuck?" Oz's voice came out a little strangled. "Are you two a for real couple? Arch, not too long ago, you had me doing our typical swindler background check. Now you're making out on a desk with this woman?"

"Sometimes, you just click with someone." Archer caught Delilah's hand. Brought it to his lips. "And you should be happy for me." He turned his head and focused his stare on Oz. "After all, you're the one who said her background check came back clean."

"I *said* I thought she was trying to prove you were guilty of murder." Oz threw his hands into the air. Frustration rolled from him. "I said she had a history of working cold cases. That's her bread and butter. I *told* you to stay on guard with her. Sleeping with her was not something I advised you to do! That was not in my game plan."

All of this was certainly interesting to hear. Though, technically, they hadn't slept *together*. Done a few other things, yes, but she'd slept in the guest room. Archer had been in his own bed.

Archer pressed a kiss to her knuckles. "You told me she had no criminal background. That her former employers had all praised her. That she'd never been involved in a scandal. That she had a dedication to finding the truth and helping the missing because of what happened to her own sister."

Delilah flinched.

"You described someone I wanted to get to know a great deal better. So I have." Archer shrugged as if he didn't see a problem.

But all the smooth and easy things he said weren't the truth. Delilah had thought for certain that Archer would bring his lawyer in on their ruse. Yet he wasn't confiding in the other man and that had to mean that Archer didn't trust Oz.

Another suspect for her list.

"Okay, fine, I can maybe buy that." Oz started to pace. Then he stopped and pointed at Delilah. "But what about you? Don't you think he might be dangerous? With your past, shouldn't you be extra wary of guys like him?"

"I've never encountered a man like Archer before." An honest response. "I believe the things he says to me. Archer assures me that he had nothing to do with Vanessa's disappearance."

"Well, of course, he didn't." Almost a huff from Oz. "He's not a murderer. His killer instinct is reserved solely for the business world."

Good to know Archer's lawyer backed him up. *So why doesn't Archer want Oz knowing the truth about our partnership?*

"Why are you here, Oz?" Archer suddenly asked. "We didn't have a meeting on the schedule."

"I'm here because I heard about the scene at the opera last night. There was a pic online of you carrying Delilah out of the place—holding her tightly in your arms. All very dramatic and protective-like. Probably very good PR for you now that I think about it...It would be a nice change for you to be viewed as the hero instead of the villain." His head tilted as he locked his focus on Delilah. "But I digress. Is the story I read true? Did someone push you down the stairs?"

"Yes."

Oz swore. "Tell me security footage caught the bastard."

"No, but I am working on the issue," Archer assured him in a voice rife with menace.

"*We're* working on it," Delilah corrected.

A quick knock sounded at the door.

"Did you hear that?" Archer drawled. "Someone *knocked* before entering. Such a novel technique. Something you should try next time."

"I did try that shit *last* time. But, I guess at least then, I didn't see anything to burn my eyes." Oz threw his body down in the nearest chair.

Another knock. Then Casey poked his head inside. The light glinted off the lenses of his glasses. "Mr. Radcliffe, sorry to interrupt, but you're supposed to go for that tour at the building site, and your project manager is waiting in the lobby."

"Dammit." Archer looked over at Delilah. His frustration was more than apparent.

"Go," she urged him. "I have things to do." Lots of items on her to-do list.

His brow furrowed.

He obviously wanted to stay close. Not happening. She truly had stuff to do. "First up, I need to talk more with your lawyer." Delilah motioned toward him. "So how about you tell Oz I should get an all-access pass to the case files you have on Vanessa?" She knew they had them. And she had been promised *all access* as part of their deal.

Jaw locking, Archer nodded. "Give her the all-access pass."

Shock slackened Oz's handsome face. "You aren't serious."

"Let me be clear. *Give Delilah whatever she wants.*"

***

Oz chased Archer to the elevator. Then he jumped *on* the elevator with him right before the doors closed.

"What the hell are you doing?" Archer frowned at him. "You're supposed to be with Delilah."

"You don't *know* her. She's here to take you down, Arch."

He hit the button for the ground floor. "Give her what she wants."

"The files we've been collecting? They are useless so far. Do you really think this woman is going to magically see something in them that we didn't? Something that all the other investigators didn't?"

"Delilah doesn't think like everyone else. It is possible that she might pick up on something that we missed." He sure as hell hoped that she would.

"Maybe..." Oz's face had gone all dark and worried. "Or she might see something to nail your ass to the wall!" Oz's breath rushed out on a frustrated sigh.

Archer tensed. "You think I'm guilty?"

"What?" A quick, almost nervous laugh. "Of course not, man. I've known you for ages. I—"

"Then you know she isn't going to find anything to nail me because I didn't *do* anything to Vanessa."

"Someone is setting you up." Low. Intense. "Someone has been all along. If Delilah connects the wrong pieces of the puzzle, you could be in for an even worse nightmare. Are you ready to risk that?"

The elevator chimed. The doors opened. *No risk, no fucking reward.* "Give her what she wants."

***

She was rifling through Archer's desk. Feeling vaguely guilty about the search, but he'd been the one to leave her in his office, and when offered the temptation...

Rifle. She'd been a snoop since age seven. Not like that was ever gonna change.

The door opened. She kept thumbing through Archer's old datebook. It had been buried in the bottom drawer, tossed down there and seemingly forgotten. Her fingers shoved through the pages. She was heading back to the weeks around Vanessa's disappearance. *Back two years.* The date book sure was a lucky find to have just been tossed under those papers...

"Discovering anything useful?" Oz asked.

Her index finger slid over the page. She'd finally found the days she wanted. "Archer had a trip scheduled for the week after Vanessa's disappearance. He was supposed to head up to Vermont."

"His family has a cabin there. Obviously, he didn't make the trip." A pause. "You're using him."

"I prefer to think that we are using each other." She looked up even as she made a mental note to check on that cabin. Vermont was very, very far away from Miami. Why had Archer planned that trip for that specific time? And had he gone up there since Vanessa vanished?

Oz's nostrils flared. "You think I haven't done everything possible to clear his name?"

Delilah considered his statement. "I think you probably have. After all, you are the Wizard, right?" She knew the nickname had been tied to him because he seemed to have a magic touch in the courtroom. At least according to the prosecutors who had gone up against him. Oz had a reputation for getting off clients when others were sure they were about to be locked away. Almost as if by magic... "But I'm not really here to clear Archer's name. I'm here to find Vanessa."

"And you think you can do that?" His hands flew into the air as he began to pace. She'd quickly come to realize that he liked to pace. The man seemed to be filled with barely bottled energy. He was quite the contrast to Archer. Archer's movements were always controlled. Oz seemed on the brink of a constant explosion. He strode to the window and gestured outside. "The ocean is right fucking there."

She was quite aware of the ocean's location.

"If someone wanted to get rid of a body, it's pretty freaking easy to do." A shake of his head. "Half the people in this town own boats. You load up the body, you go out at night, you weigh her down, and you drop her. *Done*. She won't rise up, and if she tries, hell, the sharks would probably eat her."

She maintained her light grip on Archer's datebook. Delilah intended to keep her prize. "Is that what you would have done?"

He whirled toward her. "I'm not a killer."

"I didn't say you were. I simply asked if that was what you would have done."

A cold grin lifted his lips as he stalked toward her.

She didn't retreat. Didn't move at all. Just waited.

"Do you think I had something to do with her disappearance?" Oz inquired silkily.

"Did you?"

His eyes were chips of green ice. "I defend murderers. I'm not one."

"But you were having sex with Vanessa."

He jerked back as if she'd burned him. "What?" Some of his cocky confidence faded. Gave way to shock.

She'd hoped to catch him off guard with the question. Turned out, she'd succeeded. "I said you were having sex with Vanessa."

"Who told you that?" He swiped a hand over the back of his neck.

You just did.

"Because it's not true," he snapped. "Vanessa came on to me. The woman came on to every rich man in her radius, but I turned her down. I don't care what crap you think you dug up—*I told her no*. Archer is my friend. The oldest one I've got. I wouldn't hurt him."

There was a ring of truth to his words. The full truth, though, or a partial one?

"Is this what you're going to do? Rip apart everyone close to Archer because you think someone he knows is responsible for whatever happened to Vanessa?"

One of her shoulders moved in a little shrug. "That is an option I'm considering."

His lips thinned.

Are you going to stand in my way?

"Then...good luck," Oz muttered.

"Excuse me?"

"Maybe that was why the other investigators failed. Maybe they were too busy pussyfooting around because they were scared of the power the people near Archer possess." Once more, he closed in. "Don't be afraid. Don't stop. No matter what you uncover. It's time for the full truth to come out."

*Well, well...*He'd just surprised her.

"Just watch your ass," he added grimly. "Because next time, you might not be so lucky if you take another tumble. And, no, that's not a threat. It's a warning. Bad things happen in Archer's world. You need to be ready for them."

CHAPTER TWELVE

"Did you learn anything interesting from the PI reports?" Archer asked as he lounged back against the limo's seat and lightly drummed his fingers along the top of his thigh.

Delilah sat a few inches away from him. Not surprisingly, she looked sexy as hell. His fault, of course, because he'd been the one to tell the personal shopper to get her something that would make her fit in at Club Thirty-Two.

Club Thirty-Two. A strictly VIP scene. The hottest club in town, if you listened to the rumor mills. The place to see and be seen. And the club had become Harrison's personal playground.

"Interesting?" Delilah shifted a bit as she seemed to taste the word. Her skirt—already incredibly, mind-bogglingly short—hiked up a little more. Her top was a deep red, silk, and cut with a low, plunging V that arrowed down between her breasts. When he'd first seen her, he'd nearly pounced.

He wasn't supposed to be the pouncing type.

Dammit, he could use a drink. Every man in the club would be after Delilah. It wasn't about her *fitting in* with the crowd. She was so freaking sexy that she'd be standing out and starring in every fantasy those horny bastards possessed. "Such a damn bad idea," he rasped.

"Excuse me?" Her warm voice. "Didn't quite catch that."

He growled. Cleared his throat. Tried again. "Interesting," he enunciated slowly. "Was there anything in the files that caught your attention or not?" She might be aiming to drive him crazy. If so, Delilah was certainly succeeding.

"Someone is grumpy," she murmured. "Bad day at the office?"

"You have no idea."

She reached over and gave his arm a little pat. "There, there."

Her touch electrified him. He looked at her hand. Then slowly, back up at her face. A little smile had been on her full lips, but as she held his stare, that smile faded.

"I am not in the mood to play." Rough.

Her tongue swiped over her lower lip. "I can...see that. Sorry. I was just attempting to lighten the tension."

"Touching me isn't the best idea." Because her touch didn't *lighten* anything about him. Quite the opposite. When she touched him, things got harder.

She didn't move her hand. "If the people in this fancy club are supposed to believe we're lovers, don't I have to touch you?"

Yes, she did. She had to touch him. He got to touch her. He had to put his hands all over her body because he was *not* going to let anyone else move in on her.

"But I'll save the physical contact for our audience." Her hand slowly pulled back. "And, to get back to our previous topic, what was the most *interesting* discovery was the stuff I didn't see."

She was trying to redirect him. He ignored his aching dick and attempted to focus on what Delilah was saying. "What didn't you see?" She was talking about the reports from the investigators. *Focus.*

"There were no big reports on the people closest to you. I wanted to read a file on Oz. Wanted to know where he was and what he was doing the night Vanessa vanished."

"Whoa. Hold up." Tension snaked through him. "Oz?"

"Um. Were they sleeping together?" Casual. Breezy. Like she'd just asked about the weather. But her gaze was sharp on him.

She's watching for my reaction. Playing him. Anger hummed in his blood. "You already know the answer to that."

"Would I ask if I knew?"

Probably. Just to watch his reaction.

"I know what Oz told me. But I'd like to hear what you have to say about the matter. I mean, we're on this big trip to the club right now because you're taking me to see Vanessa's ex-lover. But what if she had more than one?"

Then I'm a bigger fucking idiot than I thought.

"I see." A nod from Delilah. "Not so sure, are you?"

He'd fisted the hand on his thigh. With care, he unclenched his fingers. "Oz wasn't sleeping with her."

"And you know this because...?"

A low exhale. "You already know I have other investigators, don't you?" Others that he hadn't told Oz about.

Her head tilted. The soft lighting in the back of the limo allowed him to clearly see her face. "Well, when I looked through Oz's files and realized there was no info on the people closest to you, I did suspect that you had done other investigations—investigations that you hadn't informed him were occurring. Probably because he was one of the suspects *in* those investigations."

"You impress me."

"Really?" Surprise had her voice rising. "I've barely done anything at this point. Just gotten my ass pushed down some stairs. Not exactly something that demands a standing ovation."

His hand flew out and curved around her wrist. "That's not funny."

She looked down at his hand. Swallowed. Returned her gaze to him. "I've been told that I have a somewhat unusual sense of humor."

"A joke about you getting hurt isn't fucking funny." His thumb slid along her pulse point. He felt it lurch.

"I like it when you touch me," Delilah confessed.

That confession was the *last* thing he'd expected.

"But you probably realized that already. Seeing as how each time we touch, need quakes through me."

Need quaked through him, too. *But I'm not fucking her in the back of a limo.* Mostly because...they were almost at their destination. There wasn't enough time to do all of the things he wanted. And he had so many plans for Delilah.

As if realizing they were getting close to the club, her gaze darted to the windows, then back to him. "Not much time, so how about you hurry along the tale?"

He swallowed. Her scent was driving him crazy. She'd said she didn't like flowers, but she smelled just like them. *Lilacs...for Lila.* But he didn't call her Lila. Because they weren't friends. They were something so much more. Something darker. Hotter.

"Archer?"

"I had a team dig into the lives of those close to me, yes. I found out that Vanessa had made a move on Oz. He'd kicked her ass to the curb. And the night that she went missing? He was with a client at the county jail. Video footage showed him going in and coming out. Hard to fake that alibi."

"So it would seem." She didn't try to tug free of him.

He didn't let her go.

"What about Harrison Walker?"

"He's not exactly someone I would define as close to me."

"But he's someone you hate, and I suspect he is someone who hates you. Why is that?"

"Why indeed?"

A sigh escaped her. "I'll find out. It would save considerable time if you just told—"

"Because he's my half brother." She *would* find out. He had no doubt. She noticed things others didn't, and her online team had proven to be quite resourceful in the past. "My dad fucked his mother when she was married to Clyde Walker. When Harrison was five, he had a pretty bad accident. Wound up needing a blood transfusion. Let's just say that lots of test were run, and the truth came out."

"I don't remember reading about this truth."

"That's because the truth came out to a precious few. Clyde had an image to maintain. He wasn't going to let it be known that one of his chief rivals had screwed him over."

Her hand jerked.

"But he never treated Harrison as his son after that day. Harrison grew up hating my father—hating me, too, probably just for the hell of it. And he's let that hate eat him alive."

Silence, and then, "That's some secret."

"You wanted to know about him." He still had his grip on her hand. "That gonna wind up in your story when we're done?"

"Not everything is about my story."

"Isn't it?" The limo had stopped. He leaned in closer to her. "I'm still trying to figure out how much of you is real," he murmured against her lips. "And what is just a trick to pull me closer to you."

Her lips parted. And she said, "Bastard," with a fierce, hard snap in her voice. Then she jerked away from him and surged out of the limo.

He sucked in a steadying breath. He *was* the bastard. That was a role he was very, very good at playing.

I overshared too much with her. He'd never told anyone else that story about Harrison. Not even Oz. He needed to get his wall back in place. Watch himself better with Delilah.

The woman just might have the power to destroy him.

He took his time and followed her out of the limo. The line to get in Club Thirty-Two stretched around the block. Hardly surprising. Archer didn't head for the line. Instead, he strolled straight for the door.

Not like Harrison could deny him entry.

I bought the fucking place. Another story. Another secret.

Delilah paused to peer up at the thick, tall building. No sign outside. None was needed.

Two bouncers—both wearing black suits and earpieces—guarded the double entrance doors. Archer curled his arm around Delilah's shoulders and directed her straight for the guards. They recognized him and scrambled to open the doors. As they did, the pounding beat of music spilled into the night.

"Guessing someone comes here often," Delilah said.

No, but the guards were on *his* payroll. He liked to have his own eyes and ears around the club. As he passed the guard on the right, he ordered, "Tell Harrison I will be in VIP room number 6." His room. "He should get his ass in there because we need to chat."

The guard on the right inclined his head.

Then Archer and Delilah were in the club. The darkness inside was punctuated by glowing, neon lights that flashed and rolled across the dance floor. The DJ held court on the raised stage, pumping his fist into the air as his mixes blasted. Bodies gyrated on the dance floor. Glow-in-the-dark paint covered the skin of at least half of the dancers.

Level one. That was the bottom floor. Reserved for the rich and spoiled in the city. The people who liked to dance and drink the night away.

He didn't waste time heading for the dance floor. Not exactly Archer's scene or style. Instead, he ushered Delilah toward the elevator. His hand shoved into his pocket, and he pulled out his keycard. A quick press of the keycard to the control panel, and the elevator doors opened. He guided her inside. "We can see out," he told her as he pressed the button for the third floor. "But no one can see in."

The elevator rose. He had a perfect view of the gyrating bodies. Hands flew into the air, waving toward the DJ on stage.

"That is, um, a whole lot of energy out there," Delilah noted carefully.

"Do you like to dance?" The question slipped from him. The night he'd had her in his arms, she'd moved gracefully. Elegantly. And felt so good against him.

Before she could answer, the doors opened. There was no music on the third floor. The gyrating dancers may as well have been a million miles away. The thick carpeting swallowed their steps as Archer led Delilah toward room number six.

She cut her gaze toward the rooms they passed. "Do I want to know what's happening in there?"

"Probably not."

Door number five opened. A woman with long, curly red hair exited. Body paint covered her arms and legs, and otherwise, she was just wearing a bikini. Her breath came hard and fast, and she slid some cash under the top of her bikini.

She quirked a brow at Delilah. Smiled at Archer. "Haven't seen you in a while."

Delilah tensed.

Archer kept walking and he pulled Delilah with him. When they got to room six, once again, he used his card to gain them entrance. And as soon as the door closed behind them...

"What in the hell is going on?" Delilah stormed about five feet away, only to immediately swing back around and glare at him. "Is there some serious *Eyes Wide Shut* shit happening here?"

"What?"

One hand motioned toward the window behind her. Like the elevator's glass, the window let them see out, but no one could see in the VIP room. "Are we inside some weird sex club? A club you apparently frequent so often that employees *recognize* you? That you have your own room?" Her head shook in a rather dazed fashion. "This did not come up in my research. Nowhere did it say that Archer Radcliffe was some sort of closet freak who came to a sex club to get—"

"*Ahem.*" The shadows to the left moved.

Archer put his hands on his hips. "Delilah, my love, we are not alone in here."

She gaped. Then swung to the left.

Harrison Walker stalked from the shadows. A sardonic grin curled his hips. And his eyes glinted with—

"Oh, right. Totally obvious." Delilah took a step toward Harrison and frowned at him. "He's got your chin and nose."

Harrison's nostrils flared. He looked at her. Then at Archer. "What the hell is going on? Who is this woman?"

"Uh, I'm his *girlfriend*." Delilah swept to Archer's side, and she also looped her arm with his. "He's bringing his girlfriend to meet his brother because I am so incredibly important in his life."

Harrison laughed.

Archer didn't. He just waited for the bastard to get control of his shit again. While he waited, Archer brought one of Delilah's hands to his mouth. He kissed her knuckles. He was finding the small act was a habit he rather enjoyed doing with her.

Harrison stopped laughing. "Girlfriend?"

"Yes," Delilah affirmed. "Girlfriend. As in, the new love of his life. The woman who makes him feel complete. The woman who—"

"Who didn't know that Archer liked to get off in a sex club?" Harrison taunted. "The woman who had no clue—with her research—that Archer has a very, very dark side?"

Delilah's chin notched up. "I was teasing him."

"Were you?" Harrison's doubt was obvious.

Archer could have interrupted, but he was curious to see just where this would go. He was supposed to be trusting Delilah, and investigating *was* her job.

"Yes, I was." Delilah didn't miss a beat. "Obviously, I know exactly what this place is. Not a sex club. I was teasing him. It's just a spot for bored, rich bastards to while away their time. Archer wouldn't have backed a business if there was anything illegal happening at the facility. Not like he'd risk that sort of venture turning sour on him. He's very risk adverse."

"Is he?" A muscle flexed along Harrison's jaw. The jaw that *was* very similar to Archer's.

"Um." That sounded non-committal, but she plowed on with, "That's why so many of the employees defer to him. They know that if shit starts getting illegal, they are to report to him right away. You might act like the boss, but he's the real one in charge."

Harrison's eyes glittered. "And you know all of this because...?"

"Because it's obvious?"

"What about your *Eyes Wide—*"

"Oh, saw the movie, did you?" Delilah cut through Harrison's words to say. "Not surprised." She offered him a tight smile. "I knew you were watching us. I saw you the instant I came into the room. I figured if you were the type to watch, I'd give you a little show."

Had she seen him? Now even Archer was curious.

"Who the hell are you?" Harrison breathed.

"I told you." A long suffering sigh. "I'm his girlfriend. His dearly beloved. The sunshine of his day. His reason for breathing. His—"

"Name," Harrison snapped.

Delilah sniffed and glanced toward Archer. "You obviously got all the charm."

He smiled at her. She was rather fun when she got going. "Thanks for noticing."

"You are welcome."

"What. The. Fuck?" Harrison's patience was long gone.

Good. When he was at the edge, Harrison was always easiest to read. And manipulate. "Are you sleeping with Tiffany Lassiter?" Archer asked bluntly.

Harrison's jaw locked. It took a moment before he gritted, "Seriously? You think because you gave me some cash, you get to come in here and ask me personal questions about my sex life?"

"Sorry. I think Archer's question should have been far more specific. I'll rephrase, if that helps." Delilah locked her gaze on Harrison. "Were you sleeping with Tiffany *last* night? Did you take her home from the opera?"

"Oh." Harrison rocked back on his heels. "I see. You were the woman who got pushed." He winced. "Must have hurt like hell taking that tumble." He took a few, slow steps toward Delilah and Archer. "The fall can be a real bitch, can't it?"

Archer didn't like the glint of unholy amusement in his eyes. "Watch the tone." A lethal order. "I'm not here to play games."

"No? That's why everyone else is." Harrison's hand lifted as he rubbed his jaw. A line of neon green paint slid along the exterior of his hand. "Just what is it that you're accusing me of doing now? Do you believe I was the one pushing the, um, sunlight of your day?"

"Not accusing you of anything," Archer responded. Delilah's body pressed to Archer's side. He liked having her that close. He curled his arm around her waist. Tugged her a little closer. "I just want to know if you're fucking Tiffany." A pause. "Like you fucked Vanessa."

And it was there—on Harrison's face. A faint twitch. Yes, the sonofabitch had fucked Vanessa. *You just wanted to take something away from me, didn't you?* Because his whole life, Harrison had believed that Archer had taken things from *him.*

The biggest thing? Their asshole of a father.

A mocking smile tilted Harrison's lips. "If a beautiful woman wants to have sex with me, who am I to deny her that pleasure?"

A faint gagging sound escaped Delilah. "Oh, please." Archer caught Delilah's eye roll. "Is he serious right now?"

Harrison's smile tightened.

"Look, God's gift, or whatever you think you are..." Delilah exhaled heavily. "I'm trying to find out if Tiffany shoved me down the stairs last night. She said *you* were her alibi. That you could vouch for her. So how about we cut to the chase?

Sound like a plan? To get to the chase, just answer my questions. First, were you at the opera house last night? And, second, did Tiffany spend the night with you?"

His smile vanished completely. "Tiffany didn't shove you down any stairs. I was with her, yes, and I was waiting when she came out of the bathroom after her little chat with you."

I knew you were at the opera, bastard. But Archer didn't let his mask slip.

"I escorted her away. We were fucking in the back of the limo before we'd even left the opera house." A roll of his shoulders. "So, no, we weren't pushing you down the stairs. Does that alibi satisfy you?"

"We?" Delilah pounced on that word choice. "Don't remember accusing you. But, gee, thanks for telling me that you aren't guilty."

"Figured that's all it would take." He smirked. "A man says he isn't guilty, and you believe him. After all, isn't that why you're with Archer? He fed you a sob story. You bought it, and now, you are going where angels fear to tread." A pause. "Archer's bed."

"Oh, is that where I'm going?" Delilah murmured. "I was confused for a moment. Though being in Archer's bed does have me feeling like I'm touching heaven."

Anger tightened Harrison's features. "You're a reporter. I saw the story about the opera scene. I saw—"

"If you saw all of this, then why the whole routine about wanting my name? Seems suspicious." She made a tut-tut sound.

"Suspicious scenes make people look guilty of bad deeds."

God, he loved Delilah's fire. Archer's hold tightened on her even more. A helpless movement.

And Harrison noticed it. Hell.

"She was afraid of him," Harrison announced suddenly. "Vanessa, that is. She was terrified of Archer."

Delilah didn't change expression. Archer did not let her go.

"Why do you think she looked somewhere else?" Harrison pushed almost gleefully. "But then, if you've been in Archer's bed, you probably know what she feared, too. There's a reason he tries to cling so tightly to that control of his." His gaze shifted to Archer. Held his stare. "Got the devil inside, don't you, Archer? Just begging to get out. According to the gossip I heard, a session with you is more like hell than heaven."

Archer surged toward Harrison—

Delilah stepped between them. "It's cute that you worry about what Archer is like with me. Super cute. So sweet. Really. Adorable, almost. But no worries. I can handle him just fine. In fact, I like handling him."

Archer looked over her head. Knew his stare would promise retribution to Harrison.

Harrison's Adam's apple bobbed.

Delilah wasn't done. "I like being with Archer because truth be told, I'm no angel. Never claimed to be. And I don't fear a whole lot. But maybe *you* should be afraid, Harrison."

"Of what?"

"Of the truth getting out. It's time everyone stopped looking at Archer like he was the monster. Maybe they need to see real evil." Her hands were on her hips. "When you stare at real evil, you know what you're seeing."

He leaned in close to her. "*Are you threatening me?*" He reached out to grab—

Mistake. A terrible, terrible mistake. Because Archer's control splintered. He yanked Delilah back behind him before Harrison could touch her, and then he drove his fist straight into his brother's midsection. A hard, brutal hit that had Harrison curling over and grabbing his stomach as he let out a guttural groan.

"What...the...*hell?*"

"You don't touch her. Delilah is *mine*."

Harrison gaped up at him. "Since when do you care who I touch?"

His hand was still fisted. "Delilah isn't Vanessa. No one touches her but me. Delilah is mine, and she's staying mine. And if anyone wants to threaten her?" He leaned in close once more. He wanted this message received, understood, and taken to the grave. "*They will have to go through me.*"

Instead of replying, Harrison let out a snarl and surged toward Archer. But Archer just twisted, avoided his lunge, and then Archer hammered both of his fists down onto Harrison's back.

Harrison slammed onto the floor.

Delilah's gasp teased Archer's ears, but he didn't look back at her. "I will fight for her. Make no mistake about that. I will fight harder for

Delilah than I have ever fought for anything else in my life."

Harrison rolled onto his back. Panted. Glared up at Archer.

Archer knelt beside him. Voice dropping, he promised, "I will kill for her."

CHAPTER THIRTEEN

"When we are trying to convince people that you are *not* a killer, it would be extremely helpful if you would not threaten *to* kill people." Delilah tapped her right foot. "Do you see how that is counterproductive?"

Archer whirled toward her. He'd just none-too-gently shoved Harrison out of the VIP room door. "He's a dick. I didn't want his hands on you."

So much for the controlled Archer. "I could handle him." In her sleep. She'd dealt with plenty of jerks in her life.

"Don't be fooled. There is a whole lot more to him than meets the eye." He marched toward the bar in the corner.

She watched him, waited a beat, and asked, "Like there's more to you? I must say that getting into a fist fight hardly fits with your glamorous, sophisticated image."

He threw some whiskey into a glass. Downed it and slammed the glass onto the bar. "That wasn't a fist fight. That was me trying to teach an asshole some manners."

"Huh. Weird. It looked like a fight to me."

He spun toward her. "How did you know?"

Her eyes widened. For an instant, his face had been savage. Keeping her voice light, she queried, "Know what? That it was a fist fight? Because fists were involved. Because a man hit the floor. Because—"

"Know that the place was mine."

"Oh, that. I realized it had to be yours as soon as I heard the name." She waved one hand vaguely in the air. "Then there was the way the bouncers reacted to you. And the keycard you possessed." Every sign had been there for her. "Seriously, it didn't take a giant stretch to connect the dots. *Club Thirty-Two*. The temp that things freeze? And you, the big, bad Iceman." Now she sighed. "I think you're taking the ice thing a bit too far. You're not nearly as cold as you want the world to believe. Maybe you should stop seeing yourself that way." *And let someone get close to you.*

He stalked toward her. Delilah didn't let her shoulders tense even though there was definitely something wild about him. She could feel that wildness thickening the air around them both. He stopped right in front of her. "You're one to talk." His hand rose. His fingers slid down her cheek.

She shivered. *Oh, damn.*

"Ice breaker," Archer breathed it like an accusation. "Here to break my world apart."

Her hand flew up. Curled around his. "No. I'm not. By the time I'm done, I think you'll be thanking me." She could feel the faint calluses on his fingers.

Archer leaned toward her. "Are you afraid of me?"

Never let them see your fear. "You mean because I just saw you attack a man in front of my eyes? Don't stress over it. The scene isn't likely to turn me into a quivering bundle of nerves. Not like it's the first time I've witnessed a fight. I'm hardly the sheltered sort."

His jaw hardened.

"You should really find an outlet for all that tension, though," she murmured. "Can't be good to keep so much of yourself bottled inside. You keep doing that and one day you might just explode."

"Are you afraid of me?" Low. Burning with intensity. "Just give me a yes or no answer. Please," Archer gritted the last word.

Was she afraid? "No."

He released a breath.

Wait. Back up. Had he been *holding* his breath while he waited for her response? That was almost endearing.

His forehead pressed against hers. "Good. Because I would not hurt you. I swear it."

He felt strangely right against her. Warm. Strong.

He jerked away. "Why the hell do you trust me?"

She couldn't touch that one. Because her own feelings were such a tangled, mixed-up mess and explaining would make her do some soul-searching that she'd rather face later. So Delilah went with... "Well, I trust you more than I do Harrison because he's obviously a lying bastard."

"Excuse me?"

"You gave him the money for this place? It's been operating for about three years—I learned that much online—but you were not linked to it in any of the databases I found."

A muscle flexed along his jaw. "I figured my father owed him something. So, yes, I gave him the money, with the understanding that nothing illegal could happen here."

That explained the employees who were loyal to him but... "I think he's found a way around your watchers."

Archer's gaze sharpened. "What do you mean?"

"Unless you knew that he was monitoring everything that happened in your, uh, private room?" She glanced around. "And that he'd been coming in here whenever he wanted."

"What are you talking about?"

"When he first arrived, Harrison didn't enter through the door. Not the one we used, anyway. Because I *would* have seen him when I did my first sweep of the place. I was trained by an ex-cop to always search a room when I entered it, and he was not here." She backed away. Turned to the left. Headed for those thick shadows where Harrison had first appeared. A wall greeted her. "He came in from the room next door to this one. Room number five. The room that lovely lady in the bikini exited." Her hands lifted as she began to press against the wall. *Scooby Doo, don't fail me now.*

"The lady in the bikini? Bridgette?"

"That her name?"

"Yes. Bridgette Summers. She's one of the paid dancers."

"Um. She's also involved with Harrison. The man is very busy." Bridgette *and* Tiffany? Someone had stamina. "We should make plans to question her." She pressed down hard and—*click*. Delilah felt more than heard the sound.

The wall slid open.

"What. The. Fuck?" Archer rushed toward the opening. Peered inside.

There was a small hallway between the two VIP rooms. The walls of the narrow hallway sported computer monitors. *Video surveillance.* Damn but it felt good to be right.

He spun toward her. "How do you know he's involved with Bridgette?" The words were bitten off.

"Because she had neon green paint on her stomach. Green paint that had been smudged a bit, and when Harrison lifted his hand—"

A low curse. "He had green paint on him."

"Ah, you noticed it, too." A pleased nod. She pointed to the monitors. "I'm guessing you did *not* know this equipment was here?"

"No, and it won't freaking *be* here for long. I will shut down this damn club."

"Yes, you do that." She opened the little bag that she'd taken the liberty of bringing with her. It had been dangling by one delicate strap over her shoulder. She pulled out the flash drive that she'd tucked inside. Delilah leaned over a small computer—the only one in the hallway, a little computer nestled in a nook to the right. She started typing.

"What are you doing?"

"Accessing." Obviously. "I'm sure there is some sort of alarm that has alerted Harrison to our presence in this secret passage of his, so I want to copy any files that I can find. You know, things that might be useful to our investigation." One of the women on her team was a computer science guru. She'd taught Delilah a few quick and dirty tricks during their association.

So much that it was easy for Delilah to scan through the files. *Not even password protected. What a dumbass.* So easy for her to find the dates that she wanted. Easy for her to get that data onto her drive and—

She pocketed the drive just as she heard a nearby door fly open and slam into the wall. "*Archer!*" Harrison bellowed. *Someone is back for round two.*

Then he was charging forward.

Only...that was a whole lot of footsteps *charging.* He obviously hadn't come alone. Harrison had brought reinforcements.

Her stomach twisted. Uh, oh. "Archer?"

He pushed her behind him.

She peeked around him to see Harrison rushing toward them. She'd been right. He wasn't alone. Two hulking figures flanked his sides. The same hulking figures she'd seen at the entrance to Club Thirty-Two. The men who'd been so quick to guide Archer inside. *Because they work for him, not Harrison.*

"Drag his ass out of here!" Harrison thundered as he pointed at Archer.

Archer laughed.

She knew exactly why he was laughing. Poor Harrison. She almost felt sorry for him. *You picked the wrong men to bring up here.* He'd be regretting this choice for a while.

"No." Archer pointed back at his brother. "Drag his ass out. And make sure he *doesn't* get back in."

"What?" Shock flashed on Harrison's face.

The two men grabbed him and hauled him back.

"What the hell are you doing?" Harrison snarled. Red filled his face as he fought their hold, but he was no match for those over-muscled men. "You work for me! This is my place! This is—"

"I warned you what would happen if you did anything illegal on the premises. Recording people without their permission? You damn well know that's breaking my rules. You should have listened to me." Archer's hand dropped as he shook his head. "Consider the club permanently closed."

"You motherfuck—"

The door shut on his scream.

Archer glanced back at her. "The thumb drive was cute, but you didn't need to rush. We can go over every file here and take as long as we need."

Cute?

"Correction. We *will* go over every file because I want to know exactly what that sonofabitch has been doing."

***

He'd been kicked out of his own damn club. Tossed onto the street like trash. Rage filled Harrison as he watched Club Thirty-Two from the shadows.

Archer was inside. Archer and his new girl. A woman who seemed to be more than fine with the dark side that Archer had always hidden from so many.

You can't take the club from me.

Archer had pulled in more goons. He'd had a whole team swarming the place with just one phone call. The guests had all been escorted out. Now the entrance to the club was blocked by Archer's hand-picked men.

This is my place. It had been bad enough when he'd had to go to Archer, begging for a handout, but for *this* to happen...

No, no, it won't end like this. Archer might think he was God, but he was wrong. Harrison had his own team of lawyers. No one was going to do this to him. No one would take what was his. Harrison yanked out his phone.

And it rang in his hand.

Frowning, he looked at the screen. He didn't recognize the number. It was beyond late, his night was shit, and when he answered the call, he barked, "Listen, you fucking asshole, you do not want to mess with me right—"

"We have a common problem."

Harrison stiffened. He didn't know that voice. Was it distorted? It seemed a little robotic but—

"Would you like to help me eliminate that problem?"

He saw Archer appear in the doorway of the club. Delilah was right at his side. Swallowing, Harrison muttered, "What in the hell are you talking about?"

"You hate him. You want to hurt him."

Archer.

"If we work together, things will be better for us both. All I need you to do is set up a little meeting for me."

"I don't even *know* you, so—"

"I'm the only friend you have. That's who I am. You help me, and we can bring Archer to his knees. Think about it. I'll be in touch soon."

The caller hung up.

Bring Archer to his knees?

Hell, yes. Sign him up right now.

***

"Blackmail." Archer stalked across his den. Tension poured from his body. "Should have fucking known."

They'd reviewed the video footage captured from the club. Delilah had recognized the politicians. The attorneys. The celebrities. Harrison had definitely broken the whole "nothing illegal" rule that Archer had put in place. "Let me make sure I understand everything fully. If he owns the club—"

"Doesn't, not technically." He tossed his coat aside. Jerked at the buttons of his dress shirt. "I gave him the start-up money, but I knew how to tie things up in enough legal loopholes that if the day came when the bastard stepped out of line—"

Oh, he has stepped. She wasn't even sure Harrison understood the concept of a line.

"If that happened, I could make the club vanish. It's tied to subsidiaries that my company owns. By dawn, it will be gone."

"And, um, the people in those videos?"

He slanted her a glance. "I'll take care of them."

She slipped out of her heels. Heels were the devil. She was convinced of that. "What exactly do you mean when you say 'take care of' in that menacing way?"

The top three buttons of his shirt were undone. He'd raked his fingers through his hair, and the tousled mane just made him look sexier. This wasn't the controlled Archer. She knew it. Delilah could feel the difference in the air. See it in him.

She'd wondered what he would be like with his precious control stripped away.

Be careful what you wish for.

"You think I'm going to blackmail them?" A question laced with silky menace. "That I'll keep the videos so I have power and leverage to use against future enemies?"

Why lie? "The thought did cross my mind, yes."

His jaw hardened as he advanced toward her. "Or maybe..." Low, drawling. Dangerous. "Maybe you think this is all some big show. Maybe you think I was in on the blackmail all along. My club, my brother, am I right? And I know you recognized the DA in those videos. The same guy who decided not to press charges against me. The man who said there wasn't enough evidence for a trial. Maybe he did that because I had a video of him snorting coke with a dancer. Maybe I have been behind the blackmail all along, not Harrison. Maybe this is just another move in my game. An elaborate show for you." He stopped right in front of her. "I'm the villain, right? Isn't that the shit I would do?"

Her head cocked as Delilah considered the matter. "Well, you are certainly no Prince Charming."

His gaze gleamed.

"But we established early on that I was more the wicked stepsister than Cinderella, so I'm fine with that."

Confusion cracked through on his face. "What does that mean?"

"It means I don't view you through a fairy-tale lens. I don't think you're perfect. Far from it." She paused. "I also don't think that you're the evil villain out to destroy everyone in your path."

"Thank...you?" A choked question.

"You're welcome." Her thoughts shifted. Refocused. "We need to talk with Harrison. At this point, we don't actually know that he *has* blackmailed anyone. Could be he was just gathering his intel. Saving it to use at a later date." Doubtful, but until she knew for certain, she wanted to wait and see how this bit of drama played out.

"Fuck Harrison," Archer growled.

"I'd rather not." Her instant response.

His lips parted. "*Delilah.*"

"Yes, Archer?"

"You should be terrified of me. You should doubt me. You should be running to the cops."

A sigh. "I've never enjoyed it when people tell me what I *should* do. I like to make my own choices." She was making a choice right then and there. "You've had a lot of betrayal in your life, haven't you?" No wonder he didn't let people get close. "You gave Harrison the money for the club, then he still had an affair with Vanessa."

His eyelids flickered.

"He wanted to hurt you." That was obvious to her. "He's got a lot of rage aimed at you." A reason why Harrison was at the top of her suspect list. He had rage. He had motive. And he'd been sleeping with the missing woman. Three strikes against him.

"Harrison always thought that he should've had my life. At least, that's what he told me once. My dad should have taken him in—*our dad*. Should have claimed him. Should have given him a slice of the Radcliffe fortune." His hands lifted to indicate the house—the mansion—around him. "Only there was no fortune. That was the big lie." Bitter. Hard. "When my father died, we had *nothing* left. The business had been the last thing he cared about. He let it spiral while he was out doing whatever the hell he wanted."

Anger. Pain. She could see it in his eyes and hear it in his voice. Delilah didn't speak. She just waited. This was a story Archer needed to tell.

"I had to build the fortune back. No, I had to *make* my own fortune. Creditors were beating down the door, and I was the only one answering them. To make my money, it meant that I had to spend every single moment I had working. I had to give up evenings, nights, weekends. I had to pour every bit of blood and energy I had into the company so that all of the employees who counted on me would have jobs. My father didn't give a shit about them. I wasn't going to be the same way. I gave up *everything* for the business. *Everything.* But Harrison thought I was the one who'd had a friggin' cake walk through life. I *handed* him that money for the club, and he still screwed me over."

She reached out. Curled her hand over his.

"People think I'm some kind of machine. That I don't care. That all I do is focus on work." He stared down at her hand as it touched his. "I'm the way I've had to be. We were going to lose *everything.* I had to get it back."

So he'd poured all he had into the company. And he'd succeeded.

His hand turned. His fingers laced with hers. "I want more."

"More?"

His hand rose, pulling hers up. His lips pressed to her knuckles. The charge that was always between them heated her blood. His gaze held hers. "*More.*"

He might as well have said...*You.*

She licked her lips. They'd done nearly everything *but* have sex, so why was she suddenly nervous?

And he must have seen that uncertainty, because he let go of her hand. Stepped back. "Right." Flat. "Don't trust me so much any longer, do you? But then, I suspected that, despite what you said." Another step back. "It's late. You should go to bed."

She didn't feel sleepy. Jittery. Nervous. Needy. But sleepy? No. "What are you going to do?"

"Take a cold shower." He yanked off his shirt. Tossed it to the floor. "And try to *stop* thinking about you." Archer stalked from the room.

***

Delilah stared at the message on her computer screen.

You need to check in more often. I was getting worried.

Her fingers hovered over the keyboard. Then, she typed...*There have been a lot of developments.*

The reply was instant. *Yes, like you getting shoved down the stairs.* She could practically feel the frustrated fury in those words even before the next line appeared...*You need backup.*

Her fingers tapped again. *I'm working with Archer.* Automatically, Delilah glanced toward the closed bedroom door. Was Archer in the shower? She swept her gaze back to the computer.

Another message waited.

You are supposed to be working to bring him down.

That wasn't true. Her fingers flew. *The goal is to find Vanessa.* And about that...She wrote, *I want you to see what you can find out about an area for me. A cabin, in Vermont.* Delilah bit her lower lip as she waited for a response. There was something about the cabin that nagged at her. Why was it so important?

She didn't know. Yet. Typing once more, Delilah revealed, *Archer's family owns the place.* Actually, not true. Archer owed it. As he owned everything. Because he'd had to work to keep all that he had.

Her friend sent a fast response. *Shit. You think he dumped her body there?*

No, she didn't. In fact...Delilah nodded as she made the decision to fully reveal her thoughts. Her fingers tapped quickly. *I don't think Archer is guilty.* She'd had her doubts from the beginning. *Look harder at Harrison Walker.*

She heard a creak, and Delilah's head instantly whipped up, then to the side. But no one was in her room. It was just the house. Settling. As if that knowledge did anything to calm her nerves.

After another careful scan of the bedroom, her gaze darted back to the computer.

Are you staying objective?

Her eyes narrowed at the question. Oh, hell, no, he had *not* just gone there. Huffing, she responded, *I know what I'm doing.* Maybe. *I'll check in tomorrow.*

She was about to shut her laptop when she saw his response...

No, I will.

Dammit. The man could be exceedingly frustrating. But, he was also the best tracker she knew. Delilah closed the laptop. Slowly rose. Glanced at the bed. But in her mind, she could only see Archer. Archer with her. Tangled in the sheets. For an instant, she could feel him. Those callused fingertips of his sliding over her skin. His mouth on hers.

Before she realized what she was doing, Delilah was in front of her bedroom door. Reaching for the knob.

She stopped. What in the hell was she thinking?

***

The cold water wasn't helping. Now he was just naked and still thinking about Delilah and all he wanted to do was go to her. Strip her. *Take her.*

Hard to do when she was afraid of him. And she *was* afraid. He'd seen the flash of fear in her gorgeous eyes. *Dammit.* He wanted her to be different. He wanted her to—

Not alone.

He turned. Tried to peer through the glass door. For just a moment, Archer had thought he caught movement. His hand lifted, and he swiped his fingers over the foggy glass. And he saw her. Delilah, clad in just a black bra and black panties. Standing a few feet away. He sucked in a breath. Closed his eyes. When he opened them...

Still there.

She wasn't some dream. No matter what he might think. His hand flew out and yanked off the cold water. *Drip. Drip. Drip.* He held her gaze through the glass. He sucked in a breath. Another. The cold water hadn't helped. Deep breaths weren't helping. Driving deep into *her?* Hell, yeah, that would be the solution he needed.

He opened the door.

Her gaze slid over him. Her tongue darted along her lower lip. "Are you…um, sure that water was cold? The cold is supposed to make things shrink. Shrivel, you know?"

"*Delilah.*"

"Right." She tossed him a towel.

He caught it. Didn't use it. Just kept gazing at her. "Why the hell are you here?" There was only so much torture that one man could take.

"I could say that I'm here because my muscles were aching again, and I thought I could use some of that cream you mentioned last night but…" Her shoulders thrust back. The move made her pert breasts thrust *forward,* and he wanted that black bra—sexy as it was—gone. "But that would be a lie."

He stepped onto the lush mat. Tossed the towel away.

"You're dripping," she whispered.

Like he cared. "Why are you *here?*"

"Don't you know?"

He wanted the words. He would not touch her until she gave him the words he needed.

Delilah swallowed. "This has nothing to do with the hundred grand that you *will* be paying me. That money will go a long way to helping other people."

He'd forgotten about the money.

"But I don't want you thinking I was trading sex for—"

"Didn't think it," he growled.

"Well, yes, that's good." Her gaze darted down his body, only to fly right back up. "And it doesn't mean anything. Emotionally, that is. You don't need to worry that I'm falling in love with you or something like that. I know the difference between sex and love."

He advanced on her. "Good for you."

Her brow furrowed. "I kind of thought this would go differently."

His hands fisted. *Do not touch her yet.* "And how did you think it would go?"

"I had initially planned on slipping into the shower with you, but then you turned and saw me before I could. I'd kind of thought we'd just be kissing and the heat of the moment would overwhelm us and there wouldn't be a need for a lot of talking."

"Because talking makes you nervous?" Gravel-rough. "Talking makes you realize that you'll be surrendering to me."

Her head moved in a slight shake. "I don't see this as any kind of surrender."

She could call it whatever she wanted.

"More like seduction," Delilah amended.

"Then you're here to seduce me?" Like she had to try. He'd more than made it clear—

"I think we're seducing each other, and maybe we have been all along." A slow release of breath. "Why aren't you touching me?"

"Is that what you want?" His hands, on her.

"I want *you.*"

And those were the words he needed. He surged forward and pulled her into his arms.

CHAPTER FOURTEEN

He should use care. He should be gentle. He should worship her body with his hands and his mouth. But instead, Archer curled his hands around Delilah's waist and lifted her up against him even as his mouth took hers in a deep, hard kiss. A kiss that claimed and demanded a response. Her legs wrapped around him. Her hot core—shielded by the thin panties—rocked against his aching dick.

He wanted in her.

There would be no tender foreplay. He was way past that point. He carried her to the bed. Thrust his tongue into her mouth. Became maddened by her taste. Loved the feel of her soft body rocking against his. She was riding his dick, with only her panties in the way, and he knew he would go crazy if he didn't get inside her.

He lowered her onto the bed. Hauled away her bra and locked his mouth over one gorgeous breast.

Her breath hissed out of her as she arched against him. *"Archer!"*

His hand slid down her body. He grabbed the crotch of her panties. Yanked. Heard the fabric rip and didn't give a damn. He shoved the torn panties aside and slipped his fingers into her.

Wet. Hot. Tight.

Everything he wanted. Everything he *would* have.

He strummed her clit with his thumb, and Delilah nearly rocketed off the bed. She was so responsive to him. Her desire just fed his own, and he had to tear himself away from her as he grabbed for the nearby nightstand.

"Archer!"

He looked back at her. Spread out on his bed. Naked. Waiting. Her breath panting. Her nipples thrusting toward him. Her legs parted for him.

He couldn't get his condom on quickly enough, and his fingers were shaking with his need. All he could think about was getting inside her. Control? Hell, no, he didn't have any.

He climbed back on the bed. Pushed her legs apart even more as he settled between her thighs.

"I don't want to wait," she whispered.

He was staring at her sex. So pretty. His fingers parted her. Opened her more. He'd licked. Tasted her before. And he wanted to do so again and again. He loved it when she let go, and her body shuddered with her release. He wanted to make her come over and over again. Endlessly. Until there was no room for fear or doubt. No room for anything but the primal need and pleasure they gave to each other.

His dick lodged at the entrance to her body. He knew this was going to be different—no holding back. No controlled thrusts. No slow build.

He didn't want slow. Didn't want control. He wanted fast and deep, and he wanted her nails digging in his back as she urged him to go harder.

Her nails raked over him, as if she'd just read his mind. "I need *you*."

He drove into her and lost the last bit of his sanity. There was only dark desire. A voracious need. He kissed her as his hips pistoned hard against her. Her legs wrapped around him. Her nails dug into him, and her moans made him crazed.

The bed shoved against the wall. His heartbeat thundered in his ears. She was incredibly tight, hot enough to burn him to his core, and there was no way—no way—that he would ever be able to give her up.

Mine.

Deeper. Harder. Faster.

His hand snaked between them. Worked her clit and Archer felt her jerk and shudder beneath him as Delilah's climax slammed into her. Her delicate inner muscles clenched around him, and he threw back his head and nearly roared because the pleasure was so good. His release didn't hit— it *exploded* through his body as the pleasure burst through his every cell.

On and on and on.

Will not let go.

He never fucking planned to let her go.

***

She couldn't quite catch her breath. And her sex kept quivering. Happy, little after-shock quivers that had pleasure pulsing through her.

Wow. Delilah pulled the covers up to her chest, and even the silk felt like it was too rough as it slid over her sensitive breasts. She'd figured sex with Archer would be good. Fine, *more* than good. But she hadn't expected the insane lift-off that had made her think she'd nearly been flying.

Nothing had ever felt that sensational. The pleasure still made her toes want to curl.

A one-off. No way would it be that good again. It had to be a mix of adrenaline and need and me having gone way, way too long without—

He approached the bed. Her head turned toward him. Moments before, Archer had left to ditch the condom. His body had been wet from the shower when he climbed into the bed with her, and Delilah realized the sheets were a little damp. Not that she cared. She was too busy staring at his dick and realizing that Archer was already up for another round.

So am I.

She tucked the sheet under her arms. "Archer..."

"Can you take me again?"

Her breath shuddered out. "Yes."

He dragged the sheet off her. "Good."

But he didn't surge down onto her. Instead, he rolled them on the bed, moved so that he was beneath her, and Delilah straddled his powerful thighs. Her hands pressed over his chest—over the hard muscles just beneath the skin, and her hair fell forward as she stared down at him.

"This way, I can see you even better," he rasped.

His eyes were on her. And his hands rose to cup her breasts. To tease her nipples. To make her body ache again.

"Get the condom. Put it on me."

Right. Check. Condom. She leaned over and probably would have fallen if his hands hadn't lunged down and snagged her waist. A startled cry escaped her.

Instantly, Archer let her go. "Delilah?"

"Sorry. That was...um, near one of my bruises." She tore open the condom.

A vicious curse burst from him. Then his fingers were carefully sliding over, as if in apology. "I didn't mean to—"

"I know." She stopped the apology. She didn't need words of apology. Her mind was occupied with other things. Delilah reached for the heavy, full length of his cock. It stretched even more beneath her touch.

His hips surged toward her.

Slowly, she rolled the condom over his cock. She squeezed. Enjoyed him.

"Don't tease, baby."

She had no intention of teasing. That wouldn't be good for either of them. She straddled his hips. Positioned the head of his cock at the entrance to her body. Delilah began to slowly work him inside of her. At first, her sex tensed, the muscles straining against him.

"Delilah?" Her name seemed to rumble from behind his clenched teeth.

"It's...been a while for me." And her muscles were tight from the frantic bout they'd just had. Her spirit was more than willing, and her body would follow. Soon. "Just, ah, give me a...minute."

He tumbled her onto her back.

A quick cry came from her, but he didn't thrust deeper. Only the head of his cock stayed inside of her. "Define 'a while.'"

He wanted a definition, right then?

His fingers toyed with her clit. Started the sensual stroking that made her quiver.

"How long?" Archer pushed.

"I..." *Right there.* When he stroked that spot...Her hips flew up, and she took a little more of him inside. "At least a year. I've told you this before."

His eyes darkened. "Why me?"

He kept stroking her, but he wasn't thrusting deeper. Her body had clamped so tightly around him, that thick portion of his cock that he'd given to her...*But I want it all.*

"Why. Me?"

"Because...I want you."

"And you didn't want anyone else? In the last year, you didn't—"

Her hips drove up, hard, and took all of him inside her. He filled her completely and her frantic gasp filled the air. "I didn't want anyone else...as much as I want *you.*"

His cock lodged fully inside of her. Her core tightened around him, squeezed, and his fingers were still strumming her clit. He wasn't thrusting.

Was holding that thick dick completely still. Just strumming her...

"Archer!" Delilah's climax slammed into her.

And only then did he let go. He pulled back, nearly withdrawing completely, only to plunge into her again and again. She grabbed for his shoulders even as her release kept pounding through her body.

She held tight. She rode the waves of pleasure.

His hips jerked against her. His face went savage with his release. *"Mine."*

In that moment, Delilah absolutely felt that he was hers.

***

She should go back to her bedroom. She probably would, once her body stopped feeling all limp and sated. One of her arms was flung over Archer's chest. One of his legs lodged between hers. They were a tangle. He was warm and strong and sexy, and she should definitely go back to her bedroom.

Her eyes tried to sag shut. Falling asleep wasn't an option. Not until she was back in her own—temporary—bed. *So get moving.* She pulled her arm off him and reached for the side of the bed.

Only to have *his* arm immediately curl around her stomach. "Stay." The word was a rough growl.

"Is that a good idea?" Probably not. Tempting, but undoubtedly dangerous. *It's a slippery slope, and I'm supposed to keep my emotions separate.*

"Don't know if it is or not. But it feels right." Rough and raspy. "You feel right."

So did he. "I am sleepy."

"Um."

"And you're warm." She snuggled against him. "I also think this bed is more comfortable than the one in my room."

"Then by all means, stay here every night." He pulled her against him. Pressed a soft kiss to her temple. A tender kiss.

This doesn't change anything. She wasn't going to let her emotions get involved. This had just been about sex. Satisfying the desire that burned so hotly between them.

"It's never been that good for me before."

His low words had her tensing.

"Did I hurt you?"

"No." *It's never been that good for me, either.* But "good" wasn't the right word. Good didn't even come close to describing the maelstrom of pleasure that had rocked through her. It felt *good* to sit in the grass and have sunlight on your face. It felt *good* to dip your toes in the ocean. Having sex with Archer?

Way, way better than good.

"Tonight won't be enough." His words sounded like a warning.

But she just said, "No, it won't be." Because she wanted more, too. A whole lot more.

With his arms around her, with her body still humming because of him, she closed her eyes and slept.

***

Archer thought he had top of the line security. He thought his precious home was impenetrable. He was wrong. As he'd been wrong before.

It was too easy to gain access into Archer's inner sanctum. Too easy to slip up the stairs. Archer was playing a game, but he needed to realize—*you can't play with me.*

Delilah wouldn't be in Archer's room. Their relationship was a lie. Just another setup. As if that wasn't apparent. *You can't fool me.* Delilah was trouble, and she would be stopped.

And perhaps Archer would learn a lesson in the process.

The main guest room was right past Archer's. It was the second biggest bedroom in the house, so it made sense that Archer would put her there. He'd like the size of the room for her, and that controlling asshole would also want her close to him.

The doorknob turned easily, and the darkened room waited. The bed covers were rumpled. She would be sleeping. Thinking she was safe inside Archer's lair.

Wrong, wrong, wrong.

The backpack was a light weight. With only the low hiss of the zipper, the pack came open. Fingers reached inside for the prize. A moment later, the bottle lifted, held tightly, and it was so simple to light the strip of cloth that hung from the end of that bottle. Light it...and then toss the bottle. To send it crashing right at the wall behind the bed.

After the crash, the flames erupted so quickly...

CHAPTER FIFTEEN

Glass shattered. The faint crash had him jerking from the dream that had wrapped him up so tightly. For a moment, he didn't move. *Dream or reality?*

A beep began. Gathered strength. *Reality.* Archer could hear the shrill beep over and over, and it shoved through the clinging clouds of sleep.

"Fire." A distorted, robotic voice announced. More beeps. Then, again, *"Fire."*

What in the hell? His smoke detector?

Archer shoved upright.

"Fire." That robotic voice again. More beeps. Louder. Shriller. Now seeming to come from all over the house.

"Archer!" Delilah shot up beside him. "What's...oh, God, I smell smoke!"

He hit the lamp and light flooded into his bedroom.

"Fire!" The smoke detector's warning came again.

"We need to get the hell out of here." He jumped from the bed. Yanked on a nearby pair of jogging pants and snagged his shoes. Delilah had wrapped a sheet around her body. They were rushing for the door—but he hesitated before he reached out for the doorknob. He didn't know exactly where the fire was, but he could smell the smoke. If the doorknob was too hot...

He touched it carefully. *Not too hot.* "Stay low," Archer ordered.

"Fire." The robotic voice chimed again. The ear-piercing beeps continued.

He hauled open the door and saw thick, dark smoke coming from the open guest room. *Delilah's room.* "Cover your mouth, baby," he urged her.

The guest room door was thrown wide open. The smoke billowed out and when he risked a fast glance inside the room—

Coughs nearly choked him but there was no missing the bright orange and red flames—flames that were eating up the four-poster bed. The bed Delilah would have been in if he hadn't asked her to stay with him.

What the fuck?

He pushed Delilah away from the room, back toward the stairs, but then he realized...*The threat could be waiting below.* The fire could be designed to make them flee, and the sonofabitch who'd started the blaze could be hiding on the first floor. He wrapped his arm around Delilah and pulled her close. "Stay behind me."

"*Fire.*" The alarm kept calling out. He knew the fire department would have been contacted automatically by the system. He just had to get Delilah out of the house and to safety.

I promised to protect her.

Smoke thickened on the second floor, but as they made their way down the stairs, the air was clearer. He kept his guard up, kept looking for a threat, but he didn't see anyone as they fled outside.

Darkness waited. No threat. The ocean waves battered in the distance. Salt air pushed away the acrid scent of the smoke.

Her bed had been lit on fire.

Sirens wailed. Still far away, a faint cry.

"What in the hell happened?" Delilah asked. The sheet covered her. She looked delicate and beautiful and far, far too vulnerable.

He knew what had happened. He'd just gotten very, very lucky. If Delilah had been in that other room...

The call of the sirens grew louder. He saw a security SUV rush toward his house. The security team had beaten the fire department to the scene. Relief filled him because at least the security personnel could provide protection for Delilah. He recognized the man and woman who leapt from the vehicle. Kristin Merroco and Nico Perez.

"Get her out of here," he barked to them.

Delilah whipped her head toward him. "What?"

He scooped her into his arms and headed for the SUV.

Nico hauled open the back door of the vehicle when he saw Archer coming. "Boss, you okay?"

No, and someone was going to *pay*. "Someone set my fucking guest room on fire." He put Delilah in the back seat. She immediately tried to lunge out. The sheet also tried to drop.

He shoved the sheet back up. And pushed her gently—but firmly—back inside. "Take her to my office. Stay with her every minute until I get there."

Nico nodded. He and Kristin hurried back toward the front of the vehicle.

The fire truck's lights flashed as the vehicle appeared near the driveway's entrance.

"What the hell are you doing?" Delilah demanded.

"Keeping you safe." Because as far as he knew, the bastard was still there. Watching. Waiting. "I'll join you as soon as I can."

"Archer, *no—*"

"Delilah, *yes*. My office building has top-notch security. Guards are in the building twenty-four, seven. You will be safe there, and you *will* stay in my office until I come for you."

"This is ridiculous, Archer, I—"

He leaned in and pressed a frantic, hard kiss to her lips. "He wanted you dead." Guttural. *And I did this. I was the one who had the brilliant idea to drag you into this mess.* "You will stay safe. I *need* you safe. Please." The last part was gritted from between his teeth.

Archer surged back, but Delilah's hand flew out and caught his. "Get all the security footage you can." Her voice was low and carried the faintest tremble. "Have every room searched. If he's not out on the grounds watching us right now, then odds are high it's because he is still *in* your house. The fire could have just been a distraction to get us out. If so, then he's doing something in there. Leaving some sort of trap for you. Or taking something *from* you."

Even in the midst of this chaos, she was still plotting and analyzing, and he knew she was dead-on with her assessment.

"I want to see the footage, Archer. Promise to share it with me."

He leaned toward her once more. Ignored everything but her. For her ears alone, he whispered, "Orion. Ten. Five. Five."

She blinked. "What's that?"

"The password for the computer in my office. When you get there, use it, and you can access my security footage—for my office building in Miami and the home here. I will keep nothing from you. Hell, you might even find something in that footage before I do." Did she get what he was doing?

I am trusting you with everything I have.

Another kiss against her lips. Softer this time. "I will come to you as soon as I can." But he needed her away from the danger. Safe. He slammed the door shut. Stared into the dark glass, then marched a few feet to find Nico and Kristin standing near the front of the SUV. "Nothing happens to her." His gaze raked them. "Understand? *Nothing.*"

Moments later, the SUV pulled away even as the fire trucks raced to a stop in front of his house.

***

"I'm going to need some clothes." Delilah grimaced as she looked down at her makeshift dress. "The sheet has to go." Her head tilted as she studied Kristin. "I think we're pretty close to the same size. By any chance, do you have any extra clothes around here? Clothes that you would not mind sharing with a desperate woman?" They were in Archer's office. His inner sanctuary. She should have been feeling safe. She wasn't.

She was too worried about *him*.

"I've got some workout gear downstairs," Kristin told her with a nod. "I'll go get the stuff out of my storage locker. You're welcome to use whatever you can."

"Thank you." *A million thank-yous.* "The sheet dress isn't as comfortable as one might think." And the fact that Archer had rushed her out of the house while she was buck naked? That definitely screamed to the world exactly what they'd been doing before the fire had erupted.

If I hadn't slept with Archer, I could be dead now.

Dead...burned. Who the hell knew what could have gone down?

Kristin hurried away to retrieve the clothes, and Nico swept Delilah with a concerned gaze. "You all right?" he asked carefully.

Hardly, but she smiled anyway. "Sure. Nothing a couple shots of whiskey can't fix." A joke. Delilah had no intention of drinking anything. She also had never tried whiskey before, so she was completely bullshitting. She *did* intend to call in reinforcements and to attack Archer's computer as soon as Nico gave her a moment of privacy. "Thanks for the lift over. Appreciate it."

"The boss was clear—you are the priority." He didn't move. "Kristin is taking care of the clothes. What else do you need?"

She eased down into Archer's chair. "Just some time alone, if that's okay." Delilah hoped she looked suitably miserable. Honestly, she *felt* miserable. Mostly because she was so worried about Archer.

"Take as long as you need." He motioned toward the door. "Only one way in or out of this office, and I'll be standing guard at Casey's desk. No one will get to you, I promise."

Um, about that..."I'm going to call my brother," she blurted.

Nico frowned.

"I don't want him watching this story on the news," Delilah rushed to explain. "He'll be worried. I'll get him to come here so he can see for himself that I'm all right."

Nico pulled up his phone. "I should tell the boss..."

She forced a light laugh. "Tell him about my brother? Archer already knows about him, I assure you." Archer already knew, all right. He knew she had no brother. "I will vouch for him. I can promise you, the man who arrives will be no threat to me whatsoever."

His fingers still gripped his phone.

"Archer has enough to deal with right now." He really did. "You don't need to bother him with a story about me calling my brother."

Nico shoved the phone back into his pocket. "Yeah, you're right." Sympathy flashed on his face. "If it was my sister, I'd want to see her, too."

He motioned toward the phone on the desk. "Call him. And don't forget, I'm—"

"Right outside. Got you. Thanks."

She waited until he slipped out. Counted a few seconds after the door closed. *One, two, three...*

Delilah snatched the phone off the desk. When Archer had carried her out of the house, there had been no time to grab her laptop—if it hadn't burned—or to snag her phone. But luckily, she had *this* particular number memorized. Most of her interactions with her team were online, but for him, she always had a number in case of emergencies.

This definitely counted as an emergency.

He answered on the second ring. "Sweetheart, it's nearly two in the morning..."

"Wait...how did you even know it was me? Or do you just answer every call by saying, 'Sweetheart' first thing?"

"I know it was you because I'm awesome, and you're calling from Radcliffe Industries. Since you're the only one there with my personal number, it didn't take a genius to figure out you were on the other end of the line. Now, is there a particular reason for the late-night call? Or were you just waking me up for fun?"

"I'm sitting in Archer's office, I'm wearing a sheet, and a fire just consumed the bed I should have been sleeping in." Her voice held a hollow edge because her control was basically shot. "I need that backup that you mentioned, and I could really, *really* use it now."

"On the fucking way."

"One quick thing." A long exhale. "When you arrive at Radcliffe Industries, say you're my brother."

"What?"

"Just say it."

***

The bed had burned fast and hot. Archer stood in the bedroom doorway, his gaze on the sodden remains. The firefighters had quickly put out the blaze. A man at his side was telling Archer how lucky he'd been that the fire hadn't spread.

"What started it?" Archer asked. He couldn't take his gaze off the bed. *If she'd been in that bed...*

"I'll have to get an investigator in to be sure, but based on the burn patterns that I see..."

She would have burned. The bastard came to burn her.

"Did you hear me, Mr. Radcliffe? Sir, you really shouldn't be in here, I told you that before..."

I would have been in the room right next door, and she would have burned.

"Definitely seems to be arson. Are you sure you didn't see or hear anyone..."

What in the hell would I have done if he'd hurt her?

An arm touched his shoulder. "Mr. Radcliffe? Did you hear me?"

Archer lifted his chin. "When I first woke up, I thought maybe I'd heard breaking glass. But then I didn't know if that was a dream or reality.

The next thing I knew, the alarm started shrieking." He'd had his arms around Delilah. *I will keep her safe.* "He was in my house." Archer swung away. Stopped. Something was nagging at him...

He looked back into the guest bedroom. Swept his gaze around the scene. *Blackened wall. Peeling ceiling. Destroyed bed and...*

He rushed toward the desk on the right.

"Sir, this is a crime scene!" A woman's voice. Annoyed. Hard. She'd just swept into the room and was now trying to jump in his path. "I don't care who the hell you are, but you need to get out—"

"My house. My property." He slipped around her. "The laptop is gone. It would have been here. I saw it here earlier." A quick spin. He rushed to the closet and peered inside just to make sure Delilah hadn't moved her computer. *Nothing. Gone.* "He took it."

"You need to leave." The woman was adamant as she tugged him away from the closet. She had a badge clipped to her hip. "If you think something was taken, then we'll get you to fill out a report for us."

"The bastard was *here.* He slipped into my house. Climbed up my stairs. Came for *her.*" The rage was too strong to control. *And he took her laptop.* The laptop that contained all of Delilah's information about Vanessa's disappearance.

"Did you *see* him?" she asked as she pushed him toward the door.

No, he hadn't seen a thing other than the smoke and fire. *But you were here, weren't you?*

*Watching...*Archer marched out of the bedroom. By the time he reached the stairs, he could already see all of the lights flashing outside. So many more vehicles had arrived. When he exited the house, he seemed to walk straight into a scene of chaos. His steps were heavy as Archer headed away from the house.

A familiar figure hurried to meet him.

"What in the hell happened?" Oz demanded. His hair was slightly disheveled, and he wore black jogging pants and a white t-shirt. "I get some frantic text from you about a fire, and I swear, I thought you were dying on me or something!"

"He was in my house."

Oz scanned him. "I don't see injuries." A relieved release of his breath. "That's good. No burns?"

"He was in my *house.*"

Oz winced. "That would explain the line of cops I'm seeing around here." His gaze swept the myriad assortment of vehicles and people. "Cops and firefighters and probably some reporters slipping from the shadows, too. You, ah, might want to think about putting on a shirt, my friend."

Screw that. "He was in the bedroom right next to me. I didn't know." *If the bastard wanted me, why not come at me?*

But, no, Archer had never been his *exact* target. The SOB just wanted Archer to hurt. His hands fisted and released. Fisted and—

"Where's Delilah?" Oz asked carefully.

"Safe."

Oz cleared his throat. "Where exactly was the fire?"

"In the guest room. The one right next to my bedroom."

"And Delilah was...?"

"In my bed, in my arms, when the bastard came into the house." *Shouldn't have happened. Shouldn't have...* "The cops want to question me. That will be a useless endeavor. I don't have jack to tell them. You're here because I texted you so you could handle them." He started to rush by Oz. *Need to get to Delilah.*

But Oz grabbed him and pushed him back. "No, I'm here because I'm your friend." His expression hardened. "I'm your friend, and you're telling me some psycho just torched one of the bedrooms in your house...while you were sleeping inside?"

A jerk of his head. Yes, that was exactly what he was saying.

"Fucking hell." Oz's stunned gaze locked on the house. "This is gonna be bad."

Gonna be? It *was* bad.

"You can't just waltz away from the scene," Oz added as he raked a hand over his face. "The optics of that move won't be good."

Screw optics. "Watch me." He *had* to get to Delilah. His chest was tight and hard, and when he'd realized that her laptop was gone...

I did this. I put her in danger. He'd used her, he'd brought her into his nightmare, and now he had to keep her safe.

"The cops will need a statement! Even if you don't think you know anything, they will still want to talk with you."

"Tell them I'll come in tomorrow morning. In the meantime, they can search the whole house. Every bit of property I have." Like they hadn't done that before. They'd been so sure they'd find proof that he'd hurt Vanessa...

I didn't hurt her. He choked down his fury. "Maybe they can find some evidence that will show them who this SOB is."

"You've got security footage." Not a question from Oz.

He'd already viewed it. "Footage of someone in a dark hood coming up the stairs. He bypassed the cameras downstairs. Never saw his face." Just a figure in black, carrying a backpack.

Walking through my home like he owned the place.

"You think it was the man who hurt Vanessa." Oz's tone was guarded.

"Who the hell else would it be?" The plan had been to draw the bastard out. Archer had known he was there, waiting the whole time. He'd just needed the right bait.

And Delilah had entered the scene. She'd known the score. Using her had seemed like the perfect plan. But he had *never* planned on her getting hurt.

"Arch, are you...are you sure you're okay?"

Using her had been the plan. Falling for her hadn't. "I am going to destroy him." Flat. Cold. Lethal. "He will never get close to her again." He strode forward, and his shoulder plowed into Oz when his lawyer didn't move out of his way.

"Archer?" Oz staggered back.

Archer kept marching for the garage. He'd get his car and get the hell out of there.

Oz chased after him. "Dammit, I'll try to smooth things over here with the cops. You *will be* at the PD tomorrow to talk to them, though, right?"

Archer kept heading forward.

"Where the hell are you going?" Oz surged to his side.

"I'm not going to use her anymore."

"Use who?" Oz glanced back over his shoulder. Swore. "What is happening?"

"Delilah."

"Okay. Yes. I get it. The woman is obviously some major priority for you but—"

"I'm not using her." He plowed forward.

"Would you slow down? And dammit, seriously, you need a shirt."

He had clothes in the back of his car. A Go bag that he always kept at the ready.

"What is up with Delilah?" Oz wanted to know. "Look, I tried warning you about her before. I warned you *twice*. The woman is working an angle."

"No. She isn't." His shoulders shoved back. "*I* am."

"What?" Oz's voice rose. He caught himself. Looked toward the cops again. "Dammit, man, slow down and tell me what is—"

"She's pretend."

"Uh, no, she's a flesh and blood woman who—"

"She's not mine." *I want her to be.* "It's fake. We were drawing out the bastard. She wasn't supposed to get hurt."

Once more, Oz grabbed him. A hard grip. And yanked Archer to a stop. "*What?*"

"Take the hand off." The only warning he would give. He was not in the mood to be stopped. He had to get to Delilah. *Now.*

Oz yanked his hand back as if he'd been burned.

Delilah was the one who nearly got burned, because of me.

"Arch, man, you need to do some serious explaining. Like, now. You *are* involved with Delilah. I've seen the two of you together. I know—"

"Fake," he gritted. *Not true. Nothing has ever felt more real.* He swallowed. "Make sure word spreads. The media can say we are done. Delilah means nothing to me."

Moonlight poured down on Oz. "What are you doing?"

"I'm going to tell Delilah that I want her out of my life." He had to get her out of his life. Because being around him could very well prove fatal for her.

Without another word, he left Oz. This time, Oz didn't try to stop him.

CHAPTER SIXTEEN

"What in the hell are you talking about, Nico?" Archer threw open the door to his office. "Delilah doesn't have a brother—" He froze at the sight before him.

Delilah sat behind his desk. In his chair. She wore a black sports bra. That was pretty much all he could see from this angle. Her hair had been twisted back and wrapped in some kind of little knot on her head, and loose tendrils escaped to tease her cheeks.

Some bastard—big, with dark, shaggy hair, a hard jaw, and too many freaking muscles that bulged out his shirt—leaned around her and peered at the computer screen near her. *Archer's* computer screen.

"She—she said it was her brother," Nico hurried to say, his voice coming from right behind Archer.

Archer didn't take his gaze off the man who was crowded in Delilah's personal space. "*Not* her brother." The big bastard was way, way too close to Delilah for Archer's liking.

"*Archer.*" Delilah jumped to her feet. The guy had to jerk back so she didn't hit him. When she jumped up, Archer saw that she was wearing a pair of gray yoga pants that hugged her hips. Before he could study her more, Delilah surged around the desk and ran to him. She threw her arms around him and hugged him tight. "I was worried. I do *not* like it when you send me away. That shit is just incredibly uncool."

Then you are not going to like what comes next. But instead of saying those words, he locked his arms around her and hauled her closer. He inhaled her scent—lilacs—and buried his face in the crook of her neck.

Mine. The thought was there, whispering through him. But she couldn't be his. It was too dangerous to be his.

"Uh, boss, should I be tossing him out?" Nico asked.

Delilah pulled away from Archer. "No. I can explain." Her wide eyes met his. "Just give me a chance, okay?"

He didn't want an audience for this scene. "I've got it, Nico. You and Kristin can go home and get some rest." There were plenty of other guards in the building.

Nico hurried out. Archer kicked the door closed behind him. He also kept one hand wrapped around Delilah's wrist, as if he could chain her to him. Impossible, of course. *Let her go.*

Slowly, his fingers slid from her skin.

Delilah frowned up at him. "Are you all right?"

"Sure. Great. Why wouldn't I be? You were almost killed on my watch, but, hey, just another night, am I right?"

The dark-haired man gave a long whistle. "Someone is in a pissy mood."

"You have no idea." He glared at the jerk. "Get the hell away from my desk."

Lifting his hands in an I'm-no-threat gesture, Delilah's "brother" backed away from the desk. "Not looking to cause problems for you. Delilah wanted my help, so I came running."

Archer pretty much hated the man on sight. "Do you always come running when Delilah calls?" Jealousy bit at him. Funny. He'd never been the jealous type before but—

"Yes." A quick, easy reply. "I do."

But he was definitely jealous now. "Who the hell are you? And don't give me some BS about being her brother. Delilah doesn't have one."

"Well, not a blood brother, sure." He put his hand over his heart. "But in here, oh, yes, I am her—"

"I am not in the mood for bullshit." Archer lunged for him.

Delilah stepped in his path. "Memphis Camden."

Memphis smiled at him. A crooked grin. "That's me."

"Memphis is the best tracker that I've ever encountered," Delilah explained. "His prey doesn't get away from him."

Prey? Odd word choice.

"Former bounty hunter," Memphis supplied helpfully. "Though I do still dabble in the biz when the money is right. You have to think like the criminals in order to track them. I know the best hiding spots. I know how they like to go off-grid. And I know how to pull them out into the light."

"Isn't that wonderful for you." Why was the bounty hunter—correction, *former* bounty hunter—in his office? "What is it that Delilah wants you to do?"

"Well, covering that sweet ass of hers is step one," Memphis drawled.

Archer's muscles locked down. He managed a tight smile for Delilah. "Love, could you step to the side for me?"

Her brow furrowed, but she stepped to the side.

He sprang for Memphis. Grabbed the bastard's shoulders and thrust him back against the nearest wall. "Stay the hell away from her ass!"

Memphis just laughed. "Thought something like that might have happened. Warned Delilah that she shouldn't get too close to the target."

Delilah tapped Archer's shoulder. "What are you doing? I get that the night has been long and stressful, but you don't attack the people *on our side.*"

Memphis wasn't on his side. Memphis wanted Delilah. And he couldn't have her because—

Shit. What in the hell am I doing? Archer exhaled heavily. Made his hands release Memphis's shoulders. *This isn't me. I don't attack people. I don't want to rip a guy apart just because I don't like what he says.* Correction, normally, that wasn't Archer.

He was becoming someone different. *Get the control back.*

"Poor bastard." Memphis sounded sympathetic. "Snuck up on you, didn't she? The mistake was the partnership. You let someone like Delilah get that close, and then the next thing you know, you want the relationship to stop being just for show."

He knew about their partnership?

Delilah kept tapping on Archer's shoulder. "What is wrong with you?"

"Quite a bit." Her touch rocked through him. Always a mistake. When she touched him, he couldn't think clearly. "I've been viewed as a monster for two years. Some bastard broke into my house and torched a bedroom." *Your* bedroom. "And my plan is shit." He whirled toward her. *Do this.* "We're done," he announced flatly.

A cute little furrow appeared between Delilah's brows. "Done?" Then her eyes flared. She stepped closer to him. "Did the cops catch the person who started the fire? Is someone in custody?"

Her body nearly brushed against his. *That sexy sports bra.* The bra was not helping him concentrate. "Why do you not have more clothes?" A growl.

"Yeah, way to focus there, champ," Memphis praised him.

That guy was a dick.

"I got carried out of your house in a sheet, remember?" Delilah replied sweetly.

Memphis choked. Or laughed. Something. "Betting he has no problem recalling that, sweetheart."

Archer turned his head. Met Memphis's gleaming stare. "Stop using the endearments."

Memphis shrugged. "I'm just a friendly fellow. No harm, no foul."

"*Stop.*"

"Why? You're about to tell her to hit the road, so I don't see where you'd be bothered one way or the other."

He was bothered plenty.

"Don't be ridiculous, Memphis." Came Delilah's cool reply. "Archer and I are partners. He's not about to tell me to hit anything."

Yes, I am. He turned back to her. Clenched his jaw. Yanked the sweatshirt he wore over his head and pulled it over hers.

"What are you doing?" Delilah gaped at him as if he'd lost his mind.

The jackass Memphis was laughing again.

"You looked cold," he muttered.

She jerked back, shoved her arms through the sleeves of the sweatshirt, and glared. "And you're looking crazy." Her stare raked him. "At least you have on a t-shirt."

And at least Memphis can't stare at your chest any longer.

Oh, damn. But he had it bad. *Jealousy.* It burned like acid in his gut. "You and your friend should leave."

Delilah shook her head. Her hands flew to curl over her hips. "I'm not going anywhere."

He spun away. Mostly because he needed to put some space between them before he did anything else stupid. So much for being Mr. Cool and In Control. Delilah had swept into his life and blown his control to hell and back. Archer made his way to his desk. Glanced at the computer screen.

They'd been watching the security footage from his house. "Obviously, you couldn't see his face." *The sonofabitch.* He reached into his top drawer. Typed in the code for the small safe there. Pulled out a checkbook.

"What are you doing?" Delilah crept toward the desk.

Memphis didn't move.

"The job is over. Didn't work out as I planned." He filled out the check, aware that his grip on the pen was tight enough to nearly shatter the thing. "But you'll still get paid." He tore off the check from the book and pushed it across the table toward her. "Thanks for your performance."

And those were the wrong words.

Red filled her cheeks. "The *hell* you just said that to me," Delilah snapped. Pain flashed on her face. A sudden, stark pain that made Archer feel gutted.

"Oh, man." Memphis winced. "Wrong. *Wrong.*"

"Memphis, get the hell out for a few moments," Delilah ordered without looking away from Archer. "We need to settle a few things in here."

Memphis practically ran for the door. "Consider me out."

Delilah still didn't look away from Archer. She had slapped her hands down on top of his desk. The pain was gone from her face, but her fury was clear to see.

Archer swallowed. "We agreed that I'd pay you one hundred grand."

"You don't get to pay me one hundred grand for my *performance* after we sleep together."

"*Oh, damn.*" Memphis stopped before exiting the office. He shot a withering look back at Archer. "You're dead." Then he left. The door closed softly behind him.

Archer sat down in his office chair. It was either sit down or rush around the desk—maybe reach for her. Touch her. *No, no, no.* "The payment is for the partnership. Not for sex."

"How wonderful." Her tone said it was anything *but* wonderful. "Otherwise, you would have just called me a whore."

He jumped right back to his feet. "You know that's not the case." His hands slammed down near hers.

"No, I don't," Delilah fired right back. "I know that I spent some pretty incredibly hours with you, that I thought something special was happening, and now you're writing me a check and telling me not to let the door hit me in the ass on my way out. *That's* what I know."

"It's not like that," he rasped.

"It seems exactly like that."

He wanted her mouth. He wanted to pull her into his arms. He just wanted her. "I...made a tactical mistake." Stilted.

"A tactical mistake? What are you even talking about right now?"

"You could have died!" Too much emotion. Too much heat. He had to pull back. He straightened. Squared his shoulders. His hands fell to his sides. "The attack was in your bedroom."

"Well, yes, but it was in *your* house."

His eyes narrowed. "First the shove down the stairs at the opera. Now a bed that's set on fire."

"We have his attention." She nodded as if that was a good thing. "Exactly what we wanted."

"*No.*" A snarl. His hands flexed. Clenched. "That's not what we wanted."

She stormed around the desk. Came right beside him. Jabbed him in the chest with her index finger. "You were the one who proposed this brilliant plan. You said he'd come out if he thought you were involved with someone. That the guy has a hard-on to make you hurt."

His brows shot up. Had he said those exact words? Archer didn't think so.

"Whatever. You know what I mean. He wants you to suffer. So you made him think you'd fallen for me."

What if I have fallen for you? No, he was not saying those words.

Her index finger jabbed him again. "You got exactly what you wanted, and now you're trying to cancel the deal?"

He looked down at her finger. "I didn't get what I wanted."

"He's come out, he's—"

His head snapped back up. Rage and fear burst through the cracks of his control. "I *don't* want you in danger."

Her lips parted. Delilah blinked. "But that was part of the plan. And now I've even pulled in Memphis for extra protection."

She wasn't hearing him, and the drumming of his heartbeat echoed like thunder in his ears. "The plan is crap. It can't happen. I'm not having you dangled like a juicy worm on a hook for him."

"Archer..."

His hands flew up and curled around her shoulders. "Take the money. Leave."

She shook her head at him. "No."

"Delilah, consider yourself fired."

Her head tilted back. "No."

No? She was driving him *insane.* "Yes. Take the money." He freed her to grab the check. Then he caught her hand—the hand with the finger that had been stabbing into his chest. And he forced the check into her grip. "Take the money. Go find some lost souls. Just get the hell out of my life." The words hurt to say. They hurt more than he'd ever suspected, but he had to do this.

He'd tried to use Delilah. Thought she was just a tool in his arsenal. A way for him to finally bring his enemy into the light. To find out what had happened two years ago.

But Delilah was so much *more* than he'd ever anticipated and using her wasn't an option. Using her *couldn't* happen. Protecting her at all costs? Oh, hell, yes, *that* would happen. Step one in that protection plan was to get her out of his life. The further away she was from him, the safer she'd be.

Silence ticked past. He didn't realize he'd been holding his breath, not until Delilah slowly smiled. "I see."

No, you don't. He didn't even fully see. She'd come into his world and wrecked everything and now he didn't know what the hell he was supposed to do.

Actually, correction, he knew one thing. *Protect her at all costs.*

Delilah glanced down at the rather crumpled check in her hand. "Services rendered," she murmured.

"This *isn't* about what happened between us last night." Last night? This night? Shit, what time was it?

She was still staring at the check. "I know it's not about the sex. I think I know more than you do."

"Delilah..."

She lifted the check. Held it so he could see it clearly. Then she ripped it in two.

His jaw almost hit the floor. "You just ripped up a check for a hundred grand."

"Good observational skills."

"I'll write another," he said.

"How about before you do that, I tell you what *I* have observed? Because I've got some pretty handy observational skills myself." She let the ripped check fall between them. "Observation number one...Archer Radcliffe, you are scared."

He reached for the drawer. "I'll get another check."

"You felt too much with me when we made love. It wasn't just sex. Maybe we both tried to pretend that it was—that it could only be physical—but something else happened."

He had the check book in his hand.

"I reacted differently with you. Everything was different with you. It was about a whole lot more than just sex."

He scribbled his signature on the check. "I'll leave the amount blank. Write whatever the hell you want."

"And you got scared," she continued, as if he hadn't spoken. "Scared because you *felt* something for me. Something that was real and strong. When you realized that I was under attack—that the fire had been targeted for me— you freaked out."

"I don't freak out." Flat. He offered her the check. She didn't take it. "You're mistaken about my response."

"I'm not because I was scared, too. I'm still scared. I'm afraid that something is going to happen to you. I'm afraid that I waited my whole life to feel the way I feel about you, and I'm so, so scared that this creep in the dark is going to try and destroy us both." She licked her lips. "Worse, I'm afraid he's going to convince you to do the dirty job yourself. Because it's easier when people aren't close, isn't it Archer? It's easier when you don't have to care."

She wasn't taking the check. Her scent was wrapping around him, and her words were sinking through him. "What are you saying?" He made his words mocking. "That you fell in love with me?"

"I don't know."

He frowned at her.

"I have no idea what I feel, not yet. I just know that I *do* feel something for you. I didn't want to get wrapped up in anyone after I lost my sister and my parents. I didn't want to feel that pain ever again. But I'm here in front of you, and I'm telling you that something is different when I'm with you. That I'm different."

And I'm different with you. That was why he was trying to send her away. He wanted her safe. "You don't feel different with Memphis?"

"Memphis is my friend. I've never fucked him."

He forced his jaw to unclench. "Excellent to know."

"And I won't. You're the one I want, even if you are trying to break us apart." She didn't take the check. She did reach out and touch his chest. Her palm pressed over his heart, with only the thin t-shirt separating them. "What's your real fear? That I'll get in here and you'll have to admit that you care?"

She had to feel the frantic drumming of his heart. "It was a mistake."

"What was? Our partnership?" Her head cocked to the right. "Or us sleeping together?"

Using you.

"Or the way you feel about me?" Delilah pushed. "Is that the mistake?"

"Take the check."

"No."

"Dammit—"

"If I kissed you right now, what would you do?"

Fuck you on the desk. The thought flashed through his mind. The wrong thought. He was about to grind his teeth into dust, and his greedy cock shoved toward her. "Don't you see what I am trying to do?"

"I do, and don't you see that it isn't going to work?" She smiled up at him. "I can be afraid, but it doesn't mean I leave you. It doesn't mean I turn away. I told you we were in this together, and that's exactly what I meant. It's not over."

"You are so stubborn."

"I prefer to be called determined. Dedicated. True blue."

She was *everything* he'd always wanted. "What if you'd been in the bed?" A question he never meant to voice, not to her.

"Then I would have seen the bastard coming," was the reply he hadn't expected.

Archer swallowed. "He would have killed you."

"Maybe I would have killed him. I am not some weak flower. I fight. I always fight. Why do you think I'm standing here right now? Someone has to fight for us." Her eyes were so intense. "You're worth fighting for."

So are you. She was worth everything. Every single thing. All of his wealth. His business. His life. She had come crashing into his world, and nothing would ever be the same. The way he felt for her? Nothing compared to it. Everything before hadn't mattered. He hadn't even really been living until she'd appeared, and now he was terrified that she would be hurt.

He hauled her close. The check got smashed in his hand. His mouth swept down to take hers. He wanted to be controlled, but that wasn't happening. Too much need and fear and fury burned within him.

No one will hurt her.

His tongue thrust past her lips. She gave a moan that made him feel savage.

I can't lose her.

He would find a way. When the bastard out there was eliminated, Archer could woo her back. Somehow.

Her hands looped around his neck. Brought him even closer. Her tongue met his. Her taste had him aching and devouring her. His desire for her was too strong, Archer knew it. His feelings too untamed, too fierce. He wanted her too much. Was too possessive. Too jealous. Too protective. He wanted to lock her away and make sure she never knew fear or pain or doubt.

He wanted to put the world at her feet.

He wanted...*her.*

A soft knock tapped at the door.

"Ahem." Memphis's overly loud voice carried through the wood. "Don't mean to interrupt something important in there, but time is ticking. I like to get to crime scenes as fast as I can, so how about we do a quick group plan of attack, then I can get out of your way?"

Archer's head lifted. Delilah's lips were red and swollen from his mouth, and when her thick lashes rose, he could see the desire in her languid stare.

"We aren't over," she told him.

No, he wasn't sure they ever would be.

"And I think you know where you can stick that check."

He'd be depositing the money into her account, and she *would* take it so she could use it on her cases. Those cases mattered to Delilah, and what mattered to Delilah...now mattered to him.

"There's also some lawyer in here, really glaring at me," Memphis continued in his overly loud voice. "He wanted to barge in your office, but I explained the whole concept of manners to him. When people are having a private talk, you knock first. Basic info." He knocked again. "See?"

"He will be coming in." Delilah pressed her lips together. Then... "And we should let Memphis go to the crime scene. He could see things the cops miss."

"They have the place roped off. He won't get close."

A faint smile tipped her lips. "You don't know Memphis."

No, he didn't. "How do you know him?" He wanted her mouth again. That little smile was driving him crazy.

Another knock. Less soft. More impatient. "I have shit to do," Memphis declared.

"He's trying to find something important for me," Delilah admitted.

"What?"

"Let him in, and I'm sure he'll tell you. He's a very straightforward sort of guy. One of the things I like about him."

Right. So to be clear, Archer did not want to hear about why she *liked* Memphis.

"He doesn't lie. He always tells you exactly like it is, even when you'd rather he just give you some BS." She backed up a step. "You probably need more people like him in your life. Instead of having so many who rush to do your bidding without stopping to tell you when you're being a dumbass."

A dumbass. "Are you saying I'm being a dumbass?"

"When you try to get rid of me, absolutely." She turned her back on him. Strode determinedly toward the door. She swung it open.

Memphis flashed her a grin. "Did you sort him out?"

"I am working on that very thing, but, honestly, I could use your help."

His grin vanished. "Always."

"Make him understand he's better off with me." She started to slide past Memphis.

"No!" A quick denial from Archer.

Her shoulders stiffened.

He rushed from behind the desk, only to draw up short. "I meant...where are you going?"

"Uh, hey, split personality," Memphis muttered. "Weren't you trying to send her away a few moments ago?"

"You need a guard, Delilah." He'd planned to get some people he knew—a protection firm called Wilde—to provide surveillance for her. "I don't want you running off alone."

She glanced back at him. "I'm just going a few feet. I have some phone calls to make. I was going to make them from Casey's desk. Besides, I thought the building was secure."

"It is."

Memphis jerked his thumb over his shoulder. "Your lawyer is out there. Not like she'll be alone."

His forehead scrunched. "Why the hell is Oz here?" He'd left him to deal with the cops.

"Because we need to talk!" Oz's disgruntled voice replied.

"Yeah, take a number, buddy." Memphis gave Delilah a little push over the threshold. "Go make those calls. Talk to your reporter contacts. Do the digging I know you're itching to do. Just remember that not everyone will be as pleased as me to get a two a.m. phone call." Then he kicked the door closed.

Archer's body tensed. He didn't—

Keeping his voice low, Memphis noted, "You have it so bad. One minute, you're pushing her away. The next, you look like you're having an aneurysm because she's gone five feet away from you. Don't worry. She's okay out there." A calculating look entered his eyes. "Unless you don't trust the lawyer." A pause. "Is that it? We think he's a suspect?"

"I think *everyone* is a suspect." And since when was there a *we* involved?

"Everyone but Delilah. And me," Memphis clarified. "We're not suspects. I'm your new best friend, so you'd better not suspect me. But if we're unsure about the lawyer, then, hell, no, let's not leave him out there alone with Delilah." A decisive nod. "Okay. I'll be bad. You can be good or indifferent or really, whatever the hell you want. Whatever floats your boat."

Archer could only shake his head. "What are you talking about?"

"Follow my lead, and you'll be fine." He wrenched the door open. "Oz, get in here. We've got so much to discuss. All the things."

What. Was. Happening?

Oz hurried inside, still wearing his t-shirt and jogging pants. Still looking disgruntled and sleep deprived.

As soon as Oz crossed the threshold, Memphis poked his head out and called to Delilah, "If you hear screams, it is no big deal. Nothing to worry about at all."

Oz's face scrunched up. "Why would she hear screams?"

Archer got a bad feeling. "Memphis...?"

Oz took a step toward him. "You left me with the cops. I had to make a ton of explanations and—" His words broke off. Mostly because he couldn't speak any longer.

Memphis had grabbed him from behind. One of Memphis's arms locked around Oz's throat as he hauled the other man back. Oz's eyes widened in horror, and he grabbed at the forearm that circled his neck.

"Time for a little chat," Memphis announced, sounding cheerful. "And if I don't like your answers, I will hurt you. Consider yourself warned."

Fantastic. Delilah's friend was insane.

CHAPTER SEVENTEEN

"Let him go!" Archer barked.

Memphis frowned at him. "What part of 'follow my lead' did you miss? Or did you just miss all of the parts?"

Archer lunged toward him.

Oz drove his elbow back into Memphis's ribs. Then he slammed his foot down, obviously intending to break some of Memphis's toes. Memphis merely laughed. But he *did* let Oz go.

Oz whirled toward him with his fists up. Only to realize that Memphis had pulled out a knife.

Where in the hell did he get that?

"Archer." Oz's voice seemed high. "You understand you have a man with a knife in your office. He just attacked me—an unprovoked attack—and we need to call the cops on him."

Memphis rolled his eyes. "How boring. Why would we want to bring in the cops?"

"It's possible he is mentally unstable," Oz continued doggedly. "You need to inform the police dispatcher of that situation."

"It's also possible that I am the most awesome guy you've ever met. So there's that." Memphis flicked a glance toward his knife. "Would you like to see what I can do with this?"

"No!" Archer nearly roared.

Memphis frowned. "Wasn't asking you. I was asking *him*." He pointed the knife at Oz. "I'll show you, if you don't answer my questions."

Oz hurriedly backed up. "Who is he, Archer?"

"I'm a friend of Delilah's. She vouched for me." Memphis's stare flickered toward Archer. "Remember?"

She had vouched for him. But she hadn't mentioned that he liked to get knife happy.

Oz yanked out a phone from his pocket.

"Don't," Archer ordered him. "Don't call the cops. He's...working for me."

Oz's jaw nearly hit the floor. "You are not serious."

"He's not," Memphis returned. "I'm not an employee. Truly just a volunteer in this matter. Someone attacked my friend, I got pissy, and I decided it was time to step up and put myself into play." A shrug. "So to speak." He offered what looked like a shark's smile. A whole, whole lot of teeth. "You smell like ash."

"That's because I was inside Archer's house, trying to figure out who the hell came after him!" He still gripped his phone.

"You sure it's not because you set the fire at Archer's place?" Memphis pushed.

Oz's knuckles whitened around the phone. "I'm sure." He cut a scathing glance toward Archer. "You believe this creep?"

"You arrived at my house very quickly."

"Because you *texted* me, and I came running, like I always have when you need me!"

"It would have been easy enough to pull on a hoodie over your t-shirt. To disguise yourself." Things Archer had already considered. "You know where my security cameras are located. You could have gotten past them without any issues. Made sure you were only seen from the back. And I suspect that you can get in and out of my house quite easily."

Oz's nostrils flared. "What do I have to do in order to prove my loyalty to you? Bleed? Burn?" He faced off with Archer while seemingly ignoring Memphis and his knife. "I don't have an alibi for tonight. I was home, alone. Hell, maybe you can get someone to hack into some street cams and find footage of me *running* red lights as I rushed to get to you. I did that because I wanted to help you."

"Oh, I can absolutely do that," Memphis said. "I'll get right on the street cams. Thanks for the suggestion."

"Fuck off." His stare didn't leave Archer. "You think the whole world is against you, but I'm not. And I'm not just sticking around because you pay me too damn much money. I am your *friend*. One of these days, you'll realize it." His lips twisted in disgust. "Until then, we have a nine o'clock appointment with the police. Be at the station, got it?" With that, he stormed for the door.

Memphis stepped out of his path, but just as Oz started to pass him, Memphis casually noted, "You knew about the blackmail."

Archer frowned.

"The stuff going down at Club Thirty-Two. You knew about it." Memphis motioned toward Archer. "Delilah briefed me."

Oz glowered at him. "I have no idea what you're talking about."

"Sure, you do. Politicians, lawyers, a big old who's who of important people in this town. You had to know. There had to be someone close to Archer who was trying to make sure he didn't figure out what was happening at the club. Granted, he's been pretty distracted because he's been trying to prove that he's not a murderer and he's been trying to find his ex, but you still needed to make sure that he didn't look too closely over there, am I right?"

"No, you're wrong."

"Maybe. Really, it's just a theory I'm working at the moment," Memphis said, all modest-like. "But it makes sense. You're connected to that political world, and I'm wondering if I look closely, will I see that you magically won some of your cases when you went in front of some of the judges who visited Club Thirty-Two? Is a connection to that place where you get your *magic*, Oz?"

"I won my cases because I'm a damn good lawyer."

"And not because you use a little extra pressure when necessary?"

Archer watched the byplay between them. The tension had ratcheted up in the office. But then Oz glanced over at him, and for just an instant, Archer could have sworn he saw a flash of guilt in his lawyer's eyes.

What have you done, Oz?

"Be there at nine," Oz said. "And stop listening to this moron." With that, he left. Didn't look back.

Memphis ducked his head out of the open doorway. "Yep, keep walking to that elevator," he called. "Keep it going. And...you're inside. Nice. See you around, Oz." His body shifted a bit. "Delilah, I just need to say one more thing to your boyfriend, then you can have him again. Cool?"

Boyfriend.

"Just a sec. Promise." Memphis closed the door. Exhaled. Then looked over his shoulder at Archer. "Don't trust him."

An unnecessary warning. Archer didn't trust him.

"When you have too much money, even your own family will sell you out for a slice of the pie. They'll stab you in the heart even as they smile right into your eyes." Memphis tucked his knife back into his boot—or into a strap on his ankle, *inside* his boot. "Don't trust anyone close to you. Except Delilah. You can count on her." He straightened.

Tell me something I haven't already figured out. "And I suppose I can count on you?"

His brows shot up. "Why the hell would you think that? You don't know me. You just met me."

I already know that you're insane.

"Kidding," Memphis declared. His face suddenly looked very, very serious. His eyes glinted. "That woman sitting on the desk out there, making her phone calls to every source and contact she's got—the woman doing that so frantically because she wants to help *you*—who is she to you?"

His gaze trekked toward the door.

"Better question, *what* is she to you?"

"Everything." The answer was a whole lot easier and clearer than he'd expected.

Memphis grunted. "Then, yeah, you can count on me. She's one of the few friends I have, and I will stand with her always. Just like I'm thinking you'll do now, too. Am I right?"

Always.

"She gets beneath your skin before you realize it. Kind of like a tick that you don't see coming."

Archer crossed his arms over his chest. "I do not view Delilah as a tick."

"God, you are so formal and controlled. I bet that drives her crazy."

He wasn't always controlled. Especially with her. "I view Delilah," Archer said very deliberately, "as the most intriguing, maddening, and fascinating woman I have ever met. I want to protect her, I want to shield her, and I want to make absolutely certain that *nothing* bad happens to her. So if you truly want to help, focus your attention on keeping her safe because *she* is what matters."

"Dammit, man." A disgusted shake of Memphis's head. "I didn't want to like you. Just wanted you to be another annoying, too-rich prick, but there you go, worming your way into my heart. If you're not careful, I'll blink, and we'll truly be besties."

"I don't think that will happen." It would be a cold day in hell first.

"You never know." Memphis blew out a hard breath. "Here's the deal. I love that woman like the sister I never had. She hauled my ass out of a very dark time in my life. You get too focused on hunting the wrong things, and suddenly you're the problem. You're the person everyone needs to fear, and you don't even recognize yourself in the mirror." He chewed on his bottom lip. "Don't know if she's told you, but I'm trying to find her sister."

A surge of surprise filled Archer.

"Delilah thinks she's too close. That she can't see the truth because she's too emotionally involved. She knows that emotions screw up a case, but she still went right ahead and let herself fall for you."

"She hasn't...fallen for me."

"Sure she has. Otherwise, she never would have let me have this one-on-one with you. She'd be too worried I'd spill her secrets to someone she can't trust. But she's not afraid of that because she trusts you. Despite all the evidence and suspicions other people have, she *trusts* you. Let that sink in, my man. Absorb it and allow it to change your whole world."

"She's already changed my whole world." In too fast a time, she'd become his world. "She's in danger. I can't have that."

"Then we need to stop the sonofabitch out there, don't we?"

"He took her laptop."

Memphis made a faint, humming sound. "Because he wanted to see what she knew about him. He's worried that she's too close. That means he's gonna come after her again. Word of advice?"

"Just a word? I'd expect quite a few words from you."

Memphis flashed a pleased grin. "That was a joke! See, you are loosening up with me already."

He wasn't.

"Ready for the advice? Because, honestly, I'm giving it whether you want it or not."

Somehow, Archer had expected that outcome.

"Having her in your bed kept her safe last night. Having her *close* kept her from being harmed. Maybe don't go with some stupid-ass plan to send her away—*that* could prove dangerous. If it were me, if it were a woman I loved, I'd keep her at my side twenty-four, seven. I'd chain her to me if need be." His features had hardened. His gaze went lethal. "And I wouldn't let her go, not until that bastard was cold in the ground."

That actually sounded like very, very good advice. But... "I'm not right for Delilah."

"Right? The crazy thing is, I'm suspecting you actually might somehow be *right* for her. Good enough? Now, that's a whole other game, and I can go ahead and tell you, speaking from personal experience, hell, no, you aren't good enough. But something tells me that is not going to stop you from taking what you want."

Would anyone or anything stop him from having Delilah again? He—

The door flew open.

Something is wrong. He could tell instantly. He elbowed Memphis out of his way and reached out to Delilah. He tugged her close. "Baby, what is happening?" His hands flew over her. No injuries. *She's okay. She's okay.*

"She posted."

"What are you talking about?"

"I was on Casey's computer. He needs to change his password, by the way, it is literally, ILOVECHRISTMAS and you can figure it out because he has a tree figurine in his top drawer."

He shook his head. "Okay..."

"Not nearly as tricky as yours. But I figured out what your numbers were referring to, by the way. You were talking about the Orion constellation with your password. Ten for the stars, five for the declination, and then for the right ascension—"

Memphis coughed. "She's on a tangent. Better stop her." He grimaced. "By the way, yes, I do know your password. But like I said, you can count on me."

Archer would be changing his password. "Delilah, tell me what's going on."

She exhaled slowly. Nodded. "I remembered that Tiffany mentioned Vanessa's social media accounts had gone silent. I was waiting on you and Memphis to hurry the hell up—"

"I wish you would hurry the hell up on this retelling," Memphis grumbled.

"So I checked out her socials. She posted two hours ago." Delilah swallowed. "That was right around the time of the fire. *Vanessa posted an update on her account.*"

CHAPTER EIGHTEEN

Hello, world! Did you miss me? I missed a certain someone, I can tell you that. Time for me to come back into this great, big, fiery life once again!

And the picture posted with the update showed a smiling Vanessa as she sat perched on what looked like a rocky ledge, with a red, streaking sunrise visible behind her.

"Let me get closer." Memphis eased into Casey's chair. They'd all been crowded around Casey's computer while they checked out the update. Memphis started tapping on the keyboard.

Delilah glanced at Archer. His eyes were still on the computer screen.

"Her haircut is the same," he said, voice gruff. "That's the exact cut she had two years ago."

Delilah wet her dry lips. "Do you recognize the location?"

"He doesn't have to recognize it. I got the EXIF data." Memphis swung his head to look back at them. "Basic, you know? Downloaded the photo. Hit properties, and bam...got it." His mouth tightened. "Too easy."

Yes, it was. So easy that she knew someone had to be baiting them.

"Got the GPS coordinates, too." He peered back at the computer. Did more typing. "Huh. Would you look at that, it's—"

"I recognize the rocks and the view," Archer interrupted quietly. "It's near my family's cabin in Vermont."

The back of Delilah's neck prickled. *This will not end well.* "Archer..."

"She just showed back up there? After all this time?" Doubt was heavy in his voice.

She felt the same doubt.

Memphis cleared his throat. "The date and time this pic was taken—it's stored in here, too. I can access it, and..." He *did* access it and gave a low whistle. "Man, it's not about her showing *back* up there. The photo was taken a long time ago."

Archer leaned in closer. "How long ago?"

"Three days after she vanished. Right around the time when the cops were searching your place and *her* home had that whole look of a tornado wrecking it. I remember when all that footage hit the news..."

Delilah remembered, too. The cops had gotten a random tip about her disappearance. They'd gone to Vanessa's just to discover that the home seemed ransacked. There had been no sign of Vanessa. No sign of her in just over two years. Until now.

"What in the hell is happening?" Archer snarled.

She curled her hand around his arm. "I don't think she's *back,* Archer." But Delilah wanted to be wrong. She wanted to be wrong so badly. "I think...I think maybe she's been at your cabin the whole time."

"Why the hell would she be hiding there—" He stopped. Squeezed his eyes shut for a moment, then slowly opened them. "Fuck."

"Now you're getting it," Memphis murmured. "Delilah already suspected it might be a body dump site—shit, that was not tactful to say, was it? Sorry. I suck at tact. Delilah is always telling me that. One of the reasons why she usually reaches out to the families instead of me doing the initial contact job."

Body dump site.

"But Delilah already thought the cabin might be a potential location, that's why she wanted me and some buddies to prepare for reconnaissance up there."

Archer's stare drifted to her. "How did you know?"

"I found an old date book of yours inside of your desk."

He shook his head. "There is no date book in my desk."

Why would he say that? "Uh, yes, there *was*. I even took it with me." Because sometimes she had sticky fingers. "But I left it in my bedroom before the fire."

His eyes widened. "Then it might be gone, just like your laptop."

"My what?" Real alarm blasted through her.

"The laptop was taken," Memphis informed her. "Deal with the grief and move on. The SOB is on to us. Luckily, I know you have cloud backup."

Still...*the laptop?* Delilah huffed out a breath and focused on the cabin—and the date book. "When I found the date book, there was a notation about you visiting your family's cabin the week after Vanessa went missing. Only when I questioned him, Oz said you didn't take that trip. At that point, Vanessa had vanished and everything became chaos, so the cabin was forgotten. I asked if he remembered the last time you'd been up to the area, and he couldn't."

"I haven't been back. Not since Vanessa vanished. I was too busy with the business and hiring investigators." His jaw tightened. "Why the hell would she be..." His words trailed off.

She knew what he'd been about to ask. *Why the hell would she be there?* But Delilah wasn't saying Vanessa was there, alive. She was saying someone had dumped her body there. She knew he had to realize what both she and Memphis suspected. Just because the photo had been posted on Vanessa's social media account, it didn't mean that Vanessa had been the one to post it. Trying to be careful, knowing this would still hurt him, Delilah said, "I think that place was used because it was important to you. Something good from your past. I'm guessing it was a place where you went with your family. A place where you had happy memories." Her voice softened even more. "I'm sorry, Archer, but you told me all along that you thought this person was trying to hurt you. If the cabin was one of your sentimental places—one of the special spots where you knew some happiness, then it would hurt more to find her there. By dumping her body in that location, he would wreck the good memories for you."

"Yeah," Memphis agreed. "Plus, just looking at the maps, there are tons of places to hide the body in the area. If you wanted some privacy to play for a while—"

"*Memphis,*" Delilah snapped.

"Sorry. Tact shit again. My bad. I keep forgetting he's not in this world with us." He cleared his throat. "There was plenty of privacy up there for the killer. The trick would just be transporting her to the cabin, but, hell, for all we know, she went with the perp willingly."

"We don't have a body." Archer was obviously trying to think this through. And hold out hope. "Right now, we just have a picture."

"A picture of your missing ex on *your* property," Memphis supplied. Unnecessarily, Delilah thought. Archer already knew that.

"He's trying to draw you up there," Delilah explained.

"Then he's going to get me." A grim nod. "I'll have my plane ready to leave immediately."

"*Archer.*" She shook her head. "If the killer wants you there, you don't *race* to him. You stop. You plan. You plot." It was like detective work 101.

"Ahem." From Memphis. "Look, I already got corpse-sniffing dogs and some friends with ground-penetrating radar at the ready in Vermont. Delilah was gonna make sure we had your permission to search your land before this whole photo posting shit hit the fan, so you just give me the word, Archer, and I can get them active at first light. You can fly up there and meet them."

His head jerked in instant agreement. "Get your friends ready. I'll meet them."

Delilah's hold tightened on his arm. He wasn't going to ditch her. "You mean that *we'll* meet them. Because if you are flying straight into whatever trap this is, I will be with you. Don't even think of trying to leave me behind." Not happening.

Instead of arguing, Archer leaned forward and pressed a soft kiss to her lips. "I don't intend to leave you."

"Damn straight," she affirmed.

"We'll contact the local authorities in Vermont. Get them to meet us on the property. We will not be going in alone."

It was good that Archer wanted to include the authorities. A rather necessary step. But Delilah still had to warn him. "It's possible that they'll think you're guilty because it's your property."

"Possible?" Memphis snorted. "You mean probable. Another reason why it would be the perfect dump site. And if the team finds the body, they may just wanna lock your ass up right away. Sorry, buddy, but it being your place automatically makes you look extra guilty."

"But you're not guilty." Delilah's fast return. Memphis had never been able to sugar coat anything. He just lacked that skill. Normally, she appreciated his honesty. Right then, as tension gathered on Archer's face, she would have liked a little more care. But, now that they were going down this path... "When we find her body—I mean *if*—we could find evidence that ties us to the real killer. Or there could be planted evidence that makes you look guilty as sin."

Archer swallowed. "There's no chance she's alive?"

He'd caught her slip of *when*. Delilah sighed. "I think there's always a chance."

"I wasn't in love with her." Low. "But I never, ever wanted this to happen. I didn't want her dead. And to think that for the last two years, she might have just been dead all along and dumped in the woods...God, no one deserves that. No one."

"We don't know that she's dead yet." The signs were not good but... "We *don't* know. And I am not nearly as tactful as I like to think." Maybe she'd been hanging around Memphis far too long. Or maybe she just needed to watch her mouth. "I'm sorry about that, I'm sorry that—"

He kissed her again. Soft. Tender. "Don't be sorry about anything. You are helping me. You're helping her. From the very beginning, you said you wanted to find her."

She had. She did.

"I'll get the team moving." Memphis said. "They owe me lots of favors, so they'd better not say shit when they get this late night call from me." He rose from the chair. "Maybe it's more early morning than late night at this point?" His steps padded away.

Archer put his forehead against Delilah's.

"You aren't leaving me behind," she told him. He'd better not even try.

"I'm worried this might be a trick. Not just to get me to the cabin, but to try and get me away from you. Memphis said—he thinks it's better when you're close to me."

"Sometimes, Memphis can be a genius." A pause. "Other times, he is an asshole."

Archer's arms wrapped around her waist. "I'm sticking to you, love. As close as I can get."

***

"Archer!"

Delilah turned at the sharp cry, and she saw Tiffany Lassiter rushing toward them. Delilah and Archer had just headed out of the Radcliffe Industries building, the limo waited a few feet away, and dawn had still not yet come.

"Archer! Did you see?" Tiffany yanked up a phone as she ran toward him. She wore yoga pants and a form-fitting top. Stylish sneakers covered her feet. "Vanessa is alive!" Delight boomed in her voice and glowed on her face.

Delilah's stomach clenched.

Archer glanced toward the limo driver. "Danny, give us a minute."

Danny shuffled away.

"You can get inside," Archer said to Delilah as he motioned toward the open limo door. "I'll take care of her."

Delilah didn't move.

Tiffany ran to Archer and threw her arms around him. "Isn't it the most wonderful thing?" She pulled back and beamed up at him. "I was at my gym—it's right down the street, I was getting in my five a.m. workout, and I just—I was scrolling on my phone while I walked on the treadmill to cool down." A bubble of laughter burst from her lips. "And there Vanessa was. Smiling at me. Vanessa is back!" She gave him another quick hug.

Delilah kept standing right there.

Tiffany seemed to realize they had an audience. She bounded back and slanted a worried glance at Delilah.

Delilah didn't speak. *I'm not sure what to say.* Tiffany's joy was clear to see.

"It was all one of her games," Tiffany added with a weak laugh. She tucked a lock of hair behind her ear. "I was going to call and tell you. But then I walked out of the gym, and I saw you here and I just—" An exhale. "I told you she'd probably hooked up with someone else. I bet she was with some rich duke or an eccentric artist with too much money to burn. They were holed up some place fabulous for the last two years, and now they've broken up and she's back." Tiffany rocked onto the heels of her feet. "She's back." Relief coated the words. Tiffany's hand flew over her cheek, catching a tear that had trickled from her eye. "I had started to believe she was...d-dead, but she isn't. She's alive, and she'll be back and..." Now her gaze—gleaming still with tears—darted to Delilah. "She'll be back for Archer."

Archer threaded his fingers with Delilah's. "Your sister and I broke up before she disappeared."

Another quick laugh. "Like that will stop Vannie. You know she always goes after what she wants." Her shoulders sagged a little, as if in relief, and she looked at her phone again. Her face softened as she stared at the picture on the screen. "I did miss her." There was an echo of pain in her voice. And for just an instant, pain showed on her face, only to quickly be replaced by happiness. "But she's back." A wide smile. "I messaged her, of course. Told her to get her skinny ass back to town. I'm sure I'll hear from her at any moment."

Archer's head turned. His gaze met Delilah's.

"I should get going." Tiffany took a quick step back. "I just saw you and ran over and I—you were going somewhere." She nibbled on her lower lip. "I'll let you get back to that." She whirled. Stopped. Shot a quick glance over her shoulder at Delilah. "I do love my sister." Low. "That will never end." A tremulous smile. Then she was hurrying away. Lifting her phone to her ear and saying, "*I have the best news!*" to whoever she'd just called.

Delilah watched her disappear down the street. "You didn't tell her..."

"That we're leaving town to try and find her sister's body? No, I didn't mention that." A long exhale. "Because she looked happy."

Yes, she had.

He urged her toward the limo. Delilah climbed inside. A moment later, the door shut. Archer sat next to her. "What if...what if you had just gotten a picture that made you think Layla was alive?" Archer asked quietly as the limo pulled away from the curb. "And then you found out—"

She put her index finger to his lips. "You did the right thing with Tiffany. I would want to hold on to my hope just a little longer."

He nodded.

Her finger slid away. She leaned toward him. Brushed her lips over his. "You did the right thing."

***

"Stay alert," Memphis ordered her.

Delilah's lips twisted as she glared at her friend. He'd just rushed from the parking lot to meet her. "No, I was planning on being completely unobservant and easy prey for whoever is out there."

"Listen, smartass, I don't like this deal."

Not like she was thrilled, either. Her gaze cut toward Archer. He was having a quick chat with the pilot. The private plane was ready on the runway.

"I want to stay in town and keep an eye on some people who are sure as hell making me suspicious," Memphis added. "Since my buddies will be waiting up there—*and* the local authorities will be on scene—you should be safe. But if you would rather I come—"

"No, I want you here." There were people she wanted him watching, too. Delilah knew Oz was at the top of Memphis's watch list. They'd had to tell Oz about their plans to fly out so he could be ready to smooth things over with the local PD when Archer didn't show for his early morning appointment.

Oz hadn't exactly been thrilled by the change of plans.

Archer's head lifted. Turned toward her. "Delilah, you ready?"

She nodded. Before she could head toward him, Memphis leaned close. "You sure you know what you're doing with him?" Low. For her ears only.

She offered him a wan smile. "I have no idea what I'm doing." But Delilah suspected that she was losing her heart. "I just know that I want to be close to him."

"You trust him." Not a question.

"It's weird, but I did almost from the very beginning." Even when everyone else had seemed to think he was the monster.

Memphis retreated. "When you get to the cabin, Tony will be waiting for you."

She'd changed clothes. Archer had made sure new outfits were brought to the Radcliffe Industries building before they left. New clothing *and* a new phone for her. He'd told her that the old phone had been destroyed or else it was still buried under ash in the guest bedroom.

Her new tennis shoes squeaked a little as she crossed to join Archer. She wore faded jeans that clung tightly to her hips and legs and a loose blouse that was the same color as her eyes. A deliberate color choice, she was sure.

Archer's fingers threaded with hers. Together, they walked out of the airport. But Delilah couldn't help looking back. In that one instant, she caught Memphis unaware. A truly unusual occurrence. His expression wasn't guarded. He didn't have on the casual mask he wore so easily.

Instead, his expression was hard. Almost angry. His eyes glittered, and he stared at Archer with suspicion clear to see on his face.

CHAPTER NINETEEN

"You can take off your seatbelt," Archer murmured as his fingers curled around the armrest. "It's safe."

Delilah offered him a nervous smile. "I'm not exactly the best flyer." Her fingers trembled a bit as she unhooked the belt. She sat across from him, and her jean-clad legs stretched before her. "I have actually been known to keep my seatbelt on for the entire length of a flight, just in case."

"In case?"

"Yeah, just in case. Fear and logic don't always go hand in hand."

No, they didn't. Archer glanced out of the window. He could see the rising sun. "Does Memphis still suspect me?"

"I think part of him suspects every person that he meets. He tends to think people are more bad than good, in general. Just who he is. How his mind works."

His attention shifted back to her. She was far prettier than any sunrise he'd ever seen. "But Memphis doesn't suspect you of being bad? He trusts you completely?"

"I may have helped him out of a few sticky situations. Trouble always has a way of finding him."

Archer could imagine that it did. "He's helping you look for your sister."

Her lashes lowered to conceal her gaze. "Yes. I thought someone who wasn't as emotionally involved might see things better."

"And does he? See better, I mean?" He wanted to reach out to her. To stroke her cheek. To kiss her. To promise her so much. Everything.

One thought had been plaguing him. Trying to wreck him.

What if Delilah had been the one missing for the last two years? What if something happened to her and she just vanished from my life?

And poor Vanessa. To have been tossed away. To have been targeted. *Because of me?* God, she hadn't deserved that. She should have still been living her best life somewhere. How many times had he wished that he could find out she was dancing on the Riviera or sunning herself on some gorgeous beach?

Delilah's jaw firmed. "Memphis thinks there are others."

"Other what?" *Stay focused.*

"Victims." Her lashes lifted. "Memphis found a pattern. He believes that my sister was part of that pattern."

He did not like where this was going. His gut twisted. "Delilah..."

"People disappear all the time. Sometimes, they run away. Disappearing is their choice. Sometimes, accidents happen. People are just trying to get home, a deer runs into the path of the car...and suddenly, you're at the bottom of a ravine and no one knows what happened. That was one of my cases, you know. We could tell that a deer had hit the car because part of an antler was still stuck in the hood of the vehicle. A soccer mom just went missing and all along, she'd been trapped down there. No food or water and eventually..." She sucked in a quick breath. "Accidents take people away. And bad things—bad *people*—take them away, too."

"Who does Memphis think took your sister?"

She blinked quickly, and he realized she was trying not to cry. Shit. He immediately shot out of his seat. Went to his knees before her. His fingers reached for her hand. "Delilah, no. You don't have to tell me a damn thing. You don't have to say a word about it." He'd been trying to put up a wall in his head about what he might find when the plane landed, but he didn't get to wreck her life with his questions. He didn't get to cause her pain. He never wanted to do that.

"It's okay. I want to talk about this with you." Her lips pressed together, then released. "A serial. He found two others with a victim profile like my sister's. He thinks they are all connected."

He almost fell on his ass. "A serial killer?"

"They're out there, you know. Not just on TV or in the movies. I've got a friend at the FBI—well, he was *formerly* at the FBI. Elijah was an incredible behavioral analyst. He told me that there could be as many as fifty active serials working at any time in the US. *Fifty*. And if bodies are just disappearing, if the d-dead aren't turning up," a slight stutter that hinted at her painful emotions, "it makes it even harder for authorities to track and target the perps."

His hand lifted. He tucked a lock of hair behind her ear. "What can I do?"

Her brow furrowed.

"As much money as you need. Whatever I have—use it. Take it. Find her."

"I wish it was that easy. It's not. Memphis and Elijah are both working on her case—Elijah is building a profile on the perp, and Memphis is hunting, but..." Her head shifted a little. His hand had lingered against her cheek, and she tilted into his touch. "None of us will give up. Not ever. Not until we find her."

No, she wouldn't give up. It just wasn't who Delilah was. On his knees before her, Archer confessed his guilt. "I should have looked harder."

Her brows lifted.

"I should have done more. I should have gotten more investigators. I should have tracked *harder*. I should have—"

"Stop it."

He couldn't stop. "If she was dead this whole time, if she was at my cabin...or, what if she wasn't dead, not at first, and then later he killed—"

"*Stop*. You don't need this guilt. Trust me, I know what I'm talking about. Because if you think I don't have the same thoughts about my sister—*all of the time*—you're wrong. I do. I should have hunted harder. I should search better. If I were just smarter, I could figure it out." Her voice thickened. "I know how hard you hunted. I did my research on you, remember? You were looking for her the whole time. You were trying to prove your innocence. You didn't give up. I know you have two different agencies on retainer who are looking for her right now, *plus* you've got me. You didn't give up."

"Neither did you," he fired right back. She felt guilty? Dammit, no. "Your sister's disappearance isn't on you! It—"

"I should have been there."

"What? No, sweetheart, you—"

"You don't understand." She pushed back against the seat, shrinking away from his touch when she'd sought it a moment before.

His hand fell.

"I *should* have been there," she said again. "I was supposed to be there. She wanted to go to a club because Layla loved to dance. But I got held up at work. So I gave her the keys to my car. Told her to go without me. That I would hitch a ride with a buddy and meet up with her and..." Her breath choked out. "When I got to the club, she wasn't there. I called and called, but I couldn't get her to answer the phone. The next morning, cops found the car—*my* car—along the side of the road. The back tire was flat, like it had been slashed, and Layla was gone. Her phone was tossed in the front seat, and it was full of missed calls from me."

He surged up. Grabbed her. Wrapped her into his arms.

"I should have been there."

Fuck, fuck, fuck. "This is not on you. This is *not* your fault." He held her tighter.

"I go through it in my mind, over and over, if I hadn't given her the keys, if I'd gotten her to wait for me, if I'd been in the car with her..."

He crushed her against him. *"You can't change the past. This is not on you."*

"And what happened to Vanessa isn't on you."

He stiffened. His head rose as he peered down at her.

"We'll always carry the guilt, but you can't let it control you." There were tear tracks on her cheeks. "And you can't let it drive you crazy. You have to keep going. No matter what else, you have to keep living."

She was destroying him. She'd bared her soul because she knew what he was feeling and she'd wanted him to know he wasn't alone. She'd wanted to help him. She gave—again and again—and he was such a selfish bastard because he was there to take from her. "I do not deserve you." Memphis had been right. He would never, ever be good enough for her.

"Probably not." Even as a tear trickled down her cheek and made his heart ache, she offered him a small smile. "But you have me." She leaned up and kissed him.

It should have been a gentle, tender moment. He'd never felt more connected to anyone in his life. He should have been careful. The kiss should have been one of comfort.

It wasn't. Something else happened. When her lips brushed against his, when her arms curled around him, it was as if a wall shattered inside of him. Feelings swamped him. Desire, need, lust—yes, but more. So much more. He held her tightly. His mouth was hard and fierce on hers as he sought her response.

You have me.

Her response was electric. Consuming. Hot enough to burn him alive. Her hands clenched around his arms. Her mouth opened wider. Her tongue met his in a frantic kiss that just made him want more and more.

They were on a freaking plane.

But it was his *private* plane. No one would be coming back to that area, and if he didn't get inside of her, if he didn't have her...

She's my sanity. He knew it. Understood that she was his link. No, his world. His hands flew down her body. He shoved up the shirt.

"Archer!" A shocked cry. She stepped back, shoved the shirt back down. "The crew—"

"I want you."

She looked toward the front of the plane.

"No one is coming back here." They'd better not. "Delilah..." So much could change when the plane touched down. He just wanted this moment with her. Something to hold close. A memory that he could never lose.

I don't want to lose her.

"Sit down," Delilah told him.

Jaw locking, he did. She didn't want to be with him—

She kicked off her shoes. Ditched her jeans and panties.

He almost shot right back out of the seat.

"No. Stay." She crept closer. "But we have to be quiet."

His eyes were on her bare sex. He reached out. Slid his fingers between her legs. A moan trembled from her lips.

"Quiet," he reminded her even as his fingers dipped into her.

Delilah arched up onto her toes. She grabbed the head rest behind him. "I've...never done this before. On a plane, I mean."

"Neither have I." Hardly his style. But if he didn't get inside of her...

His fingers flexed. His thumb raked over her clit, and another ragged moan slipped from her, but Delilah immediately clamped her lips together to try and hold in any other sounds.

He hated that she had to hold back. He loved her moans and gasps. He loved *her*.

The thought reverberated through him. Destroyed him.

And it came again...stronger.

He loved her.

This wasn't about sex. This wasn't about need. This was about emotion—love. He wanted the physical act with her because he hoped to bind them together. He didn't want to lose Delilah. Not now. Not ever.

"Tell me...tell me you have a condom on you."

He didn't. A grim shake of his head even as his fingers kept working her. She was getting wetter. Hotter. "No, but I'm clear. Just had a full health check. I'm good."

Her head tipped forward. "So am I. And I'm on birth control."

He could not look away from her. She was offering him... "Delilah? Baby, I've never gone without using a rubber with a partner before." The thought of being with her that way..."I want you." Any way he could get her. Every way.

"Not sure if I can fit all the way in the seat. The arm rest—"

He pulled his fingers from her heat—*I will have more*—and hauled up the arm rest. He yanked open the top of his pants. Nearly ripped away the zipper. *No underwear.* A damn good thing or he would have shredded his own boxers in his haste. Then he hauled her down on him. Her thighs straddled him. His eager cock shoved at the entrance to her body.

Her gaze met his. The tear tracks were still on her cheeks.

No pain. No more pain ever for her.

He kissed her cheek.

She arched down on him and took his cock inside.

Pleasure. Heat. His whole body shuddered, and his hands clamped around her waist. She still had on her blouse, and he was fisting the fabric beneath his fingers as he held tightly to her. Then he was lifting her. Raising her up, only to have her arch down again. Faster. Harder. She gripped the seat behind him, using it for leverage, as she ground her hips against him.

Her sex gripped him so tightly. Bare flesh. Skin to skin. He could feel every bit of her, just as she could feel him. He was not going to last. There was no way. When something was this good, when you wanted something so much...

Her eyes were on him when they went blind with pleasure. She opened her mouth, and he knew she was going to cry out. He kissed her. Kissed her even as he surged into her one more time, as hard and deep as he could. And he let go. Archer emptied into her endlessly. He held her as tightly as he could.

The thunder of his heartbeat echoed in his ears. His grip on her had to be too hard and tight, and he would ease up. As soon as the pleasure stopped pouring through him.

Her mouth slowly lifted from his. Instead of pulling away and rising, she pressed her hips down harder on him. He felt her inner muscles clamp impossibly more around him.

"*Fuck!*"

"Shh. You don't want anyone to hear." A kiss from her. Mouth open. Tongue dipping past his lips.

And he was just lost.

***

"I should apologize." Archer sat in his seat, with the belt secured across his lap. Delilah was across from him, her clothes back in place, her hair smoothed into position, and even her lipstick carefully reapplied.

She looked beautiful. Perfect.

Delilah arched one brow. "What for?"

He blinked. "Being so desperate for you?" So desperate he'd taken her on a plane.

A shrug of one shoulder. "I rather like you that way."

"And I like you any way I can get you." Truth.

Their gazes held.

She shook her head.

"Delilah?"

"You're really the same man who once told me you weren't the type for sex on desks? Or in cars?" Soft laughter.

He much preferred her laughter to her tears. Her tears cut out his heart. "I'm different with you."

"No, I think you're just really yourself with me."

He realized she was right. He didn't have to pretend with Delilah. He just was. "I said I *should* apologize." The plane was descending. Soon, this brief respite would be gone, and a nightmare would be waiting to slide back into his life. "But I'm not sorry, so I'm not apologizing."

Her other eyebrow lifted.

"I want you more than anything in the world, and whenever I have a chance to take you, I will." Fair warning.

Her gaze drifted to the window. "Same."

"What?"

She looked back at him. "I think you heard me."

He wanted to hear her again.

"I didn't ask for an apology," Delilah told him. "I certainly don't want one."

"What is it that you do want?"

"You."

"Sweetheart, you have me." She might not realize it, but the woman owned him, heart and soul.

CHAPTER TWENTY

"Why didn't you come back here in the last two years?" Delilah asked as the rented SUV slowed to a stop near the entrance to the sprawling cabin. A thick forest surrounded the luxury retreat, stretching for miles and miles. An absolute gorgeous setting.

It truly was the perfect place to hide a body.

"I was busy." His hands tightened around the wheel before he turned it and started down the winding drive. "When I was a kid, I loved this place. My mom would bring me here, before she got sick. I swear, some of my happiest moments were here."

As she'd suspected. Delilah knew someone wanted to rip that happiness away from him.

"After Vanessa disappeared, there was so much media attention. So much surveillance from the cops. They were watching my every move. I was hunting for her, trying to keep the business going when customers were bailing left and right because of all the bad publicity and I just..." He braked in front of the house. Other cars were already there. Local patrol cars from the sheriff's office. Battered pick-ups. "Going on vacation to the cabin wasn't exactly a priority for me."

"And the authorities never searched here?"

He cut her a glance. "Why haul the body all the way up here?"

The body.

The answer was so easy. *To hurt you.*

"You think we're going to find her, don't you? You really, truly think—"

Someone rapped on her window before Delilah could answer him. She turned, peered through the glass, and saw Tony. Tony's expression told her instantly that something was wrong.

She pushed open the door even as Tony stepped back. Delilah's path had crossed with Antonia "Tony" Rossi before. Tony had one very particular skill set.

She found the dead.

Tony's long, black hair was in a loose braid that draped over one shoulder. A smudge of dirt was on her right cheek, and her faded work pants and top sported more smudges and dirt stains.

"Been too long," Tony told Delilah. "And I do wish the circumstances were different." A wry smile briefly tilted her full lips. "But then again, our meeting circumstances are usually shit."

True story.

Footsteps crunched on the gravel as Archer came to join them.

Delilah motioned toward him. "Archer Radcliffe, this is Tony Rossi. *Doctor* Tony Rossi. She's got—"

Tony waved away her credentials. "A ton of degrees that basically make me really good at identifying bodies. Morbid as hell, I know, but I am what I am." She offered her hand to Archer. Gave him a quick, hard shake, then let him go.

"I know this might take a while," Delilah began as she glanced around. She'd spent some time studying maps on the drive. "The property is massive, and then it backs up to—"

"Not gonna take nearly as long as you think." The faint smile was gone from Tony's lips.

In the distance, a dog barked.

"Delilah knows how I work, but I'll give you a quick and dirty version of my methods." No emotion entered Tony's voice. "First, I look for variations in the ground surface. We're talking about small hills. Dips in the earth. Any kind of sign that the soil has been disturbed and that a body might be underground."

The dog barked again.

"That's Banshee. Her job is to sniff around the area and help me to find human remains." A pause. "I also use GPR to help me search. That way, I'm not wasting time and digging for nothing all over the place."

Archer cut a glance toward Delilah.

"Ground penetrating radar." Sweat slickened her palms even though it wasn't warm. "But I bet you knew that, didn't you?"

Grimly, he nodded. "The dog is barking again." A slight hesitation. His gaze slid back to Tony. "Have you found something?"

"Yeah. Didn't take long at all. I began at the house and was working my way outward with the team when I noticed the ground wasn't quite so level in one area. Stood out to me. The deputies are there now. We're...we're about to start digging."

The dog's cry erupted again. This time, it seemed to hold a mournful note.

"Banshee cries when she finds the dead," Tony said. "I'm sorry." She turned away and headed for the woods.

He started to follow.

Delilah caught his arm. If they'd already made a discovery... "That's gonna be considered a crime scene now. The deputies are not going to let you get close. And you don't want to see what they dig up."

"Yes, dammit, I do."

The guilt was there. Guilt and anger and so many other emotions. She wanted to pull him close. Hold tight. She wanted to lie and tell him everything was okay. But...

It wasn't okay. "It's been two years, Archer. You do *not* want to see her right now." Because there wouldn't be much left. "Let Tony do her job."

Banshee howled again.

A deputy in uniform walked from the woods and immediately eyed Archer with suspicion.

Delilah knew the area was about to be roped off. She also knew, with a sinking feeling in her heart, that she'd succeeded in her latest case. She'd set out to find Vanessa. With help from her team, they had.

Another one of the missing had been found, but not returned to her family. Not returned alive, anyway.

***

The plane ride back was different.

Twenty-four hours later, they were returning to Miami. They were waiting on an official ID for the human remains, but Delilah knew—as did Archer—that Vanessa had been located.

She'd even been wearing the same outfit that she'd worn in the social media post.

Archer stared out of the window. The cops had asked him so many questions. Over and over again.

A full exam would be performed on the remains. Cause of death had to be determined. Teams were tearing apart the cabin. Crime scene analysts were scouring the woods.

"I have to tell Tiffany." His voice was low. Seemed so very distant. "She had her hopes up about her sister, and I-I need to let her know what has happened."

The last twenty-four hours had been hell. Archer had been grilled—*grilled*—by the local authorities. There'd been little rest, definitely no sleep. He'd answered every question and never once asked for his lawyer. A bad plan? Maybe not, considering that Delilah knew he suspected his lawyer of being involved in this mess. But with Archer's money and connections, he could easily have hired somebody else. A dozen somebodies.

The sheriff had known that. His confusion had been clear.

He hadn't wanted Archer to leave town. But Archer wasn't being charged with anything—not yet, anyway—so the sheriff hadn't been able to stop him.

"You gave him your passport."

At her words, Archer tuned.

"You didn't have to do that."

"He thinks I'm a flight risk. That I will cut out of the country and never come back. The passport was to reassure him." No emotion entered his voice. "He and I both knew that if I truly wanted to run, I could. Passport or no passport."

"You're not running."

"Hell, no. I'm figuring this out. I'm hoping like hell that evidence can be found that points us to her killer. I told Sheriff Broderick that I would give him any assistance that he needs. That I could bring in the best medical examiner, that I could have the best techs brought in to do analysis on any evidence recovered—"

"And he told you to fuck yourself?" Delilah finished.

"Yes, basically. He's worried I'm trying to 'impede his investigation' or some crap. I just want the truth." Weariness finally slipped into his voice. "Dammit, she was in the ground all that time. Bagged up and shoved in a hole."

Vanessa had been found wrapped in a black tarp, not really a bag. She hadn't even been put in the ground that deeply...

Is that what happened to Layla? Will I find her in the ground one day, tossed away like garbage? Delilah shut down the thought. As she'd shut it down over and over in the last five years. "Someone else took the picture."

His hand shoved through his hair.

"I found that outcropping from her social media post. I got up there. Got in the same position that Vanessa was in for the photo. I'm telling you, there is no selfie stick in the world that could have gotten that angle for her. Someone else took the picture. Someone else loaded it online." Obviously, the dead woman hadn't loaded her own picture.

"So we have to figure out who had access to her account." He blew out a ragged breath. "I did. I'm sure the authorities know that already. She wasn't real big on keeping her password secret. It was just the word 'star' and her birthday. She'd tell it to anyone and everyone. Hell, she even had a social media assistant for a while. Don't know why. Something about being an influencer. Getting followers..." A weary shake of his head.

"It's easy to hack social media accounts." Which made this mess all the harder to sort out. "But maybe we can start by figuring out where the person was when the photo was loaded online to Vanessa's account."

A furrow appeared between his brows. "Can you do that?"

"Me, personally? Absolutely not. To be honest, I'm not sure it can be done, but it seems like a possibility, and I do have some contacts who might be able to help us, so why not give it a shot?" She leaned forward. Her hand locked on his knee. "This story is going to break soon in the media."

"I know. That's why I need to tell Tiffany first."

She understood. She wouldn't want to find out via the Internet about Layla. "She was alive in the picture. She was smiling. She *looked* happy." All important details that could not be overlooked.

A faint line crept between his brows.

"She wasn't afraid of the person taking the photo. I think she came willingly to your cabin with that individual."

"And then he killed her?"

"Yes."

The line between his eyebrows deepened. "I got that note on my pillow just hours after we broke up. It was there. Waiting. Hell, I didn't even know she *had* vanished at first. I didn't fully understand the meaning of the note until the cops got that tip a few days later saying she'd been taken. Then they searched her place, found chaos and—and the world just exploded." His hand sawed over the stubble that coated his jaw. "The note was left so soon. When it was left—she couldn't have been dead then. The picture had a damn sunset in the background!"

This was tricky. Time to tell him about her suspicions. "No, she wasn't dead when the note was left. But whoever convinced her to go to the cabin...that person had already *planned* for her to die."

He reached down. Caught her hand. Wrapped his fingers with hers. "The press will tear me apart again."

"They will try." She knew how the people in her business operated. Some would come straight for him with blood in their eyes. Others would try to work from different angles, attempting to sneak up and attack. All would be intent on breaking the story of a lifetime. And the story?

It's the big, bad billionaire who might be a killer.

"I believe in you," Delilah told him.

His hold tightened on her fingers. "Why?"

"Do you even need to ask?"

"Yes." Gruff. "I do. Because you matter to me. Because I want to know why the hell you are standing with me when you need to be running. You don't have to be in this darkness with me."

"But I'm comfortable in the dark." True. "And I would never run from you. You didn't do this. I know who you really are."

The pilot made an announcement. They were about to descend.

She let go of his hand. Settled back in her seat. "I don't care what happens when we touch down. You are not going to be alone in this. I'll be with you every step of the way." Delilah would be standing by him.

"You still haven't told me *why*."

She smiled at him. "Because I love you." Her feelings had crystalized. Certainty filled her. *I love you.*

And as the plane descended, she had the pleasure of seeing some of the sorrow and pain vanish from his face. Instead, she got to see a flash of hope.

Hold on to that hope, Archer. Because things were going to get a whole lot uglier for him—for them—before they got better. A killer was waiting, and Delilah didn't know what that person was going to do next.

***

"Problem," Memphis growled.

Delilah lifted her brows. "Wonderful to see you, too, Memphis. Yes, the last twenty-four hours were exceedingly stressful, and we've had no sleep, but—"

He turned toward Archer.

She frowned at him. Memphis was being even more abrupt than normal. He'd been waiting for them outside of the airport, standing with Danny next to the limo. Luckily, no reporters were anywhere nearby. For the time being, she and Archer were still keeping a low profile. *And word hasn't spread yet about Vanessa.*

"I lost him." Memphis thrust up his chin. "This is completely my fault, but rest assured I will find him. There is no hole he can hide in, no place he can run where I will not find his sorry ass. I will drag him back. That's a promise."

Archer glanced at Delilah, then back at Memphis. "Who did you lose?"

"Harrison Walker. I had a man on him when I left to come and meet you two at the airport, and it was a guy I trusted." Then, muttering, he added, "A guy I will not be using on my team any longer."

"*Memphis,*" Delilah snapped his name. "What happened to Harrison?"

"He gave my guy the slip. Not an easy task, but he got it done." His hands went to his hips. "So if that doesn't scream suspicious behavior, I don't know what does."

Neither did Delilah.

"I'd been keeping eyes on him and Oz. I figured with the new development in the case, the guilty party would do something to show his hand, and now Harrison is trying to pull a Houdini." Memphis laughed, but the sound was more like a low, angry snarl. "He obviously doesn't know who he is up against. I will find him."

Delilah reached for Archer's hand. The scene at Club Thirty-Two had been bad, and they'd all had their suspicions, but...*Harrison is his brother.*

"I have to tell Tiffany." Archer's voice was tight. Emotionless when he had to be nearly bursting with emotion. She'd actually learned that the colder his voice became, the *stronger* his emotions actually were. "If I don't tell her what happened in Vermont, she'll see the story on the news. I have to see her first, and then...fuck, then I'll deal with Harrison."

Memphis tossed a quick glance Delilah's way. She knew what he was thinking. Either Harrison was running or he was planning an attack. In that brief look, she could read the question in Memphis's eyes.

Want extra protection?

Hell, yes, she did. Delilah gave an almost imperceptible nod of her head. She wanted protection on Archer because Harrison would be desperate. Desperate people would do very, very dangerous things.

"You two go pay that visit to Tiffany. I'll do recon. Check in with my team." Memphis was already backing away. "I'll get a fucking army to surround you and Delilah." He did a quick about-face and stalked away.

Danny kept standing near the limo. He'd obviously heard the conversation and his eyes were huge.

"Take us to Tiffany Lassiter's place." Again, Archer's voice was tight. He rattled off the address and guided Delilah toward the back of the limo.

She slipped inside. He followed right behind her. When the door closed, sealing them inside, silence stretched. Her hand grasped his. She didn't plan to let go.

"He always hated me," Archer said.

"We don't have proof that he's guilty yet." *But the innocent don't run.* That was a lesson she'd learned long ago.

His head leaned back against the seat, and Archer closed his eyes. "Want to hear something sad and twisted?"

She waited.

"When I found out that I had a brother, I was glad. My dad was a shit father. I'd lost my mom. And I thought—I can have a family again. He can be my family. But he never wanted that."

She *hated* his pain. Just as she hated the controlled tone of his voice when she knew he was hurting inside. So, Delilah announced, "I'd like two kids. Maybe three."

Archer stiffened. His fingers squeezed hers, almost painfully.

"A daughter first would be great, but I'm not too picky. Your mother...I read that her name was Grace Elizabeth Radcliffe."

"Yes." Low.

"So I was thinking that we'd name our daughter Layla Grace. Has a nice ring, don't you think?" The limo drove away from the airport. "We'll get her a garden, and she can spend her days with muddy hands and sweet-smelling flowers."

His eyes opened. So much emotion blazed in his stare. So much desperate longing.

"Then we can have a boy. Another girl. Whatever. We'll have kids and we'll have each other, and we will be the best family ever. I mean, sure, we'll fight. After all, have you met me?"

His lips curved, as if helplessly.

Delilah had to swallow down the lump in her throat as she continued, "I am opinionated, so are you, so we'll fight, and we'll make up, and we'll make love, and we'll sing carols at Christmas. Oh, you should know that I am completely tone-deaf. That means the singing will be very, very bad. But we'll be happy, and we'll be a family and—"

He yanked her against him. Crushed her to his chest as he buried his face in the curve of her neck. "I fucking *love* you," Archer rasped.

She held him just as fiercely. "I know. But it's good of you to say the words."

***

Tiffany Lassiter lived in a posh condominium near the beach. When Archer and Delilah exited the elevator, they were on the seventh floor. The thick carpeting swallowed their steps, and, all too soon, they stood in front of Tiffany's door.

Archer stared at the door and pulled in a deep breath. *How the hell do I break this news to her?* He didn't know the right words to say. Didn't think there *were* right words.

But he had to tell her. Squaring his shoulders, he lifted his hand and knocked.

A moment later, the door swung open. Tiffany's hair was wet, as if she'd just stepped out of the shower, and she had no makeup on her freshly scrubbed face. She wore a pair of designer jeans, a pale blue top, and an uncertain smile lifted her lips as she realized Archer was her surprise visitor. The smile dimmed a little when she caught sight of Delilah.

Or maybe it dimmed when she realized just how serious their expressions were.

"Archer. I, um, didn't expect you." Her brows crinkled. "I haven't heard from Vanessa yet, if that's why you're here. I'm sure she'll be responding to my message any time, though so—"

"She won't." Gruff. God, this was going to be hard.

Tiffany frowned. "Why not?" Her eyes widened. "Is she mad at me? Have you already talked to her and she's pissed at me because I went on all those talk shows or something?" She backed up a step. "Listen, she's the one who went radio silent for two years! She's—"

Delilah cleared her throat. "Could we come inside?"

"Why?" Tiffany shook her head. "Look, no offense, but I am more than fine with Archer visiting, but you—"

"We found her, Tiffany," Archer cut in to say. Because the words had to be said. He couldn't delay any longer. Tiffany needed to know.

"You found her?" Another smile. "Of course! Well, after her post, I knew it was just—"

"I'm sorry," Archer told her, and he was. So very, very sorry. "But Vanessa is dead."

Tiffany grabbed for the door. Her knuckles whitened. "That's not true."

"She's been dead for a while. Her body was found in Vermont yesterday, and I—"

"That's not true! I just saw her post! She's alive! She's—"

Archer shook his head.

And Tiffany fell to the floor.

CHAPTER TWENTY-ONE

"I know it's early, but would you like, um, well, no delicate way to put this...would you like a bracing shot of something strong?" Delilah frowned at Tiffany as the other woman huddled on the couch.

Archer stood a few feet away, feeling helpless. He had carried Tiffany inside, and her tears had tumbled down her cheeks. She'd finally stopped crying, but now she just stared blankly ahead.

She barely even seemed to register Delilah's words.

"Is there someone you'd like for me to call?" Delilah added. "A friend, a family member?"

"Our...our dad is dead. Vanessa and I—we lost him years ago." Quiet. "My mom...I...she's in Europe. And she's not going to care about Vannie. Vannie wasn't hers." A tremble shook her body.

Delilah squeezed her arm. "What can I get for you?"

Another tear trickled down Tiffany's cheek. "Why are you being nice to me?"

Delilah crouched in front of her. "Because you're hurting. Because you lost your sister, and I know what that is like."

Tiffany bit her lip. "I thought I was getting her back." She reached forward. Wrapped her arms around Delilah. Her shoulders shook as she cried.

Delilah hugged her and glanced over at Archer.

Helpless. He was—

His phone vibrated in his pocket. He started to ignore it, but what if it was Memphis calling with an update on Harrison?

"What happened to her?" Tiffany asked in a low, weak voice. "Was it...was it an accident?"

No, because no one ever got accidentally wrapped in a tarp and buried in a shallow grave.

He looked at his phone. Didn't recognize the number. "Excuse me." He turned away, aware of the soft, soothing flow of Delilah's voice behind him as she spoke with Tiffany. Archer took a few steps toward Tiffany's kitchen. "Hello?"

"*Archer.*" Harrison's voice. Cracking. "*Archer, man, I need your help.*"

His grip nearly shattered the phone. "Where are you?"

"I didn't mean for any of this to happen, I swear I didn't. You have to believe me."

"Harrison, where are you?"

His rough breathing filled Archer's ear. "You have to come alone," Harrison ordered him raggedly. "People were watching me, people *are* after me now, and you have to come alone."

Like that would happen. "Sure, tell me where you are, and I'll be there."

"If I see someone with you, I'll run."

The floor creaked behind him. Archer turned. Saw Delilah staring at him.

"You won't see anyone with me." He was sure that Memphis would know how to keep a low profile. "Give me the address."

"I need to...tell you some things. Really important things. Then if you want to call the cops..." A long exhale. "You can. But I just need to tell you first."

This was his brother. The man who'd spent his whole life hating Archer. And what did he want to confess? That he was a killer? That he'd spent years trying to hurt Archer? *And you truly think I will come alone?*

No, he'd go in with reinforcements. He'd hear the confession. After that, Archer and Memphis would be taking Harrison straight to the cops.

"I'll come to you," Archer promised.

Harrison gave him the address. Hung up. Archer slowly lowered the phone.

Delilah sidled closer. "I heard enough of that conversation to know that you have a very bad plan forming in your head," she accused. Worry darkened her gaze.

"Harrison wants to meet. Don't worry, I'll be taking Memphis with me."

"Memphis *and* his team. And me."

"No."

"*Archer—*"

"No, baby, *no.*" On this, he was adamant. "I don't want you anywhere near him. I'll get Danny to take you back to my office and you can stay there—with my security team—but you will *not* be put anywhere near Harrison. You're too important. I can't put you at risk, I won't."

Tiffany shuffled up behind Delilah. Tiffany's nose was red, and her swollen, tear-filled eyes blinked owlishly. "What's happening?"

I think my brother may have killed your sister. He wants to confess, and I'm going to meet him before I turn his ass over to the cops. Like he could tell her that. She seemed to be barely holding herself together.

"Archer has to leave," Delilah answered smoothly. "An emergency has come up." She turned toward Tiffany. Gave her a reassuring squeeze. "But everything is okay."

Tiffany shook her head. "No." Sad. Heavy. "It's not. I don't think it ever will be okay again." Her shoulders began to shake. "Please...please, don't leave me alone now."

Delilah glanced at Archer. He could read the struggle on her face. He could also see her sympathy. Delilah had such a kind heart. She was *good*.

I'll never be good enough for her.

"I'll stay with you," Delilah promised Tiffany. "Just let me walk Archer out."

Now he stiffened. He didn't want her to stay. He wanted her tucked away in his office where she would be protected by a building full of guards. But Delilah skirted around Tiffany and walked toward the door.

Archer hurried to follow her.

At the door, she leaned close to him and whispered, "Do *not* get hurt."

"I want you at the office. I want—"

"Yeah, well, not happening. Either I come with you or I stay here with the woman who just found out her sister is dead. Your pick."

He hated both choices. "You need guards."

"Does Harrison know I'm here? Did you tell him I was at Tiffany's? Because this is kinda the last place I think he'd expect to find me. If he's trying to lure you away from me, I don't think he'll turn up here."

If he'd tailed them from the airport, he would know exactly where she was. A possibility that Archer would not ignore. "I'll call in guards."

"Fine. You do that." Her hand reached out. Fisted in his shirt. She dragged him even closer. Voice still a whisper, she ordered, "And don't you dare get hurt while you're gone. Do you understand? You'd better have Memphis shadowing your every move. I did not fall in love with you just to lose you. This isn't one of those tragic stories, got it? This is an epic romance. Epic. Deal with it."

His heart was about to burst out of his chest. He kissed her because he had to do it. He kissed her and loved her and knew that he would do whatever it took to return safely to her.

There'd been enough tragedy for them both. Time for something new. Better.

"I will come back," he promised.

***

"What...what was the emergency?" Tiffany asked quietly as she rubbed her red nose. "God, I must look horrible."

Delilah locked the door. Before he'd left, Archer had called in more guards. He'd assured her that they'd be arriving any moment. But she didn't want the guards busting in on them. She'd told Archer to keep the men outside. Tiffany didn't need to be surrounded by armed men looking for danger. "A work situation," Delilah lied because Tiffany had enough to handle at the moment. Once they learned more about Harrison, they could tell Tiffany what was happening.

Tiffany's shoulders slumped. "Archer loves his work. Vanessa always says that he is happier at work than he is with her. She says—" Tiffany stopped. Caught herself. Her whole body trembled. "Vanessa *said*. She *said* it...she doesn't say it anymore, though, does she? She doesn't say anything." Her breath shuddered in and out.

Delilah hurried back to her side. "Try to take a deeper breath." It looked as if Tiffany was about to hyperventilate. "You're not alone. And I know this has to hurt like hell, but you will get past it." Words Tiffany probably did not want to hear. But Delilah didn't know what to say. How could she make this pain easier to handle?

"I..." Tiffany closed her eyes. "I think I'd like that drink now. Something strong. Really strong. Would you please get it for me?" A hoarse whisper. "I have some...some whiskey in the bar to the right. Bottom shelf." But her eyes opened in the next instant. "But is that going to hurt or help?"

Delilah didn't move.

"Will *anything* help?"

I'm not sure that anything will. "I'll get the drink."

***

"No, he won't see me," Memphis promised. "And did you get the gun that I slipped in the limo for you?"

Archer stared at the gun on the seat beside him. "How the hell did you get the gun in the limo so quickly? I called you when I was leaving Tiffany's condo, and by the time I got to the ground floor—"

"Dude, I hid the gun in there when you were at the airport. I like to plan ahead, and I did *not* like the fact that Harrison vanished on me. If he's coming for you, I wanted a weapon close."

"You could have mentioned the gun sooner."

"I am mentioning it now, and I am not hearing a 'thank you' tossed my way."

"Thank you," Archer snapped.

"Excellent. And don't worry about Delilah. I have a man watching the outside of Tiffany's building. Delilah won't leave without him seeing her."

"I've got a team going to the building, too."

"Of course, you do. See, that's why we are going to be besties. We both know that when something—someone—is important, you protect her."

"Delilah is the most important person in my world."

"Okay, that's sweet and adorable and all, but stay focused on the particular problem at hand.

That problem? It's Harrison. Don't let down your guard around him. And if you have to shoot...hell, *will* you be able to shoot him? Because I know he's your brother. Delilah didn't have to tell me. I know and—"

"I can do anything necessary."

Silence. Then, "Good. Because if something happens to that fancy ass of yours, Delilah is gonna be pissed."

Archer hung up the phone and reached for the gun. He stared at the gun and thought about all the things that had happened in his life. His mother's death. His father's lies and endless affairs. The press that had tried to crucify Archer...

And he remembered the note that had been left for him two years ago.

You don't get to love.

All too soon, the limo pulled to a stop. He hid the weapon at the small of his back, tucking it in the waistband of his pants, then pulling his coat down over it. When he exited the vehicle, Archer knew the weapon couldn't be seen.

He stared up at the house before him. As soon as Harrison had given him the address, he'd known where he was going. Harrison's childhood home. The place where he'd grown up knowing he belonged with a different father.

The home had been sold to new owners several years back. Currently, the massive structure sat empty. Desolate. It had been hit hard by a hurricane a few years ago, and no one had ever bothered to repair it. The veneer of beauty was long gone. Only the ragged bones of the house remained.

"Stay with the car, Danny," Archer directed his driver.

"Um, Mr. Radcliffe? This, uh, feels like a bad scene."

"That's because it is." He glanced at his driver. "If you hear gunshots, don't run toward the house."

"G-gunshots?"

"Stay in the car. The glass is bullet proof."

Danny's Adam's apple bobbed. "Should I be calling the police?"

"If you hear gunshots, I think that would be an excellent idea."

***

Tiffany finally downed the shot. At first, she hadn't touched it. She'd just spent a long time staring into the amber liquid. Looking at it pensively as if she'd discover the secrets of the universe.

"That didn't help." Tiffany put the glass down on the table before her. "I think I need another."

Delilah bit her lip.

"Can you just bring the whole decanter over here?"

Delilah rose. Headed for the bar. Her fingers curled around the elaborate glass neck of the decanter, and she lifted it up. The decanter was half-full. Tiffany had told her the whiskey was supposed to be very expensive. That an ex had given it to her, and she'd slowly savored it.

Delilah didn't know anything about whiskey. Not her area of expertise. She was also apparently not very good at dealing with a grieving family member because she didn't know what to say in order to comfort Tiffany.

"Do you do this a lot?" Tiffany asked her, biting her lip.

Delilah put the decanter down on the table near Tiffany's glass before taking a seat on the sofa. "Do what?"

"Try to comfort people who are losing their minds after you've found their dead relatives."

"You're not losing your mind."

"No?" Tiffany dug her fingers into her temples. "It feels like I am."

"You're in pain. Your emotions are all over the place."

Tiffany reached for the decanter. Her fingers shook as she poured more whiskey into her glass. The whiskey spilled, dripping onto the table. She swiped at the liquid, smearing it, and hurriedly put the decanter back down. "Oh, damn it. Can you get me a napkin or something? Vanessa and I bought this table together and—" Her words ended on a sob.

Delilah shot to her feet. "Of course, I'll be right back." She hurried toward the kitchen. It was a cheerful kitchen, decorated all in white, with gleaming appliances and—

Delilah heard a creak behind her. *Way* too close behind her.

She stilled as a sudden, instinctual shiver slid over her. What—

Delilah began to turn around, but she didn't move quickly enough. Something heavy and hard slammed into her head. She heard the thud of it hitting her. A terrible, shuddering *thud* that she heard and then felt as pain explode through her head.

She fell to the floor even as she felt wetness soaking her hair. Felt something warm and wet sliding over her cheek.

Shatter. The decanter fell before her eyes even as Delilah hit the floor, and the glass shattered. She could see it flying across the floor. The broken glass looked just like tear drops.

Or chips of ice.

CHAPTER TWENTY-TWO

"I was in this room when my father told me I meant nothing to him." Harrison's hands thrust into his pockets and his shoulders hunched as he stood in the remains of what Archer suspected had once been a den. "I'd just gotten home from the hospital. I was so happy to be back, but he was so cold to me. And when he said I didn't matter..." A sad shake of his head. "I remember crying. I remember my mom hugging me and telling me that he was just mad. That everything would be all right."

Archer didn't speak.

Harrison glanced over at him. "But my dad—the man I *thought* was my dad—told me to pay no attention to her. He said she was a liar and a whore."

Archer absorbed that information. Considered and said, "He was a bastard so I don't see where he got to judge anyone."

Harrison blinked. "What?"

"He was a lying, abusive bastard. He shouldn't have hurt you or your mother. Neither of you deserved that pain. Some people are just born mean, and there's very little good inside of them. I've learned that lesson."

Harrison pulled his hands from his pockets. Shifted his body more toward Archer. "What are you doing?"

"Standing here, talking to my brother. I came, just like you asked."

"No, *no!* Why are you being nice?"

Archer laughed. "I'm not nice. Don't make that mistake."

Harrison took a step toward him. "I know it's a lie. You're cold. Just like he was. I watched you. Watched as you kept everyone away. No one mattered to you. No one mattered to *him*. I sure as hell didn't."

You don't get to love. "You think you didn't matter to me? That I didn't care I had a brother out there?"

It was Harrison's turn to laugh. "This isn't some magical bonding moment. You don't get to tell me BS and make everything all right."

"I know I don't. We're far past the point of things being all right."

Harrison glanced down at his watch, then back up at Archer.

"Am I keeping you from something?" Archer inquired smoothly.

Harrison jerked up his chin. "I had to come begging you for money—"

"I don't remember you begging. I just remember me writing a check for whatever you needed."

"You closed down my fucking club!" Spittle flew from Harrison's mouth. "You put all those employees out on the street!"

No. "I immediately reassigned all the workers. No one who was employed at Club Thirty-Two is without a job."

Harrison's lips parted. "What?"

"I gave them all new positions at other businesses." He brushed that away. "But you didn't call me here to talk about them, did you? You said you had things to tell me. Go ahead. Tell me."

"You're an arrogant, controlling asshole—"

"Yes. Unfortunate traits that I get from our father. You might believe I was the lucky one, but living with him was its own shade of hell." Keeping his voice flat took an effort, and Archer was far too conscious of the gun resting at the base of his back. "I can assure you, I never mattered to him. Pretty much the only thing he lived for was his next good time. He didn't spare a lot of emotions or even thoughts for either of his sons."

"Oh, so now you're gonna give me your sob story—"

"We found her body." He wasn't going to waste more time. Archer wanted this painful scene done. He needed to get back to Delilah. "So why don't you just tell me what you did to her?"

"B-body?" Harrison blanched. He also looked down at his watch again.

Tension spiked through Archer. *Why does Harrison keep looking at his watch?* "Yes, Vanessa's body. We found her remains at the cabin in Vermont." He waited a beat. "Now tell me why you killed her."

Harrison's head whipped up. His eyes were huge as he stumbled back. "I didn't kill her! Why would you think I had?"

"Because you called me here to confess. Because you were sleeping with her. Because you hate me and you want me to pay and hurt, and you—"

Harrison threw up his hands. "I didn't call you here to confess that crazy shit! I called you here because I was told to keep you busy!"

Archer could have sworn his heart stopped beating. "What?"

"I-I was told to just get you here for a little while. My...my partner was going to meet us. He said he had blackmail material to use against you. That we could force you to do what we wanted. That I could get the club back but..." Harrison shook his head. "Vanessa's body? You—you really found her."

Archer pulled out his gun. Aimed it at Harrison.

"Holy fuck!" Harrison cried out. "Put that away! Put it—"

"Who is your partner?"

"I don't know! We just talked on the phone. The voice was distorted, okay? Put the gun *down!*"

"Why did you vanish earlier today?"

"Because my partner told me I had to slip away. Said that you were out to get me. That you had people following me. People who were going to hurt me because you were pissed about Club

Thirty-Two. I caught sight of a tail and realized the caller was right."

No, the caller hadn't been right. The caller had been manipulating Harrison. "When were you told to contact me?"

"Like ten minutes before I made the call! Jesus, put down the gun!" Sweat covered his forehead.

*Ten minutes...*Ten minutes before the call...Archer and Delilah had been arriving at Tiffany's place. They'd just pulled up in front of her building. She'd acted surprised when she'd seen them at her door, but...

What if she'd been looking out her window when they pulled up? What if she'd seen them?

"Answer these next questions honestly," Archer ordered him.

But Harrison's gaze snapped to the right, beyond Archer's shoulder.

He didn't whirl around. Didn't lower his gun. He just slowly turned his head until he caught sight of Memphis.

"Easy," Memphis said as he advanced. "No need for anyone to get trigger happy." He had his gun up and pointed at Harrison. "And by anyone, I mean me. But if you don't answer Archer's questions—and tell the whole freaking, honest-to-God truth—I might get mad and start squeezing this itty, bitty little trigger."

"*Memphis,*" Archer warned. Now was not the time for him to do his bad routine. Though, maybe it wasn't a routine. Maybe it was just Memphis.

"I said I *might* get mad. If he talks, I won't."

Archer slid his focus back to Harrison.

"Wh-what do you want to know?" Harrison's voice broke.

"Who was in on the blackmail scheme with you at Club Thirty-Two? I know you were recording powerful people and then you had to be using your videos against them. Who was helping you?"

"Nobody."

Memphis sighed and lifted his weapon.

"No one—shit, *shit,* don't okay...it was Tiffany, all right? Tiffany Lassiter. I didn't blackmail *anyone.* She was the one who said we needed to help you so she put some cameras in the club and videoed a few judges. It didn't seem like a big deal. Dammit, I didn't do anything wrong! I was actually trying to keep you out of jail!"

Fuck. "Tiffany?"

"Yes. Look, after the charges against you were dropped, she said I should keep other videos around, in case I needed them to help myself get some power. I never used them, though, I swear. I didn't *want* to work things that way."

"Right." Memphis's doubt was clear. "Because you're the super upstanding member of society and what-not. Dumbass, don't try to feed me shit and call it a candy bar."

Archer ignored him. "The night of the attack on Delilah at the opera, were you with Tiffany?"

"I..." He flickered his stare to Memphis. "No, I mean, I went to find her after she left the restroom, but she ditched me. I didn't know where she'd gone, so I left and I, uh, hooked up at Club Thirty-Two with Bridgette." His tongue swiped over his lips. "You can ask Bridgette, I swear she'll back me up! I was with her. We've had this thing going for a while..."

Archer's heart raced faster. "Keep your gun on him," he ordered Memphis. Then he lowered his own weapon. Pulled out his phone. Called Delilah.

But she didn't answer him. The phone just rang and rang.

"Look, I don't understand what's happening!" Harrison's voice choked out. "I was just supposed to keep you busy and—"

"You were the distraction," Memphis told him flatly. "Archer, get the hell out of here. Get to Delilah, *now*. I'll call my man outside the building and tell him to damn well make sure he can put eyes on her."

He was already running back toward the limo. She wasn't answering, so he called his guards. Ordered them to get into Tiffany's condo. *Now*. They could meet up with Memphis's guy and tear down the fucking door to the place if need be. They just *had* to get to Delilah. But when he told them that...

"Boss, we're not at the building yet. Got caught in a traffic accident." A trembling reply. "But we're on the way. And I swear, we are really, really close..."

***

"God, you weigh a ton. I thought moving Vannie was hard, but, dammit, you're a thousand times worse."

Delilah's eyes fluttered open. She saw a light above her. An elegant, white, hanging light in a...*Wait, am I in Tiffany's kitchen?*

Her memory came whispering back. Going into the kitchen. Looking for a napkin. Getting...hit?

Falling to the floor. Had she lost consciousness?

OhmyGod, how long have I been here? On the floor, bleeding, and—

"I think it might have been the tarp that made moving Vannie easier. I could just drag her on it." Tiffany yanked on Delilah's ankles and hauled her a few more feet. Glass crunched beneath Delilah's body. "Fuck, you are *heavy.*"

She didn't realize that Delilah was awake. Delilah felt nausea roll through her as the side of her head throbbed in painful spasms. Blood covered her face and drenched her hair—obviously a super bad sign. But she was thinking semi-clearly, so she'd take that as some kind of twisted win, given the situation.

And the main thought she had?

Get away from the psycho who is trying to kill me.

And she would, as soon as she could do more than move her eyes around.

"I just have to get you to the closet. There's a fake wall in there. Got the idea from Club Thirty-Two. Had the same guy who built the passage there make me a panic room. Except it's not really a panic room. It's a hiding spot for me. I can hide anything I want in there. I'm gonna hide you. I'll seal you inside and no one will know where you went and when it's safe, I'll move you. I'll dump you like I dumped her and—" She broke off.

Delilah snapped her eyes closed.

Tiffany let go of Delilah's ankles. Her legs slammed onto the floor.

"Bitch," Tiffany snarled. "Are you awake?"

Delilah didn't move. Mostly because she wasn't sure she could move much. Was it her imagination or had she just heard someone knocking in the other room?

"I didn't want more blood in this kitchen. There's already too much to clean up."

That's your own damn fault!

Delilah heard the quick pad of Tiffany's footsteps. "But if I need to just cut your throat here and now, I will—"

Oh, hell, no. Delilah's eyes flew open, and her right hand snapped out to grab Tiffany's leg. She pulled, as hard as she could, and Tiffany slammed down on the floor next to her.

And somewhere in the other room, her phone was ringing.

***

"Faster," Archer snarled at Danny.

Danny slanted him a worried look. "Mr. Radcliffe, this is a limo. It doesn't do *fast* so well, and, ahem, are you sure you don't want to be in the back?"

"Put the fucking gas down to the fucking floorboard. Get us to Tiffany's. Don't stop for anything, you understand me?" Fear nearly choked him. Delilah wouldn't answer his calls.

Tiffany wouldn't answer. The guards hadn't checked in again.

I did this. I left her.

If Tiffany had hurt Delilah...

What in the hell will I do?

He still had his gun gripped in his hand, and Archer knew that he would kill to protect Delilah. He would kill to save her. He would *kill* for her.

It seemed only fair, considering that he'd only really started to live again...for her.

CHAPTER TWENTY-THREE

Delilah flopped onto her side. Tiffany snarled and groaned next to her, but Delilah didn't look back at the other woman. Not yet. She was too busy trying to find a weapon. There had to be something that she could use...

A giant chunk of the glass decanter was just a few inches away. Her fingers stretched toward it.

"Bitch!" Tiffany jumped on top of her. Straddled her body, and Tiffany's hands locked around Delilah's throat. "You think you're going to get away? Think you're going to tell him it was me?"

Yes, I am going to get away. I am going to tell him...

Tiffany yanked with her grip—dragging Delilah's head up a few inches—then slamming it back down into the kitchen floor. Pain spiraled from the back of her head.

"He belongs to me! He should have always been mine! Vannie didn't love him. She was just using him for his money. She didn't care about Archer, just like you don't!"

"I..." Speech was impossible. Tiffany's fingers were too tight. Delilah tried to arch her lower body. Tried to buck the other woman off her. But she didn't have enough strength for that. Her body just wasn't working right. Her hands weakly slid up Tiffany's arms.

"*I loved him.* Vannie started dating him in the first place because she wanted to take something away from me. She was always doing that. Trying to take what was mine. Trying to prove she was better than me, but I showed her, didn't I?"

Oh, yeah, psycho, you showed—

"I was the one to tell her to go to his cabin. She was in some snit." Her hold was punishingly tight. "She *chose* to disappear on her own for a few days. Said she was vanishing to 'make him suffer and miss her' or some crap. I told her to go to the cabin. And then I went up there. I took that stupid picture of her sitting in front of the sunset and when she turned to look at the view, I slammed the biggest rock I could find into the back of her head."

Delilah's fingers scraped over Tiffany's jaw. *If I could just reach a little higher...*

"Would you just die?" Tiffany screamed.

Furious pounding shook the condo's front door. "Delilah!" A voice thundered. "Delilah, we are coming in!"

Tiffany's head whipped toward the direction of the shout. Her grip loosened. "Who in the hell is that?" She glared down at Delilah. "Who did you bring here?"

She hadn't brought anyone, but Delilah was betting Archer had.

In that instant, Delilah rammed her fingers toward Tiffany's eyes. Tiffany screamed and jumped to her feet. Her hands flew to her eyes.

Delilah didn't waste time with her own scream. She rolled over, snagged that beautiful chunk of glass—glass stained with her blood—and gripped the edge tightly in her hand. It cut her, but she didn't care.

Tiffany's hands grabbed her shoulders.

Something crashed in the den. Footsteps pounded over the floor.

Tiffany hauled Delilah onto her back. "I will kill you. I will erase you from his life. I will—"

Delilah drove the glass into Tiffany's chest. Once. Twice. Three times.

She was still stabbing when armed guards hauled away Tiffany's sobbing form.

"I am not in the mood..." Delilah rasped because her throat just felt broken, "to disappear."

***

The familiar guard—Nico—caught Archer before he could run into Tiffany's condo. "There's a lot of blood, sir," he said grimly. "Be warned."

The world went dark.

"But she's okay. An ambulance is coming and it—"

He shoved Nico out of his way. Later, he would give Nico a raise. Later, he would tell him how grateful he was that Nico had hauled ass and gotten in the condo. *Later*.

Now he just had to see Delilah.

He ran past the shattered condo door. It hung drunkenly from its hinges. More guards filled the interior of the condo. Kristin was there, huddled on the floor next to—

Tiffany?

Tiffany was sprawled on the floor. Kristin and a man with a military buzz cut—*don't recognize him, must be the guy working for Memphis*—had their hands on her chest. They were trying to stop the bleeding that seemed to drench her body.

Tiffany saw him. She craned her neck up. A faint smile curved her lips. Her eyes were red-rimmed and one seemed to be filled with blood. "I...knew...you'd come for—"

"Delilah!" Archer bellowed as he lunged past Tiffany. He'd just seen Delilah. In the kitchen. On the bloody tile. He ran straight to her and fell to his knees. Blood covered half her face and matted her hair, and deep, angry red marks—in the shape of fucking *fingers*—lined her throat.

"I'm not..." Her voice was weak, broken. "Not going...anywhere."

He gripped her hand. Brought it to his mouth. Kissed her knuckles over and over again. "You're sure as hell not. Because if you left, I would follow."

Her eyes were open. Bleary, but on him. Two more guards that he knew—*his men*—hovered around her.

"She needs to be at a hospital, boss," one said to him. "We're trying to keep her stable, and Nico is going to send the EMTs in as soon as they arrive..."

Delilah's lashes fluttered. Nearly closed.

"No!" The cry tore from him. "Delilah, I want you to stay with me. I want you to focus *on* me."

"Demanding." A whisper from her. "So demanding."

Yes, he was. He was also scared to death. "Please, don't leave me." The blood on her beautiful face—the sight gutted him. She'd needed him. He hadn't been there for her. All along, he'd known the attacker wanted to hurt him by taking away what he loved—

And he loved nothing—no one—as much as he loved her.

"Of...course...I'll st-stay. Got to h-have those k-kids..."

It was good that he was on his knees. Otherwise, he would have fallen. "Three of them," he reminded her. "Layla Grace. Then two more."

Her eyes had closed completely. "Just...r-resting..."

"Baby, please don't go." He gripped her hand even tighter. "I love you, Delilah. Please, please don't go."

She didn't respond.

"Delilah!" Her name was an angry snarl. "Wherever you go, I follow. You understand that, don't you? I will always follow. Don't do this, don't—"

"Told you..." Barely a breath. "R-resting...I...didn't st-stab that bitch...three times..."

"Four," one of the guards supplied. "I think it was at least four."

"Five," the other returned. "Had to be."

"Just to...d-die now," Delilah finished.

"The ambulance is here!" Nico bellowed. "EMTs are coming through!"

Archer looked back. Sure enough, the EMTs had just entered the condo. "Here first!" he thundered. "Take care of Delilah." Because he would be damned if they stopped to tend to Tiffany before her. Delilah was the priority.

She was his world.

He forced himself to let her go so that the EMTs could work on her. And when they rushed her out of the condo, he was right behind them.

"Arch...er?" Tiffany's lost voice. "Archer?"

He never glanced back.

He rode down in the elevator with Delilah. He jumped into the ambulance with Delilah. As the sirens screamed, he held her hand once again.

***

"Do...I look as bad as I...feel?" Delilah asked the fourth time that she woke up.

Archer had carefully counted each and every time. He'd been at her bedside, and he did not plan to move in the foreseeable future. Each time she'd woken, she'd managed to talk, just a bit. Mostly rambles. One mumbled, "I love you" that he'd greedily taken into his heart. This was the first time that she'd asked about how she looked.

Her head turned on the pillow. Her gaze—awake, aware—met his. "Because I feel..." She licked pale lips. "I feel like some psycho slammed a whiskey decanter into my h-head...and then tried to choke me on her kitchen floor."

"Some crazy psycho did all that." He brushed back a lock of her hair as he leaned over the hospital bed. "But you fought her off. You saved yourself."

"She...wanted to p-put me in a closet." Her brow furrowed. "I think."

What?

The furrow smoothed away. "You look tired."

Probably because he hadn't slept in...hell, did it matter? "You look beautiful."

A weak shake of her head. "I can't p-possibly."

He nodded. "You do. You look like the most gorgeous woman in the world."

The hospital door opened with a swish behind him. "Delilah!" Memphis's voice boomed. "You're awake!" He rushed forward with flowers gripped in his hands. "I know you hate these, but when someone is in a hospital, my mama always said it was good manners to bring—" His words ended in a sharp whistle. "Oh, you look like shit. Your face is swollen, you have giant bruises all over your neck, and I hate to tell you, but I think the docs cut some of your hair when they were putting those stitches in your head. You are *not* going to approve of that cut."

Archer glared at him. "You are an asshole."

"What? Have you not told her how she looks?"

"She looks," he growled, "gorgeous. And you *will* tell her that."

Memphis frowned. "You know I don't like lying to friends."

"She looks gorgeous!" Archer snapped.

"You only think that because you're in love with her." Memphis plunked down the flowers.

Tilted his head and studied Delilah. "You know what you look like?"

"What?"

"A survivor. And that's the most beautiful thing in the world." He bent to brush a kiss over her cheek. "You fucking scared us all," he whispered.

But Archer caught the whisper. He'd known Memphis was scared. They'd spent plenty of time together hovered over Delilah's hospital bed, and he had a sinking suspicion that one of Memphis's earlier predictions might well be on its way to coming true.

I do think this asshole will wind up being one of my best friends.

Memphis cleared his throat as he pulled back. "There was a little brain swelling. Gave us a scare. But I told the docs you were hardheaded, so no one was surprised when you bounced back so quickly." He pointed to her throat. "You sound like a frog for now, but they told us there was no permanent damage. And you had the *best* docs with you. Archer insisted. Hey, if you are gonna live on a pile of cash, then you should certainly throw it around in an emergency, you know? And your boyfriend was making it rain cash. Rain, I say. He was flying in specialists left and right."

He would have brought in anyone he could to help her. Paid any price.

"You're going to be okay," Memphis assured her. "So just try and be good and get released and just don't worry about anything else, got it? Archer and I have everything covered."

By everything...Archer knew he was talking about Tiffany. She'd survived, too. Been stitched up. Treated. She'd almost lost an eye, but the docs had managed—so far—to save it, though they'd predicted she would probably never see clearly with it again. She was actually still in the damn hospital, under guard. In the *same* hospital with Delilah, and that drove him crazy. He wanted her locked away.

She would be. Soon. Archer would make certain of it. Whatever he had to do, Tiffany would never have another chance to come after Delilah.

"Do me a favor?" Delilah murmured.

Archer and Memphis both replied, "Anything."

She gave them a little smile. "I...I swear, there's a secret passage..."

Her broken voice twisted his heart.

"In one of her closets. Search for me? I-I think we need to see what she's hidden."

"Sure thing, Scooby Doo," Memphis assured her. "I'll get on it right now." He saluted Archer. "And you'll continue to stick as close to her as humanly possible?"

"You know I will." As if he'd leave her. He wasn't going to be able to take a full breath until the doctors had released her and given her a clean bill of health.

"Thought so." Memphis sauntered to the door. But he stopped before exiting. "Do not scare me like that again," he ordered as he tossed a glare back at Delilah. "Friends don't freak out friends because that shit is not cool. Remember that, would you? It's an important rule to live by."

Then he was gone.

Archer was left alone with his Delilah. He looked down at her, and Archer found her gaze on his. "You have the most beautiful eyes," he told her. "I thought that, the first time I saw you."

She blinked.

"I also thought...I have to meet her. I need to know her. Then you walked toward me. Told me you were going to take my necklace, and *then* I thought..." He stopped.

"Don't leave me in suspense."

"I thought...be careful. That's the kind of woman who might just wreck your world." He forced a smile. "And you did."

"Is that good? Or...bad?"

How could she even wonder? "Good. You are everything good in my life. And I swear, things are going to be different. Better. The police are going to lock away Tiffany. She isn't going to ever threaten you again. You are going to be safe. I will give you anything and everything you want—"

"I just want you." Soft. "I will always want you."

His body shuddered. "You have me." He leaned forward and had to brush a tender kiss over her lips. "*Always.*"

She was smiling when he pulled back. "Good." *You are better than good.*

"Now tell me again that I look gorgeous..."

"You are absolutely stunning."

Her hand fluttered toward her cut hair. He caught her fingers before she could get near the stitches. "Baby, you make any style work. Short hair is extra sexy on you."

"Archer..."

"Marry me."

Her eyes widened. "What?"

Okay. Wrong place. "I'll do that again—the right way—very soon. That was not supposed to slip out yet."

"You just asked me to...marry you."

He'd kind of told her to marry him which was one of the reasons why it had been *wrong*. He needed to tenderly ask and not possessively demand. He needed to be on one knee. He needed to give her a diamond big enough to weigh down her hand. "I will do it again."

"You'd better. Because if you don't, I'll be asking *you*." A pause. "Or maybe I'll just be *telling* you."

"Tell me," he dared.

"Archer, marry me."

His heart shoved into his chest. "Done."

"That is what I...like to hear." Still rasping, but her voice was a little clearer. "I do love a man of action."

"And I just fucking love *you*."

CHAPTER TWENTY-FOUR

"Tell me again why we are meeting with a killer on the day of your wedding." Oz tugged at his collar. "Because this feels like a really shitty plan to me."

"We're meeting with her because the cops asked us for this little meet and greet." Because the cops thought that Tiffany would confess all to Archer. Not that they needed the confession to convict her, but it would be the final nail in her coffin.

Delilah had been right. There *had* been a secret room at Tiffany's condo. Memphis had found it, and in that room, he'd discovered a pile of evidence. Evidence like clothing that still reeked of gasoline because Tiffany had been the one to burn the bed in Archer's guest room. She'd bulked up, wearing thick padding under her hoodie to appear bigger, and she'd snuck inside. The padding had been found in her hidden room, too.

As had Delilah's laptop. Archer's old date book. He still wasn't sure how that thing had wound up in his desk. The last he'd seen of it, he'd tossed it into one of the garbage bins at Radcliffe Industries.

Tiffany had also stolen items that belonged to her dead sister. Clothing. Jewelry. All things that had been found in her hidden room.

And she wanted to put Delilah in that room. To lock her away. Delilah had remembered Tiffany telling her that she'd seal her inside that room.

Oz exhaled as he sat down at the narrow table. Archer sat, too. The room was cold, and a one-way mirror ran the length of the wall on the right. Two other chairs—currently empty—waited on the other side of the table. The chairs would be for Tiffany and her lawyer.

As if on cue, the door opened. Tiffany came in, dressed in a garish orange jail uniform. Her lawyer shuffled along behind her.

A police detective—Detective Waylan Smith— slipped into the room. He inclined his head toward Archer. "Thank you for coming in today."

"Well, of course, he came in." Tiffany smiled at him. "He wanted to see me." She sat across from him and ignored her lawyer. "I knew you couldn't stay away."

He could, quite easily.

"This isn't a good idea," Tiffany's lawyer groused. "I warned you—"

"Shut up. I'm talking to Archer." She never took her gaze off him. Her right eye still had a slightly bloody look. "Have you realized it yet?"

Rage burned through him. *She tried to kill Delilah.* "Realized what?"

"That no one will ever love you like I do."

"That's a good thing, if you ask me," Oz muttered. He shuddered.

Tiffany's gaze cut to him. "Where is my thanks, Oz?"

"Excuse me?" Oz shook his head. "Lady, no one will thank—"

"You weren't going to get him off in court. You would have failed, and Archer would have gone to jail. I had to step in and save him. I was the one who had to threaten all the right people so that Archer wouldn't be charged with Vanessa's murder."

"You mean that you blackmailed people," Archer corrected.

"Yes. I did what was necessary." She straightened in her seat.

Her lawyer winced. "You need to—"

"Shut. Up," Tiffany ordered him. "You're some crappy public defender that I didn't even want. I don't need you. Archer loves me, and he's going to take care of me."

"No," Archer told her clearly. "I don't. After today, I hope I never see you again."

A frown pulled down her lips. "Why would you say that? You can't live without me!"

Want to bet?

"I was always looking out for you. Vannie was in the way, so I got rid of her."

Oz sighed. "I'm thinking you got rid of her because you were jealous that she was with Archer, and in some fit of rage, you bashed her head in with a rock."

A shrug of one shoulder. "I did hit her."

How could she act so cool? "Just like you shoved Delilah down the stairs at the opera?"

"*Not another word!*" Her lawyer was sweating.

"I will say what I want. And right now—*you're fired.*" A sniff. Then she winked at Archer with her non-bloody eye. "I gave her a push. She'd infuriated me. You were *making* out with her. Right in front of me. What did you expect me to do?"

Detective Smith never took his eyes off Tiffany.

Everyone was watching her.

She seemed to enjoy all the attention.

We need to move this scene along. He didn't want to be in that room longer than was absolutely necessary. "The date book," Archer said. His fingers tapped on the table. "How did it get in my desk?"

She smiled. Lifted her hand. Curled her index finger toward him as if inviting him closer.

He didn't move so much as an inch toward her.

Her smile faded. "I got it from the garbage. Sometimes, I'd stop by your building after my workouts. I slipped your assistant some money when I learned Delilah was digging into Vanessa's disappearance, and I got him to put it in your desk."

Hell.

"Delilah seemed like the nosey type. I figured she'd be searching your desk sooner or later. I thought she might find the notation about Vermont interesting." She gave what almost looked like a happy bounce in the chair. "I knew it was time for Vannie to make her appearance again. It was like I was giving Delilah breadcrumbs to follow."

"And Harrison?"

Laughter. "He's such an idiot. A pale imitation of the original. *You're* the original." She reached out to touch Archer's hand.

He pulled it away before she could. He would have to deal with his brother soon. Harrison had been calling him almost daily, desperately trying to apologize. Delilah thought there was hope for their relationship. Archer doubted that, but...hell, at least Harrison hadn't been trying to kill him.

Tiffany sighed. "He didn't know about Vannie. Didn't know about me. He hated you, but don't worry, I would have eventually got around to killing him because of that."

She said everything so casually. So easily. A monster was in front of him, and she preened in her jail-house orange.

Tiffany's voice dropped to a dramatic stage whisper as she revealed, "Do you know that eleven different news agencies have contacted me, wanting to hear my story? Eleven. I know there will be more, too. I'm big news."

"You tried to kill Delilah."

"She stabbed me. I've got *scars* on my chest." Anger cracked in her voice. "And did you see what she did to my eye?"

"Hard to miss it," Oz drawled.

Her cheeks reddened.

"Delilah defended herself," Archer said. "Because you slammed a decanter into her head—"

"I wanted to bash her freaking brains in!" More cracks. More rage. "She was in my way. I didn't get rid of Vannie just so some low-rent whore could slide into your life."

Archer rose to his feet. "You will never see Delilah again."

"I—"

"You will never see me again. Hell, I don't think you will see the outside world again." He'd make sure of it. "Goodbye, Tiffany." They'd gotten more than enough. He was *done*. He was not going to sit there while she talked shit about Delilah. Oh, the fuck, no.

"But—but you came to see me, you came—"

"He came to hear your confession," Oz told her flatly. "That's what we were all here for. Well, except for your lawyer. *Ex-lawyer*, that is. He was trying to stop you. Maybe you should have listened to him. But, hey, when a person wants to dig her own grave, sometimes, you just have to let her do the dirty work. And we all know how good you are at grave digging."

Her glare became even hotter.

"I'd like to say it's been fun," Oz continued, "but that would be a lie. Trying to avoid those as much as I can these days. Got this new buddy named Memphis who is always telling me honesty should be the best policy."

Archer yanked open the door.

"Archer!" Tiffany cried. "Don't leave me! We belong together! I did all of this...*for you.*"

He looked over at her. "No, Tiffany. We don't belong together. And you did none of this for me. You did it all for yourself."

Her expression contorted into rage as she lunged up from her seat. "I will make you so sorry! I will make you wish that—"

"He'd never met you?" Oz supplied. "Trust me, I am sure he already does wish that."

When she tried to jump across the table, the detective locked his hands around her shoulders. "Thank you, gentlemen," he said to Oz and Archer. "I do hope you enjoy your day. Oh, and congratulations, Archer. I hear wedding bells will be ringing soon."

Tiffany's scream followed them down the hallway.

As soon as Archer was outside the building, he exhaled on a long, hard breath.

"Can we never, ever do that again?" Oz wanted to know. "Because the way she is around you—it seriously creeps me out, and I have seen plenty of creepy things in my time."

Archer slanted him a glance.

"She was one hell of an actress, wasn't she? Hiding all of that inside. But then again, I guess lots of people hide who they really are. Though not quite to her extreme."

The limo waited a few yards away. Danny caught sight of them and hurried out of the driver's seat.

"We will never, ever do that again," Archer assured Oz. There was something else he needed to say to the man, too. "I'm sorry."

Oz squinted at him. "Come again? I must have misheard. It sounded like the mighty Archer said—"

"I'm sorry. I suspected you, and I was wrong. You *have* always been at my side, trying to help me, and because I'm a closed-off prick who doesn't like to let the world know what he's really feeling, I often treated you like shit. I am sorry. I will be doing better in the future."

Oz glanced away. "You don't get it."

"Get that I'm an asshole? Trust me, I—"

"Do you remember paying for my college? I know you do, so let's cut through the BS. You did it. Somehow, you scraped the money together. And then you paid for my law school. You think I didn't know it was you, all along?" His gaze slid back to Archer. "You got the schools to say it was some scholarship program, but it was a lie. I can connect dots. I knew what you were doing. *You* knew I didn't have money. You knew my family was floating on fumes, and to save my pride, you pulled strings to hide the truth. You helped me when I needed you, just like you have always done since those assholes in grade school tried to beat me up in the boys' bathroom, and you shoved their heads under the cold water in the sink."

Archer didn't say anything.

"You had my back since elementary school. I *know* you're a closed-off prick. You don't have to tell me that. But I also know you've got a solid heart hidden deep in your chest. When Vanessa put the moves on me—shit, I knew she was going to run back to you and tell you some BS story. I felt guilty as hell, so I started pulling away. Things didn't feel right with the judges and prosecutors when you were under suspicion. I know I'm magic, but this was beyond the norm. Everything was off, and, dammit…" His cheeks puffed up. "I might have suspected me a little, too, if I'd been you. So how about we just move forward, admit that we can both be wrong, and we get your ass to the wedding that is waiting?"

"That sounds like a good plan to me." He offered his hand to Oz.

Oz stared at the hand. "Idiot." Then he yanked Archer in for a fierce hug. "You are my friend. You'll always be." He let Archer go. "Just so you know, this emotional stuff makes me uncomfortable as hell."

Archer smiled.

"You're a good man, Archer. No matter what you tell yourself. Dammit, weren't you the one who just paid for Vanessa's whole funeral? Who made sure she had people there to say goodbye? To make sure she was taken care of?"

"That was the least I could do."

"No, you did that because despite what the tabloids said for so long, you aren't the monster. Tiffany is."

I did all of this…for you. Her words rang through his mind. He swallowed.

"We need to get you to the church," Oz declared. "You need to get in your tux and—"

"I have to see Delilah first." He had a desperate desire to see her. To just be sure she was safe. *I need her.*

"Uh, you'll see her *at* the wedding."

He marched toward Danny. "No, I have to see her *now*."

"That's bad luck!" Oz rushed after him. "You can't see her *before* the wedding, that's bad luck! Everyone knows that! Don't you think we've had enough of that already?"

***

"You can't see her." Memphis crossed his arms over his chest and blocked the door with his body. "It's bad luck."

"That's what I said!" Oz chimed in to confirm.

Archer didn't look back at Oz. The guy had chased him all the way through the church to the dressing room. Delilah was on the other side of that door. Archer *would* be getting to her. Nothing would stop him. "I have to give her something."

Memphis held out his hand. "Give it to me. I'll give it to her."

"Get out of the way, and *I'll* give it to her."

Memphis sighed. "I don't want to fight you on your wedding day. Delilah will be mad if you show up with a black eye."

"She'll be even madder if we *both* have black eyes," Archer returned.

Memphis appeared intrigued by the possibility. "You think you can get a blow in? Oh, rich boy, I would like to see you—"

The door swung open behind Memphis. "What are you guys doing?" Delilah demanded.

Memphis swore.

It was too late. Archer could see her in all her beautiful glory. She already had on the wedding dress. Hugging her body, flowing at her hips, all silken and soft—she looked like a fairy-tale queen standing in the doorway. For a moment, he forgot to breathe.

Oz hit him on the back.

"Bad luck. You will regret this one day." Memphis stepped aside. "Come on, Oz. Let's see if we can sneak a drink from the bar while no one is looking."

Their footsteps faded away.

Archer remained locked in place.

Delilah tilted her head. "How did things go today?"

"Got the confession. We're done with her."

Concern flashed on her face. Delilah reached out to curl her hand around his arm. "Are you okay?"

He looked at her hand. Then back to her face. "You're marrying me today."

"Yes, that is the plan."

"Then I'm more than okay." *I'm the luckiest bastard in the world.* "Is anyone in that room? Any of your bridesmaids?" He knew Tony was probably lurking around somewhere.

"It's just me." She backed into the room. "Come in."

He slipped over the threshold. "Turn around."

Frowning a little, she did.

She'd cut her hair, shaping it all into a pixie style that made her eyes look even bigger, her face more delicate, and her just—sexier. Even more beautiful than she'd been before. With the shorter hair, he didn't need to move anything out of his way as he slipped his gift out of his pocket and then carefully draped it around her neck. The bruising was long gone. "I thought you needed something old before the wedding. Isn't that a tradition? Something old, something new..."

She whirled toward him. Her hand flew up and touched the giant, diamond tear-shaped necklace that he'd hung around her neck. "Archer?"

"The day I bid on that, I knew that I wanted to give it to you." He wanted to give her everything. "The tear is something old. Our life together will be something new." His brows pulled down. "What's next? Something borrowed?"

"I'm wearing Tony's shoes," Delilah said quickly as she lovingly stroked the necklace.

"That just leaves something blue."

"My garter is blue. You can take it off later with your teeth."

A laugh tore from him even as the hot visual filled his head. "I love you." He'd gone from hell— being in that small room with Tiffany—to heaven—standing in front of Delilah.

She was his heaven.

"I will never deserve you," he told her.

"Probably not," Delilah teased as she wrapped her arms around him. She didn't seem to care at all that she was crushing her dress. "But you have me, anyway. You have me now, and you'll have me forever."

***

"And you may kiss the bride—"

Archer didn't even wait for those words to finish before his mouth took Delilah's. He could hear people cheering and clapping, and he just kissed her even harder. Deeper. She kissed him back with sweet abandon, and he knew that as soon as they slipped away from the crowd, he would totally be making love to her in the back of the limo.

A hard slap hit his back. "Congratulations!" Memphis boomed.

Archer lifted his head and drank in the sight of his beautiful wife. Delilah smiled at him. The smile that had first stolen his heart.

Tony grabbed her and pulled Delilah into a massive hug. People were still cheering. Some were whistling. Rose petals were flying around them.

And Archer was grinning. He felt his face stretching with the force of the grin. This moment was incredible. He would never, ever forget it. He couldn't remember being this happy. Didn't know if he would ever be this happy again.

Then Delilah turned back to him. She winked.

And he thought about a little girl with her mother's smile. A future of laughter and fights and hugs and...

Delilah.

Yes, he would be this happy again. Over and over again...

Always. With Delilah.

She slid back into his arms. Fit him so perfectly. "What are you thinking?" she whispered as cameras clicked around them.

"I'm thinking the prince would have been a whole lot happier if he'd married the wicked stepsister."

At first, she frowned, and then understanding dawned on her face. When Delilah laughed, it was the best music he'd ever heard.

EPILOGUE

Delilah grabbed her Go bag. She didn't exactly know *where* she was going—Archer had planned the honeymoon, and he'd been adamant about keeping the destination a surprise. Because of that, she hadn't been sure what to pack.

Then he'd told her clothes didn't matter so much. He was hoping she'd be mostly naked. Since she was hoping the same thing about him, the news had thrilled her.

Still, she was taking *some* clothes and essentials. Thus the Go bag. She slid it over her shoulder and hurried for the door. It was time to meet Archer and rush out toward the limo as they escaped, though she had been warned that the wedding guests would be ringing bells and blowing bubbles at them as they made that escape.

Before she could reach for the doorknob, the door swung open. Memphis stood there.

"Archer didn't need to send you after me." She tossed him a quick, sunny smile. "I am on my way—"

"Archer didn't send me."

Oh. Okay. She frowned. There was something about his voice...

"You know I don't like to lie."

Unease slithered through her. He'd been smiling during the wedding, but his expression seemed so much harder now. Unyielding. "Yes. That's one of the things I like most about you."

A nod. "It's a special day for you, and I want you to be happy."

"I *am* happy."

He pushed out a heavy breath. "I don't want to ruin that happiness."

Her stomach twisted as she surged toward him. "What is it?"

"I also don't want to keep things from you. I know that you and Archer are about to go dark for the next two weeks because he told me that—"

"Do *not* tell me where we are going on the honeymoon!" Delilah interrupted to say. "I want it to be a surprise."

"Right. Sure." The faint lines near his mouth deepened. "Let's just say there won't be a lot of cell service where you're going, and I won't be able to contact you if things move fast."

That twist in her stomach got worse. "What things, Memphis?"

"I feel like an asshole telling you this on your wedding day..."

"What. Things?"

"I have a lead."

She sucked in a breath. Even before he spoke again, she knew—

"It's a good one. It's about the man I think might have taken Layla. I could be wrong, though.

We know leads have turned up jack before. But this one feels different. I think I may have a way of learning more about the guy. Of getting close to him. I believe I can draw him out."

"*Memphis.*"

"I just—I didn't want to do this without telling you. But I didn't want to ruin your day and—"

She threw her arms around him. Hugged him tightly. As tightly as she could. "Thank you." Because as she'd gone through her wedding day, she'd thought about Layla. Imagined what it would have been like to have her sister as her maid or matron of honor. Imagined laughing and smiling with her.

Imagined seeing Layla just one more time.

I think she would have liked Archer.

It had been five years. After all that time, to finally find out that they might be close to discovering who had taken Layla away? "Thank you," she said again. "And you didn't ruin a thing." She eased back. Stared up at him.

"I won't give up on finding the bastard. Even if this lead doesn't pan out, I will keep hunting him."

"You're the best tracker I know. No one can get away from you."

"Damn straight." He sniffed. "Now go run to your groom before he comes in here and finds you teary-eyed. If he sees you with so much as a glimmer of a tear in your eye, we both know he will want to *try* and kick my ass. He'll fail, of course, and then he'll just be embarrassed on his wedding day." He moved to the side, clearing her path.

And she did run to her groom. The wedding guests rang their bells, and the kids blew bubbles toward her and Archer. He held her hand, and they jumped into the back of the limo.

As Danny drove them away, Archer leaned toward her. His eyes narrowed a little as he stared at her face. "Sweetheart, have you been crying?" His features immediately tightened. "What happened? Who did it? I will—"

Memphis already knew him too well. "Sometimes, we all need to cry a little bit." She would tell him about her conversation with Memphis. She would never have secrets between her and Archer. But for now, in this one moment... "I love you," she said. "I am so, so happy that I married you today." Her hand slid over his cheek. "Kiss me?"

He did. He held her tight. He kissed her with care and passion and love.

This was their beginning. This was the start of their life.

Would things always be easy? No. But that was okay. She had Archer. He had her. Together, they could face anything that came their way.

Together, they could have an amazing future. Maybe even an epic one, as she'd once told him.

"I love you," he said. "Always."

THE END

A NOTE FROM THE AUTHOR

Thank you so much for reading FROZEN IN ICE! I hope that you enjoyed the story.

I am so true-crime obsessed. Give me podcasts, give me sleuthing—give me everything you've got! When I started researching for the "Ice Breakers" team, I got lost in a world of true cold case solvers. I am amazed and impressed by the work that these individuals do.

Delilah and Archer were such a great couple to write, and as I was creating their story, there were other characters who popped up and demanded stories. Characters like...Memphis. As soon as he appeared on the page, I had a plot for him! I love it when a story idea comes with such strong force.

Thank you, again, for reading FROZEN IN ICE— and for checking out the Ice Breakers.

If you'd like to stay updated on my releases and sales, please join my newsletter list.

https://cynthiaeden.com/newsletter/

Again, thank you for reading FROZEN IN ICE.

Best,
Cynthia Eden
cynthiaeden.com

ABOUT THE AUTHOR

Cynthia Eden is a *New York Times*, *USA Today*, *Digital Book World*, and *IndieReader* best-seller.

Cynthia writes sexy tales of contemporary romance, romantic suspense, and paranormal romance. Since she began writing full-time in 2005, Cynthia has written over one hundred novels and novellas.

Cynthia lives along the Alabama Gulf Coast. She loves romance novels, horror movies, and chocolate.

For More Information
- *cynthiaeden.com*
- *facebook.com/cynthiaedenfanpage*

HER OTHER WORKS

Ice Breaker Cold Case Romance

- Frozen In Ice (Book 1)
- Falling For The Ice Queen (Book 2)

Phoenix Fury

- Hot Enough To Burn (Book 1)
- Slow Burn (Book 2)
- Burn It Down (Book 3)

Trouble For Hire

- No Escape From War (Book 1)
- Don't Play With Odin (Book 2)
- Jinx, You're It (Book 3)
- Remember Ramsey (Book 4)

Death and Moonlight Mystery

- Step Into My Web (Book 1)
- Save Me From The Dark (Book 2)

Wilde Ways

- Protecting Piper (Book 1)
- Guarding Gwen (Book 2)
- Before Ben (Book 3)
- The Heart You Break (Book 4)
- Fighting For Her (Book 5)

- Ghost Of A Chance (Book 6)
- Crossing The Line (Book 7)
- Counting On Cole (Book 8)
- Chase After Me (Book 9)
- Say I Do (Book 10)
- Roman Will Fall (Book 11)
- The One Who Got Away (Book 12)
- Pretend You Want Me (Book 13)
- Cross My Heart (Book 14)
- The Bodyguard Next Door (Book 15)

Dark Sins

- Don't Trust A Killer (Book 1)
- Don't Love A Liar (Book 2)

Lazarus Rising

- Never Let Go (Book One)
- Keep Me Close (Book Two)
- Stay With Me (Book Three)
- Run To Me (Book Four)
- Lie Close To Me (Book Five)
- Hold On Tight (Book Six)

Dark Obsession Series

- Watch Me (Book 1)
- Want Me (Book 2)
- Need Me (Book 3)
- Beware Of Me (Book 4)
- Only For Me (Books 1 to 4)

Mine Series

- Mine To Take (Book 1)
- Mine To Keep (Book 2)
- Mine To Hold (Book 3)

- Mine To Crave (Book 4)
- Mine To Have (Book 5)
- Mine To Protect (Book 6)
- Mine Box Set Volume 1 (Books 1-3)
- Mine Box Set Volume 2 (Books 4-6)

Bad Things

- The Devil In Disguise (Book 1)
- On The Prowl (Book 2)
- Undead Or Alive (Book 3)
- Broken Angel (Book 4)
- Heart Of Stone (Book 5)
- Tempted By Fate (Book 6)
- Wicked And Wild (Book 7)
- Saint Or Sinner (Book 8)
- Bad Things Volume One (Books 1 to 3)
- Bad Things Volume Two (Books 4 to 6)
- Bad Things Deluxe Box Set (Books 1 to 6)

Bite Series

- Forbidden Bite (Bite Book 1)
- Mating Bite (Bite Book 2)

Blood and Moonlight Series

- Bite The Dust (Book 1)
- Better Off Undead (Book 2)
- Bitter Blood (Book 3)
- Blood and Moonlight (The Complete Series)

Purgatory Series

- The Wolf Within (Book 1)
- Marked By The Vampire (Book 2)

- Charming The Beast (Book 3)
- Deal with the Devil (Book 4)
- The Beasts Inside (Books 1 to 4)

Bound Series

- Bound By Blood (Book 1)
- Bound In Darkness (Book 2)
- Bound In Sin (Book 3)
- Bound By The Night (Book 4)
- Bound in Death (Book 5)
- Forever Bound (Books 1 to 4)

Stand-Alone Romantic Suspense

- It's A Wonderful Werewolf
- Never Cry Werewolf
- Immortal Danger
- Deck The Halls
- Come Back To Me
- Put A Spell On Me
- Never Gonna Happen
- One Hot Holiday
- Slay All Day
- Midnight Bite
- Secret Admirer
- Christmas With A Spy
- Femme Fatale
- Until Death
- Sinful Secrets
- First Taste of Darkness
- A Vampire's Christmas Carol

Made in the USA
Las Vegas, NV
19 June 2022

50425717R00184